ECLIPSO'S
HAPPY
QUEST

Other novels in the Four Planet series by David Taylor (all published by Virtual Bookworm):

A Tale of Four Planets trilogy:
Book One: Sessions With The Seer
Book Two: The Rejected Counsel of Oomb
Book Three: Centers of the Universe

Eclipso's Happy Quest:
Book One: Goosed By An Iguanodon?

Eclipso's Happy Quest
Book Two: Eau De Diplodocus?
A Novel by David Taylor
ISBN: 978-1-63868-125-0 (softcover)
ISBN 978-1-63868-123-6 (hardcover)
ISBN: 978-1-63868-124-3 (ebook)
Library of Congress Number on file with publisher.
Special thanks to Becca for her work on the book cover!

ECLIPSO'S HAPPY QUEST

a Post-Planets Prequel by David Taylor

Book Two:
Eau De Diplodocus?

dedicated to Big Al and Blue

Faith is to believe what you do not see; the reward for this faith is to see what you believe.

-St. Augustine

Chapter 1

"I am of the school of thought that Ambu did *not* hypnotize us into licking his unclothed behind," delicately remarked Sherman Peabody. He was addressing a genuine worry that haunted his companions while their spaciously appointed steam-powered drone, Cloud Nine, sped across the sky from Papua, New Guinea to Cameroon, on the west coast of Central Africa.

"Now there's a sentence I'd have bet good money I would easily reach the end of my life without ever hearing," deadpanned resident skeptic Stephen Feldman, the most reluctant member of the expedition seeking a surviving non-avian dinosaur. "But I agree with you, Sherman. Such a hypnotic stunt is highly unlikely. My understanding is that it's well-nigh impossible to hypnotize anyone into doing something they find completely unacceptable, such as murder."

"I wouldn't think that licking someone's, well, you know, rises to the same level of unacceptability as murder," ventured the soft-spoken Bernie Coleman, curator of a cryptozoology museum in Portland, Maine. "Wait, don't look at me," he chuckled to other's quizzical regard. "I don't even lick lollipops."

"Well I hope you haven't called us here, Mr. Peabody, to settle whether or not someone's business end has been licked," said folklore specialist Irene McDowell with her usual snark.

"Indeed I have not," responded Sherman defensively, eyes averted downward with his chin scrunched against his neck, as usual.

Back in Papua, on the island of New Great Britain, Sherman and company followed up reports of a creature bearing a remarkable resemblance to an Iguanodon, especially for its thumbs-up claw. But someone, or some group, pranked them.

Yes, Augie Matias and Irene McDowell both did hear a mysterious loud quack, like they could imagine from a monster duck. And Augie's pants were punctured by who-knows-what while he felt some unseen presence's fetid warm breath in his face.

On the other hand, a dead chicken was hung from a palm tree. It baited a saltwater crocodile into rearing up on hind legs, appearing dinosaurian at a distance. And the search team discovered a foot-track-making contraption abandoned just offshore, calling into serious question who or what left three-toed tracks on a nearby beach.

The enigmatic Eclipso Sunray Smith's reggae-dancing, pencil-sized alligator, Bonsai Gator, purportedly thought the living dinosaur search was a good idea. Eclipso plus would-be golf-course developer, Alistair Frump, were bankrolling that search with a virtual bottomless pit of funding. So Augie and company could have looked past both the chicken and the track maker. They could have kept searching Papuan swamps for either proof that Augie was goosed by a dinosaur, or that every last mysterious experience there was hoaxed.

However, dramatically decreased political and military tensions in Cameroon afforded the prospect of a fresh start to the quest.

Over the past century, an unknown force had been making off with boatloads of weapons worldwide, while leaving behind solar energy panels and other hi-tech devices that leapfrogged technological progress several decades.

What vanished from Cameroon was a warehouse full of guns and artillery intended to propel more than one civil war, including between north and south Cameroon. Mixed in with the futuristic goodies left in the weaponry's place, oddly enough, were thousands of golf clubs and a half-million golf balls. The resu tant relaxed political atmosphere promised a far safer exploration of Cameroonian rivers and swamps than otherwise would have been possible, searching for the legendary mokele-mbembe.

"I'd rather not have to repeat myself, if I could have your attention as well, Mr. Matics," Sherman pointedly addressed Dr. Augustine Matias.

Augustine or Augie, as he was known, was still re-examining a video from the night in New Guinea he believed an Iguanodon descendant might very well have been what tore a big hole in his pants with its opposable thumbs-up claw.

Okay, that definitely sounds like a "quack" we recorded, rather than the racket from two trees swayed rubbing against each other, he told himself. *But this mango tree was lit up by so many flashes of lightning. Why doesn't a giant duckbill show up there on even one split-second frame? Even though I could have sworn…?*

Once more, Augie suspected something extraordinary eluded him on a video. Previously, his final episode of *Cryptomonster Hunt* featured the same location as the first leg of Eclipso's dinosaur search. On New Britain Island, the *Cryptomonster* television crew filmed a tree and surrounding bushes in serious, waving-from-side-to-side commotion, despite little breeze. But no matter how many ways Augie analyzed that video, he couldn't pick up one single clue as to what was agitating the plants so much, while still spooked by a sense he was staring right at it. *Some incredibly advanced form of camouflage?*

"Mr. Matias," repeated Sherman, chin ever-firmly embedded in his neck, "it might comfort you to learn that very same video you are obsessing over has prompted research of significant potential benefit for our quest."

"Oh?" Augie reacted, turning away from the computer screen finally.

"Indeed. Think back to when we crouched behind the cycads, trying to catch a glimpse of our thumbs-up Iguanodon during lightning flashes from an approaching electrical storm. We heard all manner of frogs and insects with their incessant mating racket. But in addition, I could have sworn-"

"Down behind my bunk mattress!!" suddenly exclaimed journalist Laura Gómez, snapping her fingers. "That's where I stored... Excuse me, Sherman, for just one more minute. Can you join me, Irene?"

"Uh, sure."

Scant moments later, Laura came bounding back into the expedition workshop, left arm raised to display a copper bracelet. "I feared it slipped off in the thunderstorm, lost for good on New Great Britain," she explained breathlessly. "But then remembered where I put it to avoid corrosion out in the pouring rain! Oh my God, didn't know what I was going to... Well, sorry for raving like a lunatic."

"It once was lost, but now it's found," Irene practically sang, kindly intent on sparing Laura further embarrassment. *No need for Laura to let the whole world know that had the bracelet been permanently lost, she would have felt obligated to tell her sweetie-pie what happened to the token of his affection. Think his name is Tom.*

"Perhaps that's a positive omen we will also soon find a living non-avian dinosaur," suggested Scott MacDonald, their resident expert on searching for surviving dinosaurs in West Africa.

"It's not a matter of anyone having forgotten they left a live dinosaur hidden away somewhere," said Stephen drolly. "It's very difficult, actually altogether impossible, to misplace something that doesn't exist in the first place."

Sherman managed to drill into Stephen with a most severe regard while keeping his chin scrunched into his neck. "You might find yourself reconsidering your position, sir," he said curtly, "after you hear and see the evidence I am about to reveal, the product of my long hours of research and analysis. That is, of course, assuming I finally have everyone's attention?" Sherman broke off his evil eye on Stephen to sweep the room visually, chin still scrunched into his neck. "No one has to pee? No one left their coffee maker on? No other epiphanies about where a certain trinket was left hidden away that we need to sort out?"

"Where I am concerned," said Bernie Coleman, "you may as well be a grazing Triceratops. In other words, you have my full attention."

"In other words, you've made Bernie forget all about peeing, so let's have it," said Irene not a little impatiently.

"Right, yes, let's get to it," agreed Sherman. "As I was saying, we were crouched behind those cycads back on New Britain Island, amidst the wealth of noises issuing from frogs, insects, the approaching thunderstorm, et cetera. And that's when I distinctly heard what sounded like a human flatus emission."

"A what?"

"A fart, honeybun," Harriet answered her husband, Harry. "I try to keep him up-to-date on certain technical terms," she announced for everyone else.

"She completes me," Harry added.

"So I've heard," said Irene. "Okay, can we get back to where you're going with this, Mr. Peabody?"

"Ever after we returned to Cloud Nine, I couldn't stop thinking about that fart," admitted Sherman Peabody. "Then it occurred to me: Why not adapt one of those futuristic devices found left behind when a cache of arms were mysteriously spirited away by heaven-knows-who? This is an audio spectrometer." Sherman patted a microwave-sized box fronted by a small video screen. "It filters out any and all sounds in aid of isolating the particular noise you are investigating, or searching for.

"So the question became: Could I use this device to analyze the video recording made during our crouching wait? And isolate the particular human expulsion of digestion-producing gases I could have sworn I heard?"

"Could you turn it into a fart-o-meter, in other words," said Stephen.

"I prefer terming it a flatus emission detector. But yes. And here is the successful result."

Using his remote control, Sherman had his transistorized equipment replay a sound clip recorded on that fateful evening back on New Britain Island. Concurrent with that, the Richter-scale-type plotline on the detector's screen jumped all over the place with a plethora of jumbled-together night-time tropical swamp noises.

"This is audio from my camcorder, prior to filtration. At best, you can pick out a few individual frog and insect noises. But now," Sherman played with his remote again, "you hear the human flatus emission in isolation."

The lengthy noise reminded Augie of a balloon suddenly deflating.

Nearly everyone else who had been down in the swamp on that weeks-ago late evening exchanged suspicious looks. Bernie Coleman mused they might as well have all been murder suspects. *One of them must be wondering whether they will be sniffed out, so to speak, while the rest puzzle over who is really to blame.*

"It wasn't me," stated Laura Gómez plainly.

"If everyone who it wasn't declares their innocence," said Stephen, "that should leave us with-"

"I did it, okay?!" Roberta burst out, instantly regretful.

"Just a 'flatus emission,'" said Irene trying hard not to bust a gut laughing. "Don't have to be defensive about it. After all, what's a little *pfftt* amongst friends?"

"Guess I did sound too much like a confession was squeezed out of me by a murder detective," said Roberta with a forced chuckle.

"Given the subject matter, you might have made a more careful choice of words there," suggested Irene to more general chuckles, Roberta's still forced.

Laura's joy over relocating her copper bracelet feared lost forever had Roberta thinking about her last video phone conversation with her significant other, Daniela. Ergo her feigned amusement.

"I don't see you wearing your Welsh dragons," was Daniela's non-sequitur response to Roberta asking about everything back home in College Park, Maryland. True, the necklace she gave Roberta as a going-away good luck charm wasn't hanging round Roberta's neck. But was that really so big a deal, when compared to their finally being able to catch up after Roberta's incommunicado absence for so long?

"Didn't want to risk losing it in the thunderstorm I just described."

"But that was days ago, right?"

"After securing it away safely, I simply hadn't gotten around to-"

"Ruff! Ruff!"

"Ruff! Ruff!"

Dachshunds Queenie and Prince Charles came barking into videophone view from Daniela's end. Their sniffing snouts loomed large on Roberta's screen before they quickly moved off.

"Queenie and Prince Charles miss their other mommy, don't you? Don't you? Yes you do! Yes you do!" Daniela spoke to the two hot dogs on legs in an affectedly deep voice. She grabbed at them to try forcing a look into her videophone, but with no success. Both pooches wriggled free, on the trail of other scents far more interesting than any provided by the phone.

"And I miss them," conceded Roberta. "I also miss…um, have to go." Roberta clicked off the call abruptly, wishing she'd never started a sentence with *I also miss*. Roberta was feeling increasingly uncertain that whatever she thought she had with Daniela ever existed in the first place. Nostalgia for a past not all that hot to begin with? *Might I just as well have been a dinosaur in one of my past lives? Longing to return to when I had to fear daily whether a T-Rex or Velociraptor was going to leap out of the underbrush?*

"Now that we have solved *that* mystery – thank you very much, Roberta - here are flatus emissions I sonically disaggregated from a variety of other creature noises," went on Sherman, undaunted by the general hilarity. "We will start with the cockroach."

A chorus of explosive-sounding poofs accompanied the spectrometer's graph-line plot of innumerable peaks nearly all the same height.

"Additional disaggregation isolated emission noises from forty-nine individual cockroaches. Without playing the audio of each one for you, I'll display those forty-nine line plots on the spectrometer screen, piled one atop the other. Of course they were the only ones close enough to our location for the original videotape to pick up. Doubtless there were countless others going at it, too distant from our location for teasing out from the general din.

"And I employ the term, 'going at it,' most appropriately. These particular cockroaches' flatus emissions are only this loud when they are mating."

"Mating?" said Laura. "So how that odd number, 49?"

"One group must have been doing a three-way," said Irene.

"Actually," Sherman set about answering, impervious to the snickers that greeted Irene's snark, "these five here, here, here, here and here," he pointed at each of five line plots, "they were giving birth. We know this from their noisy emissions being spaced two minutes apart."

"The question begs asking," said Stephen. "What does any of this have to do with discovering a non-existent surviving non-avian dinosaur? Mind you, I'd be perfectly content to see this expedition focus on cockroach farts instead; that's sure to prove a far more productive enterprise."

"I'm getting to that," responded Sherman, too enthralled by his own presentation to find Stephen's commentary the least bit irritating. ' You see," he went on, "I also teased out a snake's cloacal popping. Which particular snake, though, I could no more hazard a guess than about which particular cockroach species we recorded."

"'Cloacal popping'?" Irene repeated as in, *Did I hear that correctly? Has this all really come down to "cloacal popping"?*

"To put it crudely," said Sherman, "female snakes fart for defense. When they fear a predator is near, they relax their cloaca, draw air into it, and then quickly contract it to make a threatening noise."

"Why would a loud fart scare off anyone? It's the silent-but-deadly you really need to watch out for!" laughed Alistair Frump.

"Perhaps I should skip over other flatus emissions we documented from New Britain Island, and focus on the one of most interest to us," suggested Sherman, finally a bit perturbed by the growing hilarity over his dissertation on "flatus emissions."

"Wait, what about frogs?" asked Roberta, still sincerely more fascinated than amused. "We heard lots of them out there, especially before the storm struck."

"Their sphincter muscles are too weak for such sonic indiscretions. They are just as likely to pass gas out their mouths instead. And most birds digest too quickly for any real gas buildup within. But now allow me to play you this particular disaggregated sound that our videos recorded only once."

What Sherman shared sounded to Augie like a loud slurp prolonged a ridiculously long time.

"Slllurrrrrrrppp!!"

"Notice how high the plotline bounced for several seconds? Now I will play you a recording I obtained of a known creature."

The noise Sherman shared next struck Augie as the baby bear version of the Papa Bear slurp. Softer and of shorter duration, it otherwise sounded very similar.

"That," Sherman said, "was an iguana's mushy flatus emission, from eating nothing more than leaves and hibiscus blooms. Probably accompanied by a most watery defecation."

"And you suspect that since the first 'flatus emission' you played for us was far louder and longer, it must have been expelled by a far larger reptile, such as a herbivorous dinosaur?" asked Roberta, by no means dismissive of such a proposition.

"Why can't it have been the saltwater crocodile?" jumped in Stephen before Sherman could answer.

"We actually did unwittingly collect a couple of saltwater crocodile flatus emissions," answered Sherman, unfazed, "if you care to hear them. They are more of the silent-but-deadly variety due to the crocodile's slow digestion of meat. No, Mr. Feldman, Dr. Quiñones has characterized most accurately what I suspect. Either a herbivorous dinosaur made that particular racket we recorded, or there was some other plant-eating reptile out and about, maybe even an iguana, of far larger proportions than the Komodo Dragon."

"So what, in Africa you propose to literally sniff around for a dinosaur like we are dogs sniffing each other's butts?" asked Stephen, equal parts disgusted and amused.

"That is exactly what I propose, in conjunction with Scott MacDonald's cogent plan to trace the mokele-mbembe's migration route until we close in on one from two opposite directions. More listening than sniffing, though; useful air samples would prove impossible to collect. Odors entwine far more inextricably than sounds."

Before Stephen could wisecrack, *I'm not certain this entire project doesn't stink*, Samuel Longbottom burst like a fart made flesh, Augie mused, into Sherman's research lab to say, "Hate to break up this pungent discussion; oh, I've been monitoring it most closely. But Eclipso is waiting on the navigation room videophone to address you on what lies ahead in Cameroon."

Chapter 2

"I couldn't help eavesdropping on your fascinating discussion of flatus-emission data as possible evidence for non-avian dinosaur survival to the present day. And I eavesdropped for quite a long while, indeed, before advising Samuel I require this audience with you," admitted Eclipso Sunray Smith over the navigation room videophone.

Eclipso cut his usual enigmatic presence, where Augie Matias was concerned. How he munched on his bitten-off, humus-drenched pretzel with a certain sluggishness, Augie couldn't help being reminded of a cow ruminating on regurgitated pasture grass. Even stranger was his mother standing at attention behind him, in her frumpily beige flower-print dress. Augie saw her jaws slowly grind away as though she vicariously experienced her son's snack.

"I am reminded of how much the typical dog relies on smell," Eclipso continued after finally swallowing his mushily rendered treat of choice, apparently. "Indeed, the first time I went away to college, my pet cockapoo, Melvin, utterly failed to recognize my voice whenever Mother called me on the phone. Without my spoor to sample with his cute little snout...Oh, Bonsai Gator, must you always become so jealous whenever I mention Melvin? Do you see the look on Bonsai's face, everyone?"

Bonsai Gator was Eclipso's associate alligator, full-grown at the size of a pencil. ("He is my associate, not my pet!" Eclipso sternly lectured Scott MacDowell on a prior occasion when Scott made the egregious mistake of referring to Bonsai as his pet.)

Expedition members aboard the steam-powered transport drone, Cloud Nine, were granted a close-up view of Bonsai Gator via the videophone. He stood incredibly upright on his hind legs beside the miniature swamp embedded in Eclipso's expansive conference table.

"Bonsai is probably thinking wistfully to himself: If only you were several times smaller so I could snap you up like a tasty beetle," deadpanned Stephen Feldman from aboard Cloud Nine.

"No, not at all," Eclipso shook his pudgy head defiantly. "I think Bonsai wants his Beatles reggae music. What's that, Bonsai? The song that contains the lyric, 'How could I dance with another'? Coming right up!"

Eclipso's conference room filled with the reggae-fied opening strains of the early Beatles classic, "I Saw Her Standing There," as performed by the tribute band, Yellow Dubmarine.

Bonsai Gator remained standing still at first. But soon enough, the song's infectious rhythms seemed to travel up his short legs, putting both them and his tail into boogiefied motion. Then "before too long," with eyes closed, he swung his skyward-lifted snout swaying rapturously from side to side.

"I've been on the phone all morning with the assistant secretary to the president of Cameroon," went on Eclipso while Bonsai Gator continued carried away on reggae Beatles in the foreground.

Did it take you that long to convince him you weren't kidding about trying to find a surviving dinosaur? Stephen wanted to ask, but figured he better space out his skeptical snark. Besides which, something else was really getting to him that he'd have to comment on soon.

Meantime, Augie reckoned Eclipso might as well have been a Buddha statue brought to life, and Bonsai Gator one of his followers moved to transcendent ecstasy.

"I've managed to calm some stormy seas, shall we say," Eclipso continued, oblivious to both Augie and Stephen's thoughts. "You see, what is making our search for mokele-mbembe's migration route safe enough to finally embark upon is also what could potentially provide our biggest headache, ironically."

"Sorry, Eclipso," said Stephen, "but my biggest headache at the moment is trying to hear you above that Beatles racket."

"Well you're in luck," said Eclipso, succeeded by a crunch from biting into the humus-lathered pretzel, a crunch that sounded all the louder for the music suddenly cutting off. "Bonsai indicated having your same difficulty. Although, I must warn you his reggae momentum might take several minutes to expire."

Indeed, Bonsai's swooning sway to the expired reggae beat did continue, not yet noticeably abating.

"Funny, Stephen Feldman," said Irene McDowell, raising her chin haughtily high. "I would have thought you would just as soon our discussion of searching for a living dinosaur was drowned out by constantly discharging cannons."

"Well, since your vain quest might nevertheless put my life at considerable risk, I do have a more than passing interest in the details. As for your little gator's persisting gyrations, Eclipso, they do seem the perfect wallpaper for a room where there are people who believe a non-avian dinosaur might still be out and about. Maybe should be a padded room, at that."

"And your attitude is what makes me so sincerely grateful to have you along for the ride, Stephen Feldman," Eclipso gestured with the uneaten portion of his pretzel, his mom standing honor-guard still behind him. "If the evidence for a surviving non-avian dinosaur passes your own smell test, going with the theme introduced by Sherman Peabody, then we can rest most assured we have accomplished at least that portion of our quest."

Had Irene, Augie and company aboard Cloud Nine been endowed with rabbit ears, they would have shot straight up. *"That portion of our quest"??*

Ignoring Eclipso's magnanimous response to his ridicule, Stephen said, "Okay, storehouses full of weapons have mysteriously vanished from near Yaounde, effectively disarming a simmering civil war. Why can't we fly directly to wherever Scott MacDonald thinks we should set up base camp? Can't we avoid dealing with the Cameroonian government and other locals altogether?"

"The same as in New Guinea, Mr. Feldman, public land is at a bare minimum in Cameroon. You could be trekking the most remote, unexplored region of the country. No matter. Some village with its own king, queen, princes and princesses will still be claiming ownership there. On your own, there is no upper limit to the amount of money and resources they might try to extort before allowing you to proceed any further."

While Eclipso appeared to savor another munch on his humus-lathered pretzel, the expedition members looked Scott MacDonald's way since he'd already done a trek to Cameroon. "Sad but true," Scott confirmed. "Try viewing us through the eyes of a Bantu chieftain, though. Here are a bunch of westerners from the land of prior slave ownership, obviously flush with wealth, able to afford chasing after a legend. Whether they're indulging a frivolity or making the find of the century, why shouldn't they, aka us, pay through the nose?"

"Accompanied by armed government security," Eclipso proceeded as though given the perfect segue by Scott, "the cost will leave your nostrils undisturbed since I am covering it."

"*Armed* security?" said Laura.

"Mysterious forces might have once more made off with truckloads of weapons, just as they've been doing for the past century. But the Cameroon people have not yet exhausted their supply from the last successful weapons run. Which brings us to another important point. Practically every citizen of that beautiful country is well aware of guns having essentially been beaten into golf clubs rather than plowshares. And so, it's going to look suspicious enough if any of them happen to notice any of you exit an unusual cloud that has sunk earthward. Add to that seeing you, Alistair, hand out toy golf clubs to their children, and or practice your seven iron shot, and they might conclude, however erroneously, that you all are the weapons thieves."

Alistair Frump's head popped up above the group crowded round the navigation room video phone as though, Augie imagined, he was a prairie dog popping out of the ground. "So no golf treats for the good little girls and boys of Cameroon? Oh well," he sighed in resignation. "Guess I can stifle myself…for now."

Finally settled down from his reggae sway, Bonsai Gator presented on the video phone screen with what Augie sensed was an empathetic regard for frowning Alistair.

"I'll put it this way," said Eclipso. "When I connected with President Booyah's assistant secretary, the first words out of his mouth concerned whether we had anything to do with the stolen weapons supplies. In fact he even suggested we might have absconded with them to make it easier, safer to go after our dinosaurs. To which I said: Imagine we really *were* capable of such an epically proportioned heist. Wouldn't we also be fully capable of extracting an entire family of relic Brachiosaurs from the swamps without anyone ever knowing we were there? I am happy to report that that point was very well taken, indeed. But still..."

Bonsai appeared to nod along, to which Stephen on the Cloud Nine end of the video phone rolled his eyes. At the least provocation, he was more than ready to argue that Bonsai was focused on a teensy gnat or some such, no nodding along about it. Other expedition members might be more suggestible, willing to believe Bonsai was reacting approvingly to Eclipso's report, but whatever. Stephen skipped over this matter entirely, to say, "Okay, then, how exactly is this 'armed security' going to work, to safely chase the mokele-mbembe myth through Cameroon?"

"You mean a myth that fatally poisoned several pygmy fishermen in 1959 when they ate meat from one that was speared to death? I have this on authority from a missionary priest who spoke to one of the few survivors," bristled Scott.

"Speared elephant flesh probably would quickly turn toxic out in a swamp, even were it flame-roasted," countered Stephen.

"I think the people who have lived their whole lives there know the difference between an elephant and whatever that mokele-mbembe is, Mr. Professional Skeptic," Irene addressed Stephen with her chin held regally high, yet again. "Far better than any of us would."

"Hopefully they would also know far better than to believe Bonsai Gator is following this conversation," a flustered Stephen tried unsuccessfully to deadpan.

"Oooooo," other expedition members reacted. *Aren't we getting testy?*

"Okay, you still have loads of time left for verbal swordplay before arrival," said Eclipso, unfazed. "But please allow me to actually answer Mr. Feldman's eminently reasonable question without any further interruption.

"This is how armed security is going to work, as you put it, Stephen Feldman. One group of you will enter the port city of Douala, to purchase bags full of sow-ready beans, corn, peanuts and mango seeds, and twenty chickens."

"Twenty chickens?" Stephen repeated with a cringing face. Where Augie was concerned, Eclipso might as well have just told him he was going to eat something really gross, such as a monkey tail with the fur left on.

"That's more than one for any of us who want them," mused Bernie Coleman whimsically.

"Though in your case, Mr. Feldman," said Irene, "there might be jealous rivalry among the chickens, over who gets you all for herself."

"So rather than a rooster cockfight,-"

"Ladies and gentlemen, please," Eclipso interrupted Stephen's effort to embrace the levity, "if I might finish,-"

Bonsai nodded his snout emphatically.

"-you will be greeted by Peace Corps members in the small town of Rouala near the source of the Dja River. They will take the farming gifts from Douala off your hands. And then you will meet the king of Rouala, and his twin princes who are also soldier guards in the Cameroon army. Those soldier princes will be your armed security. They should prove most adept at defusing any tensions as you explore the speculated mokele-mbembe migration route. They will continue to accompany you, even should you need to cross the border into the Congo Republic as you near the Likouala Swamps."

"Assisting the local Peace Corps with farming projects sounds like a very worthy venture," reacted Stephen. "Have you ever given any thought, Mr. Sunray Smith, to focusing all your energies and apparently vast resources on such an endeavor? That is, rather than frittering away so much on what is more than likely to prove a vain effort?"

Augie perceived Bonsai Gator to have done a double-take, then given Stephen a reproving look through the video phone screen that asked, *What are you talking about??*

"Ah, Mr. Feldman, despite the value I place on your jaded eye, it does grow rather wearisome at times," Eclipso sighed. "But not to make excuses, I am under the impression that all the most generous assistance in the world will not matter one twit if we don't follow through on our quest."

Augie found himself moved to recall what Ambu told him back in London. That while he regarded Eclipso's dinosaur search as doomed to failure, he still believed lots of good could come from it. Augie assumed that native of Papua, New Guinea saw his daughter earning a university education in England as a prime example of such good. But presently, he also had to wonder whether in addition, Ambu appreciated the entertainment value of Eclipso's motley crew engaging in such peculiarities as chasing after dinosaur farts.

"What you're referring to, Eclipso, is Bonsai Gator thinking our dinosaur search is a good idea?" data compiler Harry Letterman fearlessly innocently asked while wife Harriet hooked her arm in his.

Irene mused to herself that Harriet might as well have been trying to prevent Harry from floating up and away like a helium balloon. Keeping him grounded, in other words.

Bonsai Gator appeared to Augie to nod approvingly, to which the ever-observant Harry most definitively nodded approvingly right back.

Stephen could only roll his eyes, as usual.

Augie actually wasn't sure that that "most generous assistance" shouldn't take precedence over the dinosaur search, given so many people's sorry circumstances. Eclipso's enigmatic assertion made no sense to him, that such assistance "will not matter one twit if" they "don't follow through on" their "quest," as much as Augie wanted to continue it, personally. But he wasn't going to chime in with Stephen, as long as nobody else was going to. And he did still bristle at the ever-skeptical Stephen dissing the search as "frittering away so much."

"I have learned to trust Bonsai's judgment in these matters," Eclipso said by oblique way of answering Harry's question.

"Can you tell us a little about how you learned to let a pencil-sized alligator guide your life?" Stephen asked, unable to resist a mocking tone.

"It's personal," Eclipso responded curtly, accompanied by a likewise curt pretzel crunch.

"Okay, so back to this king with his twin princes," said Stephen, deciding to leave bizarre enough alone. "What's to stop them from hoaxing a dinosaur for us? To have us coming back for more? We saw in Papua New Guinea what absurd lengths someone was willing to go to, just to fool us."

"Ahh, but here's the thing, Mr. Feldman. I told President Booyah, in no uncertain terms, that the second half of my generous compensation for their indulgence of our quest is not at all contingent on our success. That is, just so long as your safety is secured throughout the expedition. Whether we succeed in verifying the survival of non-avian dinosaurs in their rainforest basin, or not, my payment to them will not change one iota."

"Here's the other thing, if I might," Sherman Peabody if-I-mighted. "I think we can assume with near absolute certainty that any prospective hoaxers have no idea I'm seeking flatus emission data to corroborate whatever other evidence we might gather."

"To put it more crudely, in other words," said Irene, "no dino-farts, no dino."

"An excellent point indeed, Mr. Peabody," zestfully affirmed Eclipso, to Bonsai Gator's eager-looking nod.

Stephen kept wishing Bonsai would stop doing that. But he nevertheless added, "A point that could cause our princely guards to bust out laughing."

To which Bonsai appeared to shake his head reproachfully, how Stephen wished even more fervently he would stop doing. *Yes, yes, yes, that nuisance of a miniaturized gator is simply eyeing insect prey too minute for us to notice.*

Chapter 3

Curriculum adviser Diane Mueller entered Vicky Copplestone-Matias's classroom at Green Pastures Elementary School the same as always. Her high heels clicked ominously like the monster crab claws in a recent horror film. And her lips puckered like she'd just been sucking on the sourest lemon imaginable. At least those would have been Vicky's descriptions.

Vicky was preparing for a summer school remedial reading and writing class starting late June. She'd just finished posting a large map of Central West Africa beside the chalkboard at the front of her classroom. Diane's noisy arrival saw her turn away from admiring it.

"Vicky, I wanted to run a few possibilities past you," said Diane.

"You know what's going to make this extra special fun for everyone," Vicky half-enthused, half-prattled nervously. Based on past experience, she couldn't help suspect Diane on a quest to prove Vicky incompetent. "Just last week," she bravely proceeded, "a family from Cameroon registered their daughter for fifth grade this fall."

"Oh."

"She's from the northern part where they speak English in the classroom. Political unrest caused numerous disruptions to her fourth grade school year, so her parents want her enrolled in our summer program to make sure she's caught up. When I overheard this, I mentioned my husband working in Cameroon, and that I would weave that into my lessons."

"Mmm-hmm," Diane mm-hmmed. She strained not to explode, appearing merely nonplussed instead.

"Just last night, Augie told me they will be assisting a Peace Corps project. Add that to lowland gorillas, medical plants and of course my husband's cryptozoology research, there are so many topics for our children to investigate. Then with all the insights Giselle – that's her name – might bring to the table..."

"I don't suppose you've checked for any overlap with approved reading materials in the curriculum guide?"

"Descriptive and persuasive writing goals will be a major emphasis, which I understand was the point of those approved materials."

"But how will you assess..." Mueller looked away from Vicky for a sighing pause. Then she resumed in a calculatedly more conciliatory manner, "Look, I really do appreciate that for Jonathan, who none of us could possibly have known..." A brain aneurysm took Jonathan's life only days prior to his conclusion of fifth grade. "His parents claim your class was a positive experience for him, and I have no reason to doubt that. But the fourth grade graduates coming here next week, their parents are sure to be really concerned over reading and writing assessments early this fall. It feels almost too cruel to point out, Vicky, that Jonathan won't be facing any of those."

"Well I intend to tell parents this fall not to sweat standardized exam results," plainly stated Vicky. Even though Diane towered over her in high heels, Vicky's unflinching bluntness came easily for how offensive she found the reference to Jonathan. Diane acknowledging the cruelty of that reference did nothing to mitigate how callous it came off for Vicky.

"'not to sweat standardized exam results,'" Diane repeated with barely contained contempt. "Ms. Copplestone, do you realize-"

"I realize from mountains of research that teacher-made assessments based on what was actually taught yield far more useful data on student academic progress than one-size-fits-all exams. Besides, we never receive results until months later! But I suppose that as long as exam manufacturers make their profits…"

"I guess you're also not too keen on thermometers, and setting 98.6 degrees Fahrenheit as a one-size-fits-all ideal body temperature," said Diane with a smirk as in, Vicky gathered, she thought she'd made a checkmate move.

"Apples and oranges," Vicky nevertheless responded dismissively.

"Mmm-hm; how so?" Diane asked, her smirk sustained.

"A person's temperature is a single, isolated, easily measured and quantifiable characteristic of good health. It enjoys broad consensus regarding the ideal temperature range based on literally centuries of data. Reading and writing competence, however, involves a multiplicity-"

"I really don't have time for this," Diane interrupted, smirk evaporating. "It's really all about the basics. You cannot deny there is broad consensus over what goes into good writing, and evidences excellent reading comprehension."

"But zero consensus the present perfect should be introduced the third week of the second marking period. Or that such grammatical carts should go before the motivating horses, especially with children."

"The basics!" Diane couldn't help shouting in a girlishly hi-pitched voice as she stamped one hi-heeled shoe on the linoleum floor. "Without the basics, students will be at a loss when it comes to all your supposedly compelling content!"

"Without topics that stir genuine interest in reading and writing about them, your basics might as well be fishing equipment for a drained swimming pool," Vicky found herself able to observe calmly, ever more calmly the more agitated Diane became. Probably didn't hurt that Vicky's hubbie, Augie, was receiving an even million just for his participation in Eclipso's expedition. Vicky could be fired on the spot, no hair off her chinny-chin-chin financially.

Diane might have come unglued altogether, removed one shoe to hurl across the classroom in a fit of exasperation. But she forced herself to take a slow, deep, calming breath. Then she scanned the classroom, though unable to help fantasizing a happy wade through translucently emerald, bathtub-calm seas at Paradise Beach in the Bahamas. The multiple learning stations Vicky had already arranged were lost on her. "This really has been a taxing year for both of us," she ended up saying, her version of turning down the heat.

"What happened with Jonathan is still especially upsetting," said Vicky, not averse to a bit of cooling off, herself. "I feel just horrible for his parents."

"Look, Vicky, despite our differences, I know you work hard at what you believe is in the children's best interest. But it has been a long school year, and I could have someone take your place for the summer school session, like that!" She snapped her fingers. "You'd have plenty of time to unwind, maybe take your daughter to Disneyworld, followed by a week at Fort Lauderdale Beach watching the cruise ships go out while sipping on the best strawberry margarita I, um, well, or not, if you'd rather join your husband on one of his expeditions. Whichever, you could decompress, consider whether or not you can keep living with, um, what you really want to do with yourself from here on out."

Vicky Copplestone smiled sympathetically. Would have been too cruel to suggest the curriculum adviser was talking more about her own self. Vicky had heard whispers to the effect all was not well in the Mueller household between Diane and her decades-older husband. Nevertheless, Vicky did pointedly remark, "My heart has always been set on teaching children. As for tagging along with Augie on his cryptozoology quest, I do appreciate your offer. But our daughter would not be safe. And she'd also be too much distraction for the expedition, as much as she would love to join a living dinosaur search."

"'A living dinosaur search,'" Diane sighed.

"But later this summer, once summer school is done, Augie told me he is expecting a multi-week break. That's when we will take Liz to a dolphin research center or some such."

"Okay, well I just thought to spare you from, uh, might throw off reliability if I share with you what we're not telling the others," concluded Diane Mueller with a twisted grin before she spun around on her high heels and click-click-clicked back out the door.

Vicky imagined, from her hubbie Augie's colorful descriptions, Bonsai Gator disdainfully shaking his long snout over Diane Mueller's vague threat. Diane obviously planned to stage some "gotcha" moment. Also, how Diane had loomed over her, thanks to her high heels, left Vicky imagining them both as dinosaurs. Diane would have been a young Tyrannosaurus Rex, perhaps, her sharp stiletto heels in place of that prehistoric creature's rooster-like spurs. And Vicky herself would have been a young duck-billed Trachodon. They would have been hissing at each other until finally the T-Rex attacked.

Well, guess this is progress from old dinosaur days, Vicky told herself. *We've evolved to civilized debate, albeit Diane still plotting to have me removed from the profession. Far better that, though, than her tearing open my stomach with one of her high heels, then feasting on my entrails!*

Chapter 4

"She's back again," Augie couldn't help expressing as a frustrating fact rather than a question.

"So you do know you have a chicken walking beside you?" Laura asked.

Augie, Irene and Scott were returning to Cloud Nine's navigation room after storing away their purchases from Douala. Inside the enormous steam-powered drone's all-purpose room, they left canvas bags full of beans, corn seed, unshelled raw peanuts and mango seeds, plus a cage full of nineteen chickens. Augie reckoned said room was fully half the size of the assembly hall in the public school where Vicky taught.

"I've had all kinds of experience grabbing small dachshunds to clip their nails," said Dr. Roberta Quiñones.

"Please don't grab the chicken," pleaded Augie.

"He's serious," warned Irene. "Take one step towards her, and she'll fly up top Augie's head, and hold onto his scalp for dear life."

"Again," added Augie. "And dig her claws back in."

"We've had to bandage him," nodded Scott.

"Ah, I would expect nothing less from an elf-sized descendant of a theropod dinosaur," said Stephen. "Yes, I know it's a dinosaur survivor of the non-avian variety you're really after."

"So how did she escape from the cage-"

"Twice," Augie interrupted Bernie Coleman's gentle query. "Took us a while to confirm she was actually inside there at the outset."

"We still have no idea how she made her jail break after we locked her back up," said Irene. "It's like she's the Houdini of chickens."

Roberta found herself in a stare-down with the chicken. That fowl's beady eyes seemed to dare Roberta to make even the slightest move her direction.

Ultimately, Roberta turned away, and shut her eyes over the absurdity of having gotten into a stare-down with a chicken in the first place. *It's not as though either one of us wanted to beat the crap out of the other!*

Nevertheless, Roberta's simple motion was all it took to spook the chicken. With a "Buk-buk-BUK!" and frantically flapping wings, she lifted herself just far enough off the ground to alight on Augie's bandaged scalp.

Augie instantly regretted not having thought to find a cap to cover his bandaged head after the earlier incidents, for added protection.

"Buk-buk-buk!" the chicken flapped her wings once more as she settled down on Augie's head like it was an egg she was protectively keeping warm, Irene mused.

"I told you not to try grabbing her!" Augie complained.

"I didn't!" protested Roberta. "Making eye contact must have spooked her, sorry!"

"Maybe she's a mind-reader as well as an escape artist," said Irene. "Your mere thought of grabbing her was provocation enough."

"What puzzles me is why this particular chicken seems so committed to accompanying you, Dr. Matias," Sherman Peabody remarked into his chin. "Maybe your showers have not been thorough enough to remove all traces of Bonsai Gator spoor? So that like a dog sniffing out someone has been around another dog...the chicken is reconnecting with her reptilian ancestry. Anyway, I propose to soak her grain in a bit of tranquillizer. If one of you can direct me to the chicken feed..."

"Got it, Sherman," said Scott, leading Sherman Peabody out of the room.

"I'm really disappointed that chicken hasn't noticed Bonsai Gator spoor on me instead," lamented Harry Letterman.

"I would never allow you in bed with a chicken on your head, dear," Harriet Letterman warned her husband with a lecturing tone.

"I think that's the kind of at-a-minimum, baseline requirement all of us can get behind for our significant others," Irene MacDowell managed to spit out without laughing. "Better be careful, Augie; Vicky might become jealous if she sees you like this. Or wonder whether you have one of the weirdest fetishes, ever."

"She's my voice of reason," said Harry pointing at Harriet standing right beside him.

"And he's my silly boy," Harriet pointed right back. Then she planted a slobbering kiss on Harry's cheek that lasted long enough for Irene to want to remark, *I hope she's not about to go Shakespeare on us, making all the world her bed instead of a stage.*

"Sherman better hurry back soon with that tranquillizer-soaked bird seed," Augie couldn't help whining. "But at least Houdini Chicken is grasping my head where she grasped it before. The bandages are preventing her from digging into my scalp any further."

"How exactly did this happen?" Laura Gómez asked. "A story I can pass along for Tom to use in our *Puffington Post* woo-woo column? Without revealing the rest, of course…"

"Oh, now it's 'our' column?" Irene asked, unable to help trying to embarrass Laura again. She did refrain from commenting on Laura gently fondling her copper bracelet, though. *Are you rubbing that like Aladdin's Lamp, to make Tom magically appear before you?* "Okay," she went on instead, "I suppose you could use an excuse to get back in touch with him, and this should be as good as any. It started in Douala. We were lugging the bags of seeds and grain, plus the cage full of chickens, down to seaside where we docked our cigarette boat."

"At no small cost, of course," Scott interjected.

"Yep, we had to bribe people right and left to leave the boat alone until we returned. Didn't matter that Samuel Longbottom stayed at the helm babysitting while we went into town," detailed Augie.

"Buk-Buk-BUK!"

"I think she's complaining over your ignoring her," deadpanned Stephen.

"Okay, so you were lugging bags of what-all, plus a cage full of chickens…"

"Buk-buk-BUK!" repeated Houdini Chicken firmly settled on Augie's head, even flapping her wings.

"She really must resent not being the constant center of attention," Irene remarked.

"Yeah, please hurry up, Sherman." said Augie forlornly. "Every cluck she makes, I can sense her claws piercing ever deeper through my bandages. Pretty soon…"

"Anyway, we were hustling to rejoin Longbottom," said Scott. "The pervasive scent of roasted local coffee beans did have us wanting to stop for a cup. However, we lost our appetite with all the grilled monkeys and beheaded gabon viper carcasses that crowded tables nearly everywhere we turned."

"That's when I noticed women preparing python stew," continued Irene. "They gave us funny looks. But the real tell something was up was when two guys started following us. They cupped their hands over their mouths like they were trying not to laugh."

"That's when I looked behind me," said Augie, "and saw the grain bag I was hauling sprang a leak. And that a chicken was keeping pace with us, gobbling up the spillage."

"Keeping pace with you rather than with the rest of us," corrected Irene.

On Irene's utterance of that simple word, *us*, Scott got a dreamy look in his eyes. But he did snap out of it quickly enough to add in a timely manner, "At first I wasn't sure whether that chicken escaped from the cage, or was wandering freely about the market. But when I made a move her direction, that's when she hopped on Augie's head."

"By then, the two guys following us had offered to seal the grain bag leak," Augie added, cringing as Houdini Chicken resettled on his head, tightening her grip.

"For a price, of course," said Irene. "They just happened to be carrying the perfect kit for patching grain bag leaks. Was tempted to ask them to show us the tool they used to puncture the bag in the first place."

"Buk-buk-BUK!!"

"Hurry up, Sherman," said Augie through gritted teeth.

"They also offered, for a few dollars more, to provide security the rest of our way back down to the quay," said Scott.

"To protect us from them puncturing more of our bags," snarked Irene.

"They also offered to remove the chicken from my head," said Augie. "But by then Scott had counted nineteen chickens left in the cage, confirming Houdini was one of ours. So I was fine with a delay on dealing with that until we returned to the boat."

"Wait," said Stephen Feldman, hand to forehead as though he had yet another headache, just from following this unusual narrative. "Why so many chickens? The town we are flying out to, did they eat up all the ones they had?"

"Don't know if you noticed something about the cage," which was awkwardly long and rectangular. "Has a collection tray underneath the grillwork where the birds perch," pointed out Scott. "When they poop, their stuff drops in between the grill bars, for later use as fertilizer."

"President Booyah told Eclipso that what little agricultural land the town of Rouala has been able to carve out of nearby jungle swamp is being rapidly depleted, nutrient-wise," added Augie. "They're going to require all the manure these chickens can provide, and more, if they are to have any luck with the seeds we're bringing."

"The peanuts planted around the bean and corn crops should inject nitrogen back into the soil," Irene also added.

"The townspeople will be so grateful for your help, they'll evolve a non-avian dinosaur for you right on the spot if they have to," playfully concluded Stephen. "I think another opportunity for gathering fertilizer you should not overlook is Augie's head."

"Buk-Buk-BUK!!!" Houdini Chicken reacted to Stephen merely glancing her way.

"Oh, but if our feathered escape artist were to take a dump there, why remove it? Mr. Matias's scalp might prove as fertile a location as any for growing corn stalks," gently chuckled Bernie Coleman. "Very good," he went on to compliment himself.

"Buk-Buk-BUK!!"

"Ouch!"

"Ah, looks like I've returned none too soon," Sherman Peabody commented as he rushed to Augie's side with a small metal bowl brimming full of corn meal. "I'd lift this to Ms. Chicken myself, but am guessing you should do the honors, Dr. Matias. She seems enamored of the notion that you are her prime benefactor, that you might as well have been the one who punctured the grain bag to spill a yummy trail for her in the first place. Moreover, she might regard anything offered her by anyone but you with a great deal of suspicion."

"If your wife ever saw this," said Irene while Augie slowly lifted the small bowl towards Houdini Chicken nestled on his head, "she might become awful jealous."

"The last time I tried preparing Vicky a meal," said Augie while to his relief, he could hear the chicken pecking away at the tranquillizer-soaked corn meal, "the boiled eggs came out too watery."

"Hmm, maybe I should take a picture to squeeze a healthy ransom- Oh, forget it; Eclipso is paying us enough already."

Just then, Augie felt Houdini Chicken's tight hold on his scalp totally relax. Next thing he knew, she literally tumbled off his head into his lap.

"You and Elvis, both, really know how to make women swoon," Irene quipped.

That should have been the end of what Augie would have been the first to concede was a minor inconvenience, especially considering the risky adventures that might lie ahead. Houdini's fellow chickens erupted in clucks and fluttery wing-flapping as she was returned to their cage. Yet the tranquilizer proved so potent, their racket wasn't enough to rouse her to even the least groggy extent. Plus, she wasn't merely returned to imprisonment. True to how her namesake used to be bound up for his most amazing, death-defying escapes, Sherman improvised miniature manacles for her legs, and chains for those manacles to the chicken cage grill bars.

All for naught.

The steam-powered, football-field-sized drone, Cloud Nine, quietly made its way inland from Douala towards the source of the Dja River. For any observers at ground level, it looked like an unusualy fast-moving cloud in comparison to the sluggishly lowering overcast that foretold afternoon downpours. Meanwhile, Augie and company on board enjoyed amazing views of numerous swamps and rain forests they passed over. Always so tantalizing for Augie to wonder what marvelously unique, hitherto undiscovered creatures might be wandering about there, directly below his feet. Included foremost, of course, was that long-sought-after surviving non-avian dinosaur. Hopefully the last of its kind wasn't already sold, chopped into bits at some meat market.

These thoughts went for only so long before Augie had the creepy feeling someone was watching the navigation room screen alongside him, someone not a fellow human being. Rather, it wcs a much much smaller creature who had just landed on the end table beside where he sat.

Augustine Matias slowly turned his head towards who also slowly turned her head his way...Houdini Chicken, with not even one of Sherman's improvised manacles left on either leg.

Bernie Coleman said, "Oh my goodness!"

Irene asked, "You know why the chicken crossed the road? To get to Augie's side."

Houdini's "Buk-Buk-BUK!!" concluded with a peck on Augie's cheek.

Chapter 5

"So none of our videos reveal how Houdini Chicken made her most impressive escape, yet," remarked Sherman, his chin scrunched against his Adam's Apple in extra-contemplative mode.

"I for one made the not-unreasonable assumption that manacled to the cage, she couldn't possibly achieve such a feat," said Bernie in his typically soft voice. "I really didn't think we needed to monitor her every move."

Stephen rolled his eyes in head-shaking frustration over how Houdini Chicken, settled on the end table beside where Augie Matias sat, gave every appearance of following the conversation as attentively as anyone. "Of course, we're assuming one of us didn't secretively liberate her," he still managed to speculate.

"A saboteur in our midst," said Irene melodramatically, arching a suspicion-laden eyebrow. "Augie, for instance," she went on like some detective solving a murder mystery, Augie mused despite being made the target of accusation. "Do not think it went unnoticed back in New Guinea, your version of pretending to have gone under the betelnut's hallucinatory influence."

"He did flap his arms and bob his head about like a chicken, didn't he?" chimed in Scott.

"Maybe Houdini Chicken offered to slip him an egg or two on the side," Stephen couldn't help adding.

"Look, people, this is ridiculous," complained Roberta while beside her, Laura Gómez scribbled furiously fast in her notebook. "For the cigarette boat ride back out to Cloud Nine from Douala, there were only four of you. Correct?"

"Correct," Samuel nodded.

"Samuel, of necessity your attention was fully focused on the steering the boat."

"Correct again."

"Irene, Scott, and you, Augie, presumably were focused on- Well who was in charge of the chicken cage? Didn't Houdini Chicken make her second jail break halfway back to Cloud Nine?"

"That's when we noticed her landing on Augie's head," said Irene. "And yes, I was in charge of the cage. But I was also busy locking my eyes on various objects around the harbor to keep from becoming seasick." *And Scott was busy sneaking googly eyes at me.*

"The motor boat bounced across the surf like a skipping stone or bucking bronco, it seemed," said Scott. "So with the seed bags piled one atop the other, my full, uh, most of my attention was on keeping the top bag from sliding off into the harbor."

"I have to admit my mind having strayed from the matter at hand," said Augie, "despite the turbulent ride Scott so accurately portrayed. I wondered what Vicky and Liz were up to back home. Had we lost a bag or the cage, even, overboard, I would have had to share a big part of the blame."

"Alright, I confess," deadpanned Stephen. "I hid myself at the bottom of the cigarette boat, waiting for just the right moment when everyone else was distracted. That's when I liberated Houdini Chicken, to make her legend grow. No, not really."

"So we're saying Houdini Chicken is some other-worldly kind of escape artist," concluded Dr. Roberta Quiñones with a frustration she couldn't hide. How many times had her significant other pretended a paranormal phenomenon was to blame for the mess made by one of their too-numerous dogs?

"My pet hamster was also an escape artist," Harry noted. "I thought he had only one way out of his cage: the top. But even heavy books piled there didn't stop him."

"But that's not really the same thing is it, dearie?" asked Harriet rhetorically, gently patting Harry's hand to take some of her sting out. "You didn't ever chain one of his little legs to his cage, did you?"

"She explains reality to me," Harry waved towards Harriet, yet again as though he was introducing her to everyone for the first time.

"And he entertains me," Harriet waved right back.

"None of you happened to notice any golf clubs left in place of Houdini Chicken, small enough for a chicken to use? No? I suppose that is a silly question," conceded Alistair Frump, feeling a barrage of withering looks.

"The real question is whether we try to imprison our avian escape artist anew," Sherman spoke into his chin, making eye contact with no one. "Or whether, instead, our Mr. Matias should keep her by his side when we are received by the king of Rouala."

"Imprisoning Houdini Chicken again runs the risk she will barge in on that meeting with the king to most disruptive effect," dispassionately observed Samuel Longbottom.

"Think about when President Roosevelt met with Churchill and other European leaders at Yalta, to confer over next moves after the weapons for what was building towards world war suddenly vanished," said Stephen. "The last thing they would have needed would have been a chicken landing on someone's head."

"Maybe we package Houdini as our mascot!" Alistair said with a snap of his fingers and a slap of his hands. "Doesn't that make sense, since we all acknowledge birds evolved from theropod dinosaurs?"

Augie turned Houdini Chicken's way, to ponder her as some latter-day, more compact, feathered Allosaurus. And he wished she didn't turn his way the exact same time, like they were somehow in tune, simpatico with each other.

"I almost hate to bring Eclipso into this," said Irene. "But I think we should alert him to this Houdini Chicken business. Whatever he advises, we go with that. Then, if Augie's clucking stalker still causes grief, at least we avoid blame."

"Agreed," said Stephen. "I don't want to hear Eclipso complain, 'Well, if it wasn't for that chicken, you would have already discovered a living non-avian dinosaur.'"

*

"I call your attention to issue 47 of the original *Turok Son of Stone*," said Eclipso Sunray Smith over the videophone. He'd just made a show of leafing through a thick-bound volume of comic books like he was some scholar consulting a highly-revered, centuries-old text, Augie imagined. "In the story, 'Outcasts of the Flood,' Turok's presumed nephew, Andar, easily befriends an eagle-sized long-necked theropod dinosaur. That dinosaur not only proceeds to warn Turok and Andar of imminent danger; he ultimately sacrifices his life for them. Initially, Turok was not too keen on Andar having a pet dinosaur, no matter its small size. He ultimately had to concede, however, that that decision saved their lives."

"The word of Turok, Amen," Stephen couldn't help snarking.

"There's a name for what it sounds like has happened with your so-called 'Houdini Chicken,'" Eclipso went on to gesture like Augie remembered one of his college professors gesturing. On this occasion, though, it was with a half-eaten, humus-dipped pretzel rather than an unlit pipe. "Imprinting. Essentially, Dr. Mctias, the leaking grain bag in your wake has led her to believe you want to keep her well-fed, like you are her mother. In fact, she probably does feel you actually are her mother."

"Well that's something, Augie," Irene managed to say without snickering. "At least when she looks at you, she isn't expecting you to jump her for fertilizing her eggs."

"What I take from the *Turok* story," went on Eclipso, oblivious to snickers the other end of the videophone over Irene's remark, "is that your so-called 'Houdini Chicken' might yet benefit us in ways not currently anticipated nor understood. But there's something important to remember, as surely as what Turok warned Andar to remember whenever a dinosaur seemed too chummy. At the end of the day, your Houdini is not at all human. So don't ever expect to be able to reason with her.

"Ah, what's that, Bonsai? I believe Bonsai says he is in the mood for more Beatles reggae. Mother, please put on, 'She Loves You'; I think its particular beat should prove the perfect accompaniment to his current snout and foreleg motions."

"He's raised irony to a high art form," Stephen muttered under his breath while Augie realized Bonsai was eyeing Houdini Chicken over the videophone.

Houdini Chicken remained oblivious to Bonsai, watchful instead for sudden moves by anyone in her immediate vicinity as she strutted her ruffled-feather stuff. She never knew when someone might make a sudden grab for her.

Meanwhile, the pencil-sized, biped-standing gator had taken to flapping his forelegs and bobbing his head, clearly imitating Houdini Chicken.

"She loves you, yeah, yeah, yeah..."

*

"So I understand you have had previous dealings with this King Payasoboo?" Augie mumbled at Scott as the king's two royal princes, brothers presumably, led them, Irene, Stephen, Alistair, Laura and Sherman down a red-clay path towards downtown Rouala, Cameroon.

Mumbling, moving his mouth as little as possible, served Augie two purposes. He hoped to sneak his question under the princes' radar. And the less mouth motion when Houdini Chicken was mounted on his head, the better. In other words, the less that bird tried digging her sharp talons through his protectively deployed shower cap.

"My father is like the dog in that wise old Cameroonian proverb," Prince Englebert looked back at Augie to say, so much for Augie's effort to make his question about the king for Scott's ears only. "Do not step on his tail, and he will not bite you."

"King Payasoboo is an interesting man," said the other prince, Prince Angelbert, in what Augie found a curiously detached assessment. "Which I am certain he will waste no time making clear to you."

Meanwhile, chief adviser Camounui, who looked to Augie like he could have been Englebert's twin brother, added, "For as long back as I remember, King Payasoboo has insisted on speaking French only. He's left the rest of us to assure he is understood in English, Bantu dialects, et cetera."

"My minimally functional French received quite the workout from him," Scott finally answered Augie, loud enough for general consumption. "But I always found the king eminently reasonable. He never ran any of the bribery scams like we've had to navigate so far. Still can't get over that guy in Douala extorting us to plug the hole he or someone with him punctured into our grain bag."

"My father is like Kumba in that wise old Cameroonian proverb: Tiko drink, Kumba drunk," said Englebert. Despite him and his fellow prince carrying small machine guns slung over their backs, Irene wasn't able to completely stifle a chuckle over his umpteenth proverb. So he added, affecting a most severe tone, "It means he feels so much for others, he could never steal from them...or laugh at them."

Irene's countenance turned fearful, melting Prince Englebert's fierce regard into a wry, happy-eyed smile as he added, "But he is also not adverse to playing the occasional practical joke, *mais oui?*"

"Oui," nodded Scott, red-faced over sudden concern Englebert might be able to see through him to his crush on Irene.

Earlier, a fog bank of Cloud Nine's own steam-powered making concealed it from view while landing in a clearing outside Rouala. Then Scott and company emerged most dramatically from its persisting, billowing mists like they'd magically materialized there.

Houdini Chicken had already long since been spooked on purpose into mounting Augie's head. Better that, than risk her making another of her impossible escapes to seriously disrupt sensitive negotiations with the locals. The away team needed approval for a dinosaur search of waterways the locals claimed to own, starting with the Dja River.

"What makes her so special, she does not need to join her sisters cooped up in that cage?" King's adviser Camounui asked in a curiously resentful-sounding tone. Later on, Augie found himself oddly imagining Camounui as one of those "sisters" himself, full of jealous resentment. *To rewrite the Kumba proverb: Tiko Chicken imprisoned, Kumba Fox resentful that Houdini Chicken goes free.*

"As a descendant of certain meat-eating dinosaurs," Irene was quick to answer, having long since conjured a response to the expected question about the chicken on

Augie's head, "she serves as mascot for our living dinosaur search."

"She should be served as your dinner instead, mais oui. But as that wise old Cameroonian proverb goes," said Prince Englebert, lending Augie a sympathetic regard, "every man has his own kettle."

"Meaning burden," clarified Camounui, "but a mascot is not a burden, n'est pa? Any mascot I have ever known has been regarded as a pleasure to be responsible for carrying along, mais oui monsieur?"

"Correct," Augie mumbled, in his continuing effort to move his mouth the minimal amount, given how easily Houdini Chicken could be spooked into hanging onto his scalp that much more painfully tightly.

Prince Englebert's Cameroonian proverb shtick soon became an irritating nuisance. Fellow Prince Angelbert and adviser Camounui helped expedition members lug the seeds, grain and chicken cage over to the clearing set aside for delivering farm supplies to Peace Corps volunteers, who in turn distributed them more generally. But then right in front of volunteers Jeffrey and Susan, Englebert said, "I am reminded of that wise old Cameroonian saying: Only offer to the orphan what has gone bad."

"C'mon man!" Camounui complained in Englebert's face, prince or no prince, while Augie continued to be struck by how much they looked like twin brothers. "They just paid good money for all these 't'ngs' in Douala! None of it would have gone bad!"

"Well we have an expression too," said Jeffrey as he grabbed one of the seed bags. "Beggars can't be choosers. And begging is the position we find ourselves in. We are very thankful, whatever the condition of your offerings."

Presently, the two princes and Camounui led Augie and company on a mud-packed, red-clay trail leading directly into the village of Rouala, lined by crowded food and clothes stalls.

No mystery for Augie who King Payasoboo was; up ahead sat a man topped by a beaded red cap, and wearing robes adorned with some of the brightest "pagne" designs he'd seen yet. They were more than a match for the yellow, brown, purple and red stripes of the robes worn by the princes. Lime-green squiggles crisscrossed angles and circles like so many prowling snakes, Augie would have said.

King Payasoboo occupied a wooden throne, three-toed claws carved into its front legs, and - But before Augie could take in much else, said king shouted at them, *"Tourne le dos pour m'approcher! Tourne le dos pour m'approacher!"*

"'Turn your back to approach me' is what he's ordering," said Scott as he already obliged.

"This is true," confirmed Camounui.

"Buk-Buk-BUK!" Houdini Chicken clucked with a commotion of flapping wings, protesting how quickly Augie spun around.

"Is this different from when you were here before?" Irene asked Scott under cover of the ruckus from villagers laughing at and commenting on the chicken camped on Augie's head.

"Had to do the same thing then. Nothing different."

"And you didn't think to give us a heads up?"

Scott couldn't bring himself to say he forgot all about it, as that would have been a lie. But he was spared any response at all by Englebert interjecting, "We have a saying about mokele-mbembe: The river god can approach man, but man cannot approach the river god. A similar 'ting' applies to my father: King Payasoboo can approach anyone he likes, head on, but all visitors must back towards him until he says they may turn around."

"Tu dois aussi remuer tes lesses en t'approchant de moi!"

"Now what is the king shouting?" Irene asked Scott.

To Scott's relief, Camounui answered for him, "King Payasoboo says you must also wiggle your butts to approach him."

Stephen Feldman wanted to suggest Sherman should have no problem butt wiggling. That is, after all his practice swaying in the expressed hope, one day, to thereby hypnotize a dinosaur out of chasing them.

Irene wanted to exclaim, *You've got to be kidding!*

But the princes wielded small machine guns at the ready as they scrutinized expedition members' efforts to butt wiggle while walking backwards. That stifled any pushback from Stephen or Irene.

When the king shouted in French at the away team again, Camounui translated, "He complains you are not wiggling your butts with enough fervor."

The market-goers had been delightedly chuckling to one another in various Bantu and other local dialects. But they suddenly grew very quiet.

The resultant tense silence inspired Augie and company to butt wiggle like their lives depenced on it.

"Arrêtez! Arrêtez!" shouted the king.

"He wants you to cease all activity at once," advised Camounui, "aside of course from standing and breathing."

Oh-oh; if he was not pleased by our butt wiggles, Irene worried, *what is he going to have done to us? Can't tell from the expression on Scott's face whether he's ready to cry, or bust out laughing. Either way, if we make it out of this situation alive, I'll kill him!*

Even the ever-present birds stopped chirping. And King Payasoboo's exhalation sounded to Augie as forceful as he imagined a T-Rex's exhalation would have sounded, on the hunt. Finally, however, the king engaged Camounui in hushed conversation.

"He asked Camounui about the chicken on your head," Scott whispered. "Camounui explained about it being our mascot."

"Turn around and face me! All of you!" was how King Payasoboo's next exclamations translated according to Camounui.

After another unnervingly long silence, King Payasoboo pointed at Houdini Chicken and said in a most severe tone what Scott translated as, "That chicken on your head..."

Oh-oh, worried Augie, *have I offended him coming here with Houdini Chicken like this? Does he feel mocked?*

"...she should have been wiggling her butt as well! Especially since she didn't even clothe it for this solemn occasion! She's lucky I'm not going to feast on her!"

Once Scott finished translating from French, Augie and company thought the king must be kidding around. But the severe countenance remained on his face while his royal subjects remained blank-expression hushed...

...until he couldn't stand it any longer, and exploded with laughter. In fact, King Payasoboo even rose from his ornately carved mahogany throne to twirl around stamping his sandaled feet in ecstatic amusement.

The locals laughed in a manner that struck Augie as their being genuinely amused, while his own ha-has were more relief than anything else. And he noticed Irene giving Scott a most severe glare.

"So you knew this was going to be some big hardy-har-har at our expense, Mr. MacDonald?" Irene asked in an accusatory tone. "Again, why couldn't you have given us a heads up?"

"There is the whole matter of tickles," Camounui translated for the king, adding in a confidentially low voice, "He understands far more English than he permits himself to speak."

"There is also what we learned from a wise old Cameroonian proverb: It is far easier to take advantage of the sweet potato than the taro root," Prince Englebert quickly added. "You people on your dinosaur search are like the sweet potato that has been roasting for hours; very soft indeed," he concluded, making eyes at Irene,

Who bristled, "So is there a wise old Cameroonian proverb for those who recite too many wise old Cameroonian proverbs? For example: Those who speak in proverbs might find their mouths stuffed with coconut husk?"

Prince Englebert looked down ct his small machine gun, then up again at Irene, more puzzled-looking than threatening.

"About those tickles," interposed Stephen, especially anxious to defuse any further tension given the weapons brandished by the two princes.

Before he could go on, though, Camounui announced, "Our king asks you to attempt something he had your Mr. MacDonald try on his first visit to our village."

"Okay," said Stephen, taking the situation in stride.

"Try to tickle yourselves. Now!"

Expedition members looked to one another as in: Who's going to tickle who?

"Tickle your own self, not another," Camounui clarified.

Augie and company obliged, Augie self-conscious of maybe looking like a chimpanzee as he went at his belly and armpits to no actually ticklish effect, as expected.

King Payasoboo strained to curtail his resultant booming laughter to say, as Camounui ever-reliably translated, "You see? You cannot tickle your own self. And yet your vain effort tickles me even without your making any physical contact with me. There is also your fear what I might do to you, or have someone else do to you, after I had you approach me backwards wiggling your behinds. That tickled me as well. But had *Monsieur* MacDonald there given you any forewarning, that would have been a bad 'ting.' Pretending not to already know would have been drowned out by the looks on your faces shouting that you do know, indeed. And then my fun would have been less, so much less that I am not sure I could have allowed you to use the source of the Dja River for resuming your dinosaur quest. You see, ladies and gentlemen, I live for the tickles.

"Observe those talons carved into my throne's legs, and many-headed snake carved into the backrest. Had I carved those myself, they could not have delighted me, tickled me, anything close to how they have entertained me, carved by someone else. That is the way of the universe, and incidentally proof of God's existence. We could never have tickled ourselves into existence how God has tickled us into existence."

"Before we forget," said Scott absentmindedly as he handed over a bag full of cockle shells and bean beads.

"Ah!" King Payasoboo let out a clipped exclamation, eyes grown wide, when he peeked inside the bag. Looking up he went on, as Camounui translated, "You see? Any such shells and beans I harvested for my own self could not have tickled and delighted me nearly as much, if at all, as those you have just gifted me. In that same spirit, I will await being tickled by any results of your latest expedition."

"As that wise old Cameroonian proverb goes," said Prince Englebert, giving Irene a defiant look in tandem with giving his machine gun an emphatic shake, "If everyone dances, who watches?"

"Excuse me, your highness." Alistair stepped forward to say, pausing for Camounui to translate into French. "Might golf clubs, golf balls, and your own golf course set up alongside the Dja River, might those tickle you also?"

King Payasoboo gave Alistair a stern regard just long enough to make him cringe. Whereupon, a smile slowly stole across the king's face as he finally answered, translated by Camounui, "Perhaps, but not nearly as much as Madamoiselle Chicky on Mr. Sweet Potato's head here continues to tickle me."

"Buk-buk-BUK!!" clucked Houdini Chicken over Payasoboo's eyes having settled on her.

"Very well, then," Camounui had King Payasoboo having said next. "I sense you are anxious to put your expedition underway, to continue Monsieur MacDonald's search for a living dinosaur, a dinosaur whose flesh has not yet left its bones, an endeavor that also tickles me no end. But first you must accept a special insistence by my princes who will be accompanying you.

"We are well aware of the mysterious disappearance of warehouses full of weapons meant for distribution to conflicts all around Central West Africa. So it should not tickle you in the least to learn that when we first noticed your cloud-concealed aircraft descend just outside our village, we had to wonder. Did you not have a hand in the weapons confiscation? And I must say, Monsieur Whoever-You-Are," he looked upon Alistair again, "that your talk of golf equipment, plus transforming part of our land into a golf course, certainly raises extra questions along that line, ticklish questions indeed. Is it mere astounding coincidence, the multitude of golf equipment left in place of weapons, as though a civil war could be fought with nine irons and three woods?"

"Ah, so you do know something about the game," said Alistair feigning upbeat engagement, versus the nervousness he still felt. "Listen, I only wish I could tell you how all those clubs and balls got there. At least then, I could have coordinated that with my Lost World Golf Links plans. In fact, I am curious to see how those mysteriously gifted clubs compare to our latest state-of-the-art masterpieces. I'm assuming if any known brand names were involved, that would have gotten out by now."

"*Bien*," Camounui left not translated from King Payasoboo's resumed exposition of his non-negotiable requirement, "if what you say is true, you should have no problem accommodating my princes searching the interior of your cloud-cloaked aircraft."

"But first," said Prince Englebert, handing off his gun to Camounui, "would *Monsieur* Sweet Potato like me to have *Madamoiselle* Chicken finally rejoin her friends in the cage you left with those Peace Corps volunteers?"

"Please be my guest," agreed Augie, though thinking to himself, *Rots of ruck!*

Most surprisingly where Augie was concerned, when Prince Englebert made a grab for Houdini Chicken, she didn't flap her wings furiously and cluck like crazy to fend him off. Rather, she quietly settled comfortably, it seemed, into his large gentle hands. Although, she did give Augie what he couldn't help intuiting was a look of betrayal.

Englebert only took two steps away from Augie with the unexpectedly acquiescent Houdini Chicken before he ground to a halt and said, "I do not know what is going on with this particular chicken. But whatever it is seems to have something to do with you, *Monsieur*," he nodded at

Augie. "I am reminded, whether you like it or not, of another wise old Cameroonian proverb, in its most literal sense: A bird that allows itself to be caught will find a way of escaping. So I am going to spare this creature from having to once again return to your side by whatever means possible, *Monsieur*, whether natural or supernatural. And do not deny that would not be the first time!"

Prince Englebert returned Houdini to her perch on Augie's shower-capped head, where with what struck Scott as a most regal-looking ruffle of her feathers, she settled back in for the long haul.

Meanwhile, Sherman Peabody found himself wondering, *To repurpose that proverb, will a dinosaur that allows itself to be seen by us also find a way to escape our proving it was seen?*

"Now show us the way into your cloud craft," Prince Englebert motioned as he re-slung his machine gun strap over one shoulder. "We will follow you."

Colorfully attired well-wishers lined the narrow red-clay path Augie and company trod on the way back to Cloud Nine. Some pointed at Houdini Chicken while Augie imagined her regally waving a wing from side to side, as though she was the queen of England.

In short order, Eclipso's away team flanked by the armed princes reached a clearing of matted-down swamp grass. There, a fog bank continued to be shed by Cloud Nine hovering mere inches off the ground with an amazingly soft whooshing noise, like it could have been the quietest clothes washer Augie had ever heard.

That's when Sherman leading the way halted their progress, to turn around and say, "If I might, Prince Angelbert and Prince Englebert: I don't think the folks on board our drone away from home are going to be comfortable with those machine guns on board. Are they really necessary? Any compelling reason they can't be left behind with Camounui while you conduct your search of our premises?"

"We will not be comfortable without them, you see," bristled Englebert.

On a more diplomatic note, Prince Angelbert added, "This really should not be a problem, especially assuming you have nothing to hide."

Apart from common sense, perhaps, but I'm not sure we have any of that to hide, Stephen refrained from saying.

"Well okay, then," Sherman seemed to Irene as usual to address his belly more than anything or anyone else, for how he kept his chin scrunched into his neck. "Unless another of my fellow expedition folk would rather do the honors, let me say that inside this fog bank, we are going to encounter the airlock to our steam-powered vessel. However, it is not large enough to accommodate all of us at once."

"Wait," Englebert gestured with his machine gun, "why do you need an airlock? We are not underwater or in outer space. And why does your vessel become engulfed by the very steam it generates? This never used to happen with steam-powered locomotives."

"That is true," Sherman readily conceded. "However, the amount of moisture our four-cornered drone must draw upon from the surrounding atmosphere is vast, so vast. It has to be, just to remain hovering a foot off the ground as it is at the moment, and also to keep it comfortably cool and dry inside. And it remains engulfed in this foggy fuss even when in flight, as you could see when we landed. Too much of that moisture let inside could damage some of our more sensitive data-collecting devices, as well as counteract the air conditioning I referred to. That's the reason for the airlock.

"But as I was about to say, we need to break up into two separate groups. If you like, us expeditionary team members could enter first."

"Oh no, man," Englebert laughed, tossing his head back. "Then you fly off without us. What I propose instead is that one of us enters with half your group, and the other enters with the other half."

"I suppose that would also work."

*

Harriet and Harry Letterman, Bernie Coleman, Dr. Roberta Quiñones and Samuel Longbottom all heard the airlock hiss. That caused them to look up from poring over a river system map speckled by bright green thumbtacks. Each thumbtack represented a mokele-mbembe sighting from the last fifty years.

As Prince Angelbert preceded the first group into the steam-powered drone, his gun at the ready, the Lettermans clung to one another apprehensively.

Roberta gripped Samuel's shoulder, Samuel seated beside her at the table where the map was spread out.

"Allow me to introduce Prince Angelbert and Prince Englebert," said Sherman. His chin still ever scrunched into his neck, looked to Irene like he was introducing them to his navel rather than the team members seated round the map. "They are here for a bit of a search, to make sure we're not the ones who made off from Yaounde with all those mysteriously vanished armaments we heard about."

In another wing-flapping commotion, Houdini Chicken leaped to the floor off Augie's head. She might as well have just gotten off at her bus stop, Bernie Coleman mused.

Both princes turned slowly around, eyeing the navigation room with awe, until Prince Angelbert left to look elsewhere on board.

"What is that map about?" Engelbert asked, motioning at it with his gun.

"You see," Bernie Coleman ventured in his always-gentle voice, "Mr. Scott MacDonald over there-"

Scott waved a here-I-am hand.

"-entertains an intriguing hypothesis about a certain beast some of your locals call mokele-mbembe-"

"One who stops the flow of rivers," Englebert inserted. "From our Lingale Bantu dialect, although other locals have other names for it in other dialects; yes, I have heard of it."

"Well, yes, most interesting," said Bernie, anxious not to lose the thread of his narrative. "So Mr. MacDonald's hypothesis is that these creatures, whatever they might be, actually follow a particular migration route along thousands of miles of Central West African rivers. If we could only discover that route, we could also locate where these creatures are at any particular time."

"My husband and I documented more sightings to the north in spring and early summer," said Harriet. Her interest in supplementing Bernie's remarks emboldened her to rise above fear of the prince's machine gun.

"And more sightings to the south in late summer and early fall," continued Harry Letterman like his wife handed him a relay baton.

"The dry season runs from late fall through early winter," said Scott. "So it seems these creatures are on the move during the rainy season. Might go back millions of years to when there was more savannah here than anything else, and the dry season was much drier."

"This strange aircraft is huge," Prince Angelbert broke in, having returned to the navigation room from snooping about Cloud Nine. He felt no need to segue from what he heard Scott explaining. "I did locate a closet full of golf clubs and golf balls. No sign of any military equipment, though. And for certain, *certainement*, there is not nearly the room available on board to have stored away warehouses full of tanks and guns. '

"With your expressed interest in hunting for dinosaurs," chimed in Prince Englebert, "I mean, why as thieves would you return to the scene of your crime so soon afterwards? And risk detection?"

"Does that mean you two can leave us to get back to try proving a negative?" Stephen asked, unable to help his snark.

"As that wise old Cameroonian proverb goes, When you ask the question, you cannot avoid the answer," said Englebert ominously.

Less ominously, though, and more diplomatically, Prince Angelbert proceeded, "We never actually expected to find you having had anything to do with that massive trade-out of weapons for golf clubs and solar panels. What we are really here about is this: Around the time of the epic theft, military radar in Yaounde spotted a UFO that made a steep, perhaps crashing descent well northeast of here, into part of the Central African Republic." Letting go his machine gun, allowing it to swing freely from its strap round his shoulder, Angelbert produced and unfolded a map from amidst his colorfully designed robes. "Best as we can determine," he went on, pointing, "it touched ground here, along the edge of a feature named Lake Tele."

Harriet and Harry Letterman turned to each other excitedly, and Harriet said, "Lake Tele?"

"Where there have been so many mokele-mbembe sightings!" exclaimed Harry in his always-hoarse-sounding voice.

Harriet and Harry slapped one another a hi-five.

"You can see where we marked them on this map," said Harriet. She lifted it, and pointed at certain bright-green thumbtacks.

"They go back over a century," observed Bernie Coleman.

"Mostly from early to late summer," said Harry.

"You see?" said Englebert turning to Angelbert. "This is an entire aircraft full of sweet potatoes."

"Whether we are sweet potatoes or harvested legendary Mandrake Roots, for that matter," said Augie Matias, "so what if-"

"Buk-buk-BUK!!" Houdini Chicken interrupted.

Laura and others sensed Augie's indomitable avian sidekick saying, in her own special way, *Shut up, and stop drawing so much dangerous attention to yourself!*

"I think what Mr. Matias wanted to ask was what you plan on doing if you discover that UFO had something to do with the weapons theft," said Irene. "Of course, I'm assuming you want us to fly there to check it out."

"You assume correctly," confirmed Prince Angelbert.

"As for what we plan on doing," continued Englebert, "we have yet another Cameroonian proverb: What happens to fresh cocoa happens to dry cocoa."

"Which means…?" asked Stephen somewhat wearily.

"Hopefully we will have the pleasure of showing you," said Angelbert trying to sound upbeat.

"But what if we were to have no particular interest in learning what that proverb means, and simply said 'No'?" asked Samuel Longbottom, to the relief of Irene and Stephen not wanting to carry the burden of pushback all on their own.

"'No' is not really an option, you see," answered Prince Englebert testily, brandishing his machine gun.

"Please, E-bert," said Angelbert. "There is no need to threaten them."

"But look at them!" protested "E-bert." "They really are sweet potatoes, feeling so easily endangered!"

"So what if, as Mr. Longbottom here suggested, us sweet potatoes really are not interested in learning what happens to either the fresh cocoa or the dry cocoa?" Stephen asked.

"Please, people," pleaded Angelbert wanting to remain amiable. "We really don't want to need to shoot you."

"Very well," said Samuel. "Shoot me, shoot Sherman here, and you have exactly no one left who knows how to fly this thing."

"Ahh, but if we shoot this young lady over here," Prince Englebert swung around his machine gun to aim it at Laura. Along the way, he swept it past Augie, seemingly prompting Houdini Chicken to leap in front of Augie, and go, "Buk-Buk-BUK!!" at the prince as though to warn him off.

Stephen could only roll his eyes over anyone actually believing that was what Houdini Chicken was actually up to.

Just then, Prince Englebert's cell phone went off, and he quickly flipped it open from a robe pocket. Past his initial *"Bonjour?"* and without Camounui aboard to translate, Augie and company could make little sense of the conversation. Not even Scott, as the prince spoke mostly in a Bantu dialect this time.

However, the sense was of Englebert having to assure someone the other end that something was being handled in an appropriate manner.

No sooner was this call ended than Englebert's phone rang a second time. But that conversation sounded more routine.

"Please, people," Prince Angelbert took the opportunity presented by the phone call interruption to reboot the conversation. "Simply cooperate with our investigating what transpired with that UFO. Perhaps it will turn out to have been nothing. And then we promise full cooperation resuming your dinosaur expedition."

"One way or another," Irene grumble-whispered Scott, "I'm going to have a word with Eclipso for putting us in this situation."

Chapter 6

Over her six years at Green Pastures Elementary School, Vicky Copplestone-Matias learned something unpleasant about curriculum specialist Diane Mueller. Whenever Diane approached her with a big smirk on her powdery pale face, she was invariably up to no good.

So it transpired this particular time. Vicky was tidying her classroom after her morning summer school session, before she would retrieve daughter Elizabeth from daycare.

Diane's smirk teetered on the edge of stifled laughter, like she might tumble there any second. "Ms. Copplestone," she said with a severity she absolutely delighted in conveying, "there is a parent here to see you urgently. And given the nature of one of his many concerns, I've taken the liberty of inviting Mark Waltzer to join us."

*

"Ms. Copplestone," Giselle's father, Peter George, made a point of standing to say. He welcomed Vicky into the conference room with a slight bow, adjacent to the front office viewable through a panoramic window.

Vicky's heart did flip-flops; Giselle was her new student from Cameroon, West Africa, where her hubbie continued the search for a living, non-avian dinosaur.

Giselle's father was dressed in a dark woolen suit, uncomfortably warm-looking for late June; Vicky didn't think the school air conditioning made the indoor temperature *that* cool.

Diane led Vicky to sit directly across the conference table from Giselle's father, herself intent on sitting beside him.

Already seated with Peter George was the ESOL teacher, teacher of English for Speakers of Other Languages, Mark Waltzer. Mark gave Vicky his usual eyebrow raise which always struck her as part-flirtatious, part *well-here-we-are-with-who-knows-what-the-powers-that-be-will-throw-at-us-next.*

"I really don't mind Mr. Waltzer's presence," said Vicky, buttoning her blouse's top button. "But I didn't think Giselle required any ESOL support."

"She doesn't," confirmed Diane. "Part of what Giselle's father told me definitely touched on ESOL, though."

"In addition to my other concerns I didn't get to explain to Ms. Mueller before she called you here," clarified Peter George in his very deep voice.

Vicky's heart flip-flopped all over again. *You really don't need this job,* she reminded herself to try settling down. *I can always do volunteer tutoring.*

"That's quite alright, Mr. George," Diane said to Peter George in one of the happier voices Vicky had ever heard her employ.

"I'm so glad you agree," said Peter turning to Diane, finally seated beside him. "Because I do truly believe it is best for me to share what I have to say directly with Ms. Copplestone. Although I am sorry my wife could not excuse herself from a World Bank meeting to join us, as I know she would have loved to have been here."

Diane gave Peter George a reassuring pat on his table-resting hand as she said in her most sympathetic voice, "I am sure you will do an excellent job on her behalf."

"I don't doubt that either," chimed in Mark seated to Mr. George's other side.

"So shall I?"

"Please, Mr. George," insisted Diane, thereafter turning away, once more trying to keep her smirk from devolving into a chortle. "We are all ears."

"Thank you, Ms. Mueller. Ms. Copplestone, there is something that must be admitted directly up front, with absolutely no hesitancy whatsoever. When our Giselle came home two days ago from her first session in your summer school program, my wife and I met what she had to report with the most profound concern imaginable," stated Giselle's father, Peter George, with one of the stronger British accents Vicky had ever heard. "The bit about your husband working in Cameroon was clearly neither here nor there. You already told me as much when we registered our daughter here. But according to Giselle, you announced he was on an expedition in search of a living dinosaur. And moreover, that all your summer school reading and writing activities pertain to his search, including occasional live feeds from the African rainforest...Well I'm not sure the word, appalled, does proper justice to how my wife and I reacted, on several different levels."

Diane Mueller made a strange noise she covered her mouth to suppress.

Vicky gathered there otherwise would have been an all-out giggle.

"Excuse me," Diane said. "Something caught in my throat."

"Might I secure you a cup of water from over there?" gallantly asked Peter, pointing out the panoramic window at a water cooler in the front office.

"No, no, I'm fine. You go on ahead."

"Very well, then. Going on ahead, indeed, we worried this dinosaur search might paint ugly pictures of our fellow Cameroonians, scurrying about in loincloths, pursued by prehistoric beasts. We found that prospect awful enough."

Diane took notes at a furious pace. That kept her giggle reflex under control, watching Vicky receive the ultimate comeuppance, Vicky figured.

"But there was also the crucial question: How were reading and writing activities about a dinosaur search going to bring our Giselle up to snuff? The answer did not look promising."

"Um...," ummed Vicky, raising her hand.

"Let him finish," Diane lectured Vicky.

"Yes, Ms. Mueller is correct," sternly advised Peter. "You most definitely *will* want me to finish. Now in addition to the issues I've already raised, there was also this disturbing matter, Ms. Copplestone, of your not keeping proper control over our daughter. You see, she can be very headstrong at times. Well, she told us that when she wanted to teach your entire class a few phrases in French and Bantu, you simply said she could go ahead. And even more time was run off the clock, allowing another of your students, I believe her name is Myriam..."

"Myriam Ramirez, she's one of mine learning English as a second language," interjected Mark Waltzer.

"Well there you go. Apparently Myriam was allowed to teach a few Spanish phrases."

"And practicing Spanish is not exactly what Myriam needs the most at this particular moment," Mark interjected anew.

Diane refrained from lecturing Mark to let Mr. George finish like she lectured Vicky, to which Vicky was not insensible.

Curiously, however, Peter George gave Mark a look that, if Vicky didn't know better, conveyed being nonplussed. And he said, "Well I suppose you would know more about that than I do.

"In any event, debriefing our daughter left me feeling I must come here yesterday, Ms. Copplestone, to object to your methodology in the very strongest manner, in no uncertain terms. If possible, I was going to have our Giselle transferred out of your classroom into a sounder pedagogical environment."

"But you gave it an extra day for reflection," Diane suggested, smirkier than ever where Vicky was concerned.

"My wife counseled that we not act too precipitously," Peter nodded. "I'm so very glad we waited. When Giselle started telling us about her second day of Ms. Copplestone's class, my initial reaction was: Good God, is this like in that Shakespeare play when someone cries, 'This is not the worst when we can still say: This is the worst'?"

"I don't want to interrupt," said Diane, maybe a little less smirk, "but can we sum up Giselle's second day in Ms. Copplestone's class like this: You were left even more bothered than after her first day?"

"That was precisely the situation... initially. Our Giselle fairly burst through the door, to announce she'd seen a photo of your husband, Ms. Copplestone, with a chicken on his head. And that she and Myriam had proceeded to teach French and Spanish, and Bantu, for 'The chicken is on the head.' *Le poulet est sur la tête*,' for example. And that they got even sillier, about the chicken under the foot, in the mouth...Anyway, it would seem there's a chicken in Cameroon with a special affinity for your husband, Ms. Copplestone."

"Houdini Chicken, as she's also an escape artist," Vicky nodded knowingly. "I should be jealous, but she'll tire of him quickly after she sees the messes he makes."

"Yes, very good," laughed Peter George. But then like the power just went out, the expression on his face turned remarkably grim for going on, "You cannot imagine how angry we grew after that, Ms. Copplestone, to hear of the video you played your students."

"A video you say, Mr. George?" Diane asked perkily. *What damning new evidence might THIS be??*

"Indeed I do say, Ms. Mueller! A video Ms. Copplestone's husband produced, of one of his fellow expedition members explaining in great detail the flatus emissions produced by various animals!"

"'Flatus emissions'?"

"Farts, Ms. Mueller. Farts."

"Oh," Diane reacted as she resumed her furious note-taking, the full smirk returning to her countenance.

"Frog farts, iguana farts, even lightning bug farts: Our daughter could describe them all. She also described breathlessly how this Mr. Peabody planned on listening for dinosaur farts in aide of actually tracking one down. A dinosaur, that is. Not a dinosaur fart, although I suppose they'd go hand in, um, whatever. You can't imagine how absolutely appalled my wife and I found ourselves, initially!'"

"Well Mr. George," said Diane in her happy voice, despite wanting to convey deep solemnity, "this certainly does sound like a matter of the gravest-"

"But if you will, Ms. Mueller, I am not quite finished yet. There remains for me to elucidate the most important aspect of all."

"Do go on, then, please."

"Thank you. And so, we had this business of various 'flatus emissions' enumerated in the cause of an absolutely absurd expedition! My wife and I thought: This should be the very last thing for remediating students in preparation for their next school year. And that was that for us. We sent Giselle to her room while we discussed our plan of action, as there was no reason to bother her with such details. But on her departure, we realized there was one last piece of information we required. There was one last what we expected to be that bonus nail in a damning coffin, that special reassurance we were on the right track. In short, we resolvec to examine what was inside Giselle's backpack after her first two days of summer school.

"Together, we entered Giselle's bedroom, intent on exploring every last nook and cranny of her backpack. We might as well have been security agents for a museum, about to go through tourists' purses and bags, checking for explosives and the like.

"Well imagine our surprise when we found Giselle at her desk, writing away furiously on a notepad like we'd never seen her write before! My wife took the liberty of stopping her, to take a look at what so consumed our Giselle with such passion, if you will.

"Reading through Giselle's journal was a real eye opener, as they say. Indeed, that experience forced us to totally recalibrate everything we were thinking about your pedagogical style, Ms. Copplestone. Yes, at the moment we entered, Giselle was busily describing at length the peculiar quality of flatus emissions made by lightning bugs. But there was far more she wrote before that: a stunning revelation, one must admit."

"Umm-"

"Please, Ms. Mueller, let's allow Mr. George to finish," Vicky jumped in before Diane could proceed any further with her interruption.

"Thank you, Ms. Copplestone...in more ways than one. What our Giselle wrote about prior to the lightning bug flatus emissions was a Peace Ccrps project assisted by your husband's expedition, is that correct?"

"Innovative farming techniques that replenish soil nutrients, for example using chicken litter as fertilizer," confirmed Vicky. "Although my husband's new friend seems more interested in making his mop top suitable for growing, oh, I don't know, maybe Brussels sprouts?"

"Very good, Ms. Copplestone," chuckled Peter George, his demeanor considerably relaxed from how he first entered the conference room. "But here's the best part of all: Our Giselle expressed on paper a growing interest in learning enough agriculture to return to Cameroon and mount what she termed 'a big campaign to rejuvenate farm soil across the country, from north to south.'"

"That's wonderful!" enthused Vicky.

"Good stuff," nodded Mark with an approving, how-about-that frown. "Using a word like 'rejuvenate' at her age, wow!"

Diane Mueller merely looked aside, scratching at the nape of her neck.

"Thinking further, Ms. Copplestone, many other positive benefits occurred to us that might well accrue from your unique education approach. Yes, one might quibble that revolving a fourth-grade-level remedial class around a search for living dinosaurs is foolishly irresponsible. But the multiplicity of themes that arise during such an endeavor…"

"The space program led so many different directions for breakthroughs in medicine and other aspects of everyday life," agreed Vicky. "I think about it like that. Of course, those breakthroughs complement the myriad gifts we've already been receiving from heaven-knows-who in exchange for mysteriously confiscated weapons."

"Exactly!"

"But-But weren't you saying, Mr. Waltzer, that children teaching one another Spanish and French was not exactly helping poor Myriam catch up on her English?" Diane asked, in one last-ditch effort to steer the dialogue back towards a severe critique of Vicky Copplestone's instruction.

"Well I was thinking about that as well," barged in Peter George, leaving Mark Waltzer with his mouth hanging uselessly wide open. "And it occured to me: What better way to encourage children's education than to promote them teaching each other?"

"In fact," chimed in Vicky, "there's lots of research strongly suggestive the best way for anyone at any age to memorize something is to share it with someone else."

"You know," said Peter like he was confiding a secret to Vicky, nobody else around, "there are certain topics always bound to capture any child's attention and imagination. Animal flatus emissions? I must confess having been personally most fascinated and amused to learn from our Giselle how fireflies synchronize their farts with their sexual activity!" he ended up chuckling. "To summarize, Ms. Copplestone, my wife and I want to thank you so much, not simply for warmly welcoming Giselle to your class, which is no small thing in and of its self! You've made her proud to be from Cameroon, and in just two days inspired her to do more writing than we'd seen her do the previous two months! We can only imagine how you will benefit her over the coming weeks. So as a small token of our already high esteem for you, I should like-"

Diane rose abruptly to her feet, and muttered, "Well, I'm glad you've been able to sort things out." Darting an if-looks-could-kill glare Vicky's way, she added, "We will see how matters develop over the coming weeks," before storming out of the conference room on her ever-clicking high heels.

To Peter's worried look, Vicky explained, "Ms. Mueller really does have a lot on her plate." *She'd far rather be nursing a strawberry marguerita in the Bahamas.*

Mark Waltzer nodded along.

"To not keep you any longer from your own busy schedule, Ms. Copplestone, my wife and I just wanted you to have this special Cameroonian belt. You wrap it twice around your waist, and tie it in front."

"This is beautiful!" exclaimed Vicky, standing to follow Peter's advice for wearing the belt. "Giselle's clothing is always so very colorful like this!" she went on to rhapsodize over the belt's cheery bright orange-yellow and burgundy, with black outlines. "Is this what Giselle termed 'pagne' about her clothes' designs?"

"She's teaching you well," said Peter while Mark comically shielded his eyes like the belt's colors were blinding him, though remarking, "Wow! That looks very becoming on her!"

Peter darted his eyes quizzically from Vicky to Mark and back again, and said, "I better allow you to resume whatever you are doing."

"Maybe if Giselle can forget enough English, she can also join my ESOL class," Mark called after Peter George. But Peter did not acknowledge him, kept his back turned away to continue walking out.

"So Augie has been off on this dinosaur expedition for how long?" Mark asked Vicky.

"Long enough," she laughed. "The good news for me is: Whether or not they succeed in Cameroon, he said their ringleader is insisting they take a break the first few weeks of August. That's when we've promised our daughter Liz a dolphin experience in the Florida Keys."

"Well she should love that. Say," Mark went on like it just occurred to him, rather than having been rehearsed mentally over the past several days. "I'm stopping at Starfinkles for an espresso on my way home. Care to tag along?"

"Thank you, but I need to pick up Liz from day care for her piano lessons," Vicky responded firmly. She wanted her tone to convey innocent distraction by her daily routine, while concealing her distaste for what she suspected the guy was about.

"She could join us after her lesson. Think the place serves ice cream. Does her piano instructor allow an audience?"

"There is no 'us,'" Vicky couldn t help snapping as she turned to leave.

"O-kay," said Mark like Vicky's reaction was completely unwarranted. "Uh, by the way, you really do need to keep Giselle from teaching Myriam any more French, with all the catching-up she still needs to do in English."

"Myriam has already started writing some interesting things in her journal. In English. I'll see if she'd like to share them with you."

"You do that." *Soon enough I'll have you begging for me.*

Chapter 7

"Okay, guys," said Sergeant Fred Frankly, setting aside his 3-D goggles. "Not sure I haven't finished watching every super-hero movie of the last fifty years. So to hell with the risk of extreme redundancy I don't really give a fried fish about. I'm asking for the thousand and umpteenth time: Just how much longer are we going to sit here and wait before we finally take matters into our own hands? Isn't the food going to run out soon?"

"Even worse," responded Officer Kevin Smith-Park, beyond uncomfortable strapped back into his chair at the shuttle pod control console. Kevin once again found himself sitting tilted to one side at a ninety degree angle. But this was the only way he knew how to periodically check on the tear-drop-shaped shuttle pod's steadily deteriorating condition.

If only whatever-it-was would stop nesting atop the hybrid air and space vehicle, as it had been doing for weeks after rolling it partway over. Opening the airlock exit, moved to the ceiling by the partial rollover, might reveal its belly...or a monstrous reptilian head ready to pillage the shuttle pod for the first body it could sink its teeth into.

"Our solar cells are about to run out," went on Kevin. "Sat on by who-knows-what in this lakeside swamp, they're denied access to the necessary sunlight."

"You're still guessing 'who-knows-what' is a relic prehistoric monster, Ali? Jesus Pachycephalosaurus Christ!"

"I don't know any hippo, elephant, or other creature large enough to have treated us like an egg, and sat on us for so long," counselor Ali Magabu responded. "Unless maybe there's some monstrously proportioned turtle roaming these West African swamps."

"Well whatever," grumbled Kevin, "once our solar power runs out, so does our air conditioning, not to mention shower room mists."

"And it's not like you've been running the ventilation on frigid," said Fred.

"To extend how long we can endure these conditions until we are rescued, or wake up on a new timeline," testily explained Kevin for what seemed to him the thousandth time.

"Those scented mists are so piss-poor for keeping us clean and refreshed," complained Fred. "I'll bet you a bag full of Chris's chocolate chip cookies that once we return aboard the Smoke and Mirrors, we'll realize just how bad we actually stink, even if the rest of the crew doesn't pass out."

"That wouldn't surprise me," agreed Ali. "But what are you saying, Kevin? Is it finally time to take a chance on opening the airlock?"

"I believe it is. Like you said, Sergeant, it's not simply about avoiding suffocation. It's also about our food running out. We need to gather fruit and nuts, whatever we can find out there. At least our data base on wilderness edibles will be helpful, so we don't accidentally poison ourselves."

"As I've mentioned before," said Ali, then found himself paralyzed by the sheer ridiculousness of reiterating that. He, Fred and Kevin had been cooped up for weeks on end inside the shuttle pod, ever since the auto-pilot crash-landed it on the edge of a lake, Lake Tele, rather than the Sahara Desert dune on which they'd originally planned. The quantum wave put Kevin asleep before he could finish loading in the desired coordinates. So there was really nothing left for any of them to mention not already mentioned before.

"Okay," Ali finally went on, "let's say our presumed prehistoric monster is instinctively treating our shuttle pod as its adopted egg. When the airlock opens, it's likely to react as though the egg is hatching. So shouldn't it move aside at that point, give the next generation a chance to pop out, not suffocate?"

"Not necessarily, Maggybu," Fred shook his head. "That rhythmic thing it was doing to the shuttle pod after we first woke up, sure did feel like it was getting jiggy rather than providing maternal incubation."

"So she rested atop her mate for weeks afterwards, the world's longest afterglow?" Kevin asked, just like he asked days ago when Fred made the same point.

"Actually," said Ali, this time something brand new for a change having occurred to him, "alligators can sleep days on end after a meal. Wouldn't that fact make it not the most unbelievable thing in the world, truly, if dinosaurs wallowed one atop the other for weeks after intercourse?"

"Well Jesus Mamasaurus Christ!" exclaimed Fred. "So you really and truly believe some prehistoric monster is sitting up there, right over our heads? This is a question that bears all kinds of repeating!"

The shuttle pod suddenly lurched violently, throwing Fred and Ali off their feet. There was a screeching noise from the pod's stressed hull that grew so intensely shrill, Ali and Kevin felt nauseous.

"We need to leave now, or we might be entombed here forever!" Kevin shouted above continued screeching and loud thumps as he hurriedly unbuckled himself from the cockpit.

"Don't forget to grab your backpacks, gentlemen!" Ali added while securing his own.

"The pod has rolled partway back to upright! When we open the airlock to outside, swamp water is probably going to pour in!!" Kevin warned as he braced himself against handholds to open the airlock manually since its electronics weren't working.

"Something must be going on with whatever has been sitting on us!" shouted Fred. "Damn! Wish we had a firefly donut or some other means to see exactly what's outside! I mean, apart from a bunch of muck suspended in swamp water!"

"Our mystery beast might be feeling restless!" Ali speculated. "So we must hang on tight when you open the outside airlock, Kevin! As that is truly liable to rile it even more!"

"Unless it's simply some huge-ass log that a sudden surge of lake water is rolling about!" said Kevin, desperate to posit some more prosaic explanation for what entrapped the shuttle pod than a sedentary prehistoric monster. "Now be ready to dive through the exit if water floods in!"

"Or not, if we're facing a dinosaur belly!" Ali added. "Either way I'll have my camcorder on, strapped to my headband!"

"3...2...1!" Kevin counted down.

The outer exit started to slide open.

At first, the airlock remained dry, not even a trickle from outside. But as the exit widened, there was a sudden gush of sulfurous-smelling, peat-infused, diarrhea-brown swamp water. Accompanying that was a tremendous lurching-about of the shuttle pod, plus the deepest, loudest groan the time travelers from Earth's future had ever heard.

Clearly produced by some beast, Ali was certain. Aided by light finally from outside the shuttle pod, he did spot a massive, pale, lime-green-tinted surface lift away from the airlock exit. *A sauropod dinosaur's whale-sized belly?* He had to wonder.

Ali, Fred, and Kevin scrambled their way out of the shuttle pod against swamp water gushing in. Ali as the last one out experienced the worst of it. He found himself totally submersed, disoriented, unsure which way was up, taking him back to when he was a kid in Alexandria, Egypt, and rough surf tossed him head over heels.

Fred pulled Ali to the surface, towards squishy swampland, to escape the water trying to suck him back inside the shuttle pod.

All three time travelers were safe from drowning, if mired in mud. They could afford looking up to realize they were caught in a tropical rainforest downpour, one of those daily mid-afternoon events at Lake Tele.

"You see there?!?!" Ali shouted and pointed through the soaking torrents. "That large shape moving off?!"

"Not sure what I'm looking at there, Maggybu!" Fred responded.

SPLLLUURRRRRRRRRRRP!!!

"What the fried fish was THAT?!?!" Fred shouted.

"If I didn't know better, I'd say it sounded like a truly behemoth flatus emission!" shouted Ali, awestruck.

"Are you talking about a *fart*, Ali??" Kevin asked incredulously.

Before Ali could answer,

"Ewwwwww!!" went Kevin, holding his soaking wet nose. "I thought it was supposed to be 'silent but deadly,' not 'noisy and putrid'!"

"So what the- You actually think a dinosaur fart is what's stinkin' up this joint?!?! I mean what the hell!!"

"There is that especially wet quality to the sound, Sergeant," said Ali Magabu, no longer having to shout since the rainforest downpour had already subsided. As blazing hot sun re-emerged in deep blue sky featuring fluffy cumulus, he continued, "Reminds me of when I watched an iguana fart. Only this was thunderously louder."

"Are you sure some kind of weird local thunder didn't accompany the downpour?" Sergeant Fred Frankly asked. "I'm not."

"But what about this truly amazing stench?"

"Could have drifted over here from a nearby elephant herd for all we know, Maggybu," Fred dismissively suggested.

"Either way, time we move to more solid ground," said Kevin. He couldn't help noticing his boots were already sunk ankle deep in the swamp mud. At first he found this comfortingly anchoring, especially with the whirlpool nearby from water gushing into the submerged shuttle pod. But as he kept sinking…

"Um, I'm truly having a bit of trouble lifting either my left or right foot out of this muck," noted Ali, trying to keep his cool. "If one of you guys…"

"Cripes, I'm having the same issue here!" Fred shouted, not caring whether or not he kept his growing panic under wraps.

"Afraid that makes all three of us," admitted Kevin.

"So what, now we're going to drown in quicksand?!" shouted Fred. "I repeat: Jesus Pachycephalosaurus Christ!!"

"First thing we need to do is lighten our load. I suggest we toss our backpacks at that more solid-looking ground near those cycads," said Kevin still trying to remain calm.

"Wait; if any of you are carrying a rope in your backpack…" Ali said hopefully, though horrified over how he had sunk down almost to his knees.

"Yeah, Maggyboo, let me see if I can find a rope in here, hidden underneath the ladder, shovel, wheel barrow, and lawn mower," muttered Fred. He held his own backpack up high while struggling frantically to lift just one leg out of the muck that was inexorably if slowly sucking him downwards.

"Actually, I do carry a special cable during spacewalks in case I or anyone else drifts off untethered," said Kevin as he tossed his backpack towards shore. "So Ali's question isn't that outrageous. But you need to stop fighting the quicksand so much, Freddy. You're just accelerating the suction."

"It sucks, alright!" complained Fred as he tossed his backpack the same place as Kevin's.

Both bags practically disappeared into the swamp grass where for all the time travelers knew, more quicksand awaited.

"So this is how it ends?" Fred continued complaining. "After all that other crazy shit we've survived?"

"It's important to focus on an escape plan," Ali counseled. His voice cracked, though, over grieving fear of his own possibly imminent demise, without even a last goodbye to Tanya. "With strong enough string we might have lassoed that cycad, or that small palm, to pull ourselves out. But I realized this too late, tossed my backpack too soon. Anyway, in case some puddle-jumper passes overhead, we ought to activate one of our com-device lasers, and one only, so if it runs out before-"

"Already done, Ali," interrupted Kevin. "See that?" He motioned skywards with his right hand, where he'd securely bound his special laser beam device.

A distinct red circle moved across a fluffy cumulus cloud, in sync with Kevin's hand motion.

"Okay," said Sergeant Frankly grateful for the distraction, however fleeting, from dread. "And I've just activated a repeating SOS signal on multiple band widths."

"Then we simply wait, gentlemen, remaining as still as possible," advised Ali.

"But this probably is how it ends," Fred came back to emphasizing, "drowning in muck the middle of nowhere, eighty years in the past, after for all we know the last living dinosaur fart on us. Shit!"

"What was that?" whispered Kevin, right after a distinct rustle from a bamboo stand near shore.

"Oh, shit again!" cussed Fred anew. He noticed long, spindly legs emerge from between two bamboo stalks. "Jesus Arachnoid Christ, I thought we left the monster spiders back on Fafama!"

A spider with torso segments the size of two coconuts, furry brown, and with legs each several feet long climbed out from amidst the bamboo stand. It raced from side to side across the shoreline swamp grass. Clearly, the three humans down to their upper hips in the quicksand had it all hot and bothered.

"Truly fascinating, that the 'ch-bah foo-fee' is real," commented Ali. His marvel at the creature temporarily superseded his terror over his quicksand-imprisoning circumstances.

"The 'shake-ah yah boo-ty'?" Sergeant Frankly mockingly mispronounced the creature's name.

"My parents shared this Bantu legend when I was a child. They said the 'ch-bah foo-fee' would get me if I didn't go to sleep. Not exactly the most successful tactic, as that kept me wide awake even later, constantly checking under my bed. But as I grew older, I realized the physics of exoskeleton anatomy- Oh, I see; the way its abdomen inflates and deflates as it respires, its shell must be plenty thin enough to successfully lug about."

"Guess it's a good thing none of us did have, or keep, a rope or something to sling across to there," said Kevin. "It would have easily made its way over to us."

"Oh, that makes me feel so much f-n' better!" cussed Fred, beyond spooked by how the ch-bah foo-fee appeared to have all eight of its eyes peeled on him while it scurried excitedly side to side across the swamp grass.

Suddenly, though, just as Ali, Kevin, and Fred sank nearly up to their waists, the giant spider froze. Then it had a stare-down with Kevin, and shot a web filament at him that sailed all the way across the intervening swampland, alighting on his shoulder. When the ch-bah foo-fee subsequently gave that line a tug, it nearly made Kevin fall face-down into the peaty quicksand.

Chapter 8

Were the three time travelers not so preoccupied with being up to their waists in quicksand, and under siege by a giant spider, they might have noticed something peculiar overhead.

As sunlight broke through after the daily downpour, a rectangular-shaped cloud floated the opposite direction from all the fat, fluffy cumulous fleeing the scene, and came to a hovering halt.

"I see exactly where that laser beam emanates from," announced pilot Samuel Longbottom from the cockpit of the steam-powered drone, Cloud Nine. "A chap directly below us, he and two others are in a spot of trouble. They're rather stuck in swamp muck, quicksand perhaps, and are entangled as well in something I can't quite make out. No wonder they're waving their arms about so frantically. And- Check that out: Not far from them, a silvery dome, the top of- Well there it goes, sunk out of sight!"

Significant looks were exchanged all around, including by Houdini Chicken presently perched on Augie's shoulder.

"It can't be we've found what happened to those vanished weapons, just like you princes were hoping for, can it?" Scott asked Prince Angelbert and Prince Englebert, their machine guns ever at the ready.

"If it is, we're looking at the answer to a decades-old mystery," Sherman Peabody seemed to Augie to tell his belly, the way he kept his chin tucked into his neck, surprise surprise.

"So that swamp just finished swallowing up a warehouse-full of military hardware? Highly unlikely," Stephen Feldman shook his head.

"Hold the presses!" exclaimed Irene, raising up her hand as in, *Stop*. "You're expressing skepticism over something that would be utterly amazing if true? I'm shocked!"

"What's far more likely," said Stephen, undaunted by Irene's snark, "is that a small biplane crash-landed there. Those three people struggling in that muck are the survivors, who we should concern ourselves with rescuing sooner rather than later."

Augie found himself looking at Houdini Chicken on his shoulder, the same time Houdini Chicken looked his way. On a lark he asked, "What do you think, H.C.?"

"H.C." didn't make a sound, but she did bob her head even more than usual.

"Looks like she's feeling the r-e-s-p-e-c-t over simply being asked, Mr. Matias," Irene commented.

"That's ridiculous," scoffed Stephen.

"Actually, this would have been the perfect time for filming, sending a film feed to my wife's summer school class," said Augie. "Alas, those guns you keep aimed at us…"

"I don't see that as a problem at all," Prince Englebert reacted in his very deepest voice. "The odds have turned vanishingly small we will have to shoot anyone here."

"But it's not a good look…"

Angelbert lectured Englebert in French. Something to the effect of, Scott MacDonald figured out with his limited French, *You can be so dense at times, you know that?*

The tone reminded Scott of his mom lecturing his dad, way back when.

"Well," said Irene still addressing Augie, "maybe for your wife's class, you could pass off our princes as security guards for Houdini Chicken."

"Ladies and gentlemen," spoke Samuel as mild-manneredly as he could, given his growing impatience, "like Mr. Feldman indicated, we better attend to rescuing those three hapless creatures out there sooner rather than later."

"Well what do I see there, *mon Dieu!*" exclaimed Prince Englebert. He even lowered his machine gun aside to point at the view-screen transmission from Cloud Nine's underbelly.

"Phew!" whistled Prince Angelbert. "Ch-bah foo-fee; I wasn't sure any were left. That large spider, ladies and gentlemen, the last known sighting I'm aware of was from the early days of my great grandfather."

"Was he a prince also?" asked Harry Letterman while Stephen squinted his eyes nearly shut.

Out the corner of Augie's eye, Stephen appeared to be in distress. And out the corner only; no way could Augie help being transfixed by the creature on the transmission screen moving manically fast from side to side. It did indeed appear to be some unusually large spider, seen from so far off the ground, even taking into account the camcorder's magnification.

"Wait," Stephen said finally. "Are you sure that isn't just a regular-sized spider, or even a small one, crawling across the camcorder lens?"

"So tell me this, *monsieur*," said Prince Englebert. "The last time you were robbed, did you convince yourself you were never in possession of the stolen items in the first place?"

"I've never been robbed."

"*Mon Dieu!* Your state of denial is even more profound than I imagined!"

"Bertois!" Angelbert shouted reprovingly at Englebert.

*

Prince Englebert, Sherman, Scott, and Irene climbed down out of Cloud Nine's oddly rectangular fog bank extra quietly. They tested the ground's firmness between cycad and palm tree before letting go the rope ladder. As they hoped, the spider named ch-bah foo-fee in Bantu lore didn't pay them the least attention. But they weren't so keen on how it launched, cast out a new steel-strong web filament at the quicksand-bound strangers.

"What is it you're going to do with Spidersaurus there?" Irene whispered to Prince Englebert.

"Sh! You will see soon enough," Prince Englebert whispered harshly as in a crouch, he crept up on the running-about, web-launching ch-bah foo-fee.

"Help!" cried Kevin, noticing the new arrivals.

"Help us, please!" cried Ali, ever politely.

"Yeah, help! Okay?! I got it! Help us, you f-ers!" complained Fred over Scott making circular hand motions for the three men to keep calling out.

As hoped for, Fred and company's frantic sounds distracted the spider from noticing Prince Englebert creeping ever closer.

Meanwhile, Sherman Peabody stood aside, carefully monitoring wiggly graph lines on the noise sensor he hauled along.

But back to the time travelers, none of them needed any further encouragement to keep crying out for rescue. All three had sunk down to their armpits in the quicksand, in addition to their heads becoming increasingly entangled in spider web.

Prince Englebert made his big move just when the time travelers' predicament looked most dire. With a leap, he grabbed hold of the ch-bah foo-fee's abdomen.

From where he was sinking ever deeper, Ali was reminded of a soccer goalie holding a caught ball to his chest.

Anyway, the prince proceeded to play his fingers with lightning speed across bristly hairs on the giant spider's mouth. That caused it to roll itself into a big ball, legs and all, which the prince cupped in cne arm. Then he turned round and round until finally letting go the creature like he was throwing an oversized discus.

The curled-up spider sailed through the steamy jungle air, and on its descent skimmed the water like a skipping stone until with one, unceremonious plop, it splashed sinking below the surface of Lake Tele.

"He would have shattered to pieces had he fallen on solid ground," explained Prince Englebert. "And do not worry; in water he can safely swim away, rowing his legs like oars."

"What exactly did you do to him?" Scott asked in such shock, he was practically oblivious to the increasingly frantic nearby cries, the worsening plight of Ali and company.

"I simply tickled his mouth until he curled up in his futile effort to stop me."

"How did you know where it was ticklish, or that it was even ticklish in the first place?" asked Irene.

"Every creature is ticklish, *mademoiselle*," chuckled Prince Englebert. "I made an educated guess where the ch-bah foo-fee's tickle zone is, and so you see..."

"Excuse me, people," said Sherman, though making no least effort at eye contact with anyone. Rather, he remained intently focused on his recording device's brightly lit display screen monitor, his chin continuing tucked firmly into his neck. "I've teased out a most interesting noise from amidst all the cries for help..."

"Cries for help?!?!" Fred Frankly screamed. "You mean like this?: HELLLLLLP, YOU M-F-ERS!!!!! HELLLPP!!!"

"But you see, I think that for one fleeting instant, we might have recorded the flatus emission from one of our target beasties, headed that way," Sherman pointed. "Roughly south, southwest."

"'Flatus emission'?" Prince Englebert repeated, puzzled.

"Popularly referred to in our common parlance as a fart."

"Ohhh," Englebert nodded knowingly. "A fart; well that is a very ticklish subject, indeed."

"HEY?!?!? WE'D ALL BE EXTREMELY TICKLED HERE IF YOU'D FINISH RESCUING US!!! OR EVEN BEGIN!!!" complained Fred in full-on panic. "WE'RE ALMOST UP TO OUR NECKS IN THIS SWAMP MUCK NOW!!! CAN'T KEEP OUR ARMS RAISED MUCH LONGER!!!"

"Sorry this took so long," apologized Samuel Longbottom, grabbing Fred's wrists from a rope ladder. It was one of three rope ladders that dropped down out of Cloud Nine's fogbank without the hapless time travelers noticing them, or the oddly rectangular-shaped cloud that had lowered to within a mere fifteen feet over their heads.

"What?!?" Fred complained anew, though allowing Samuel to tightly lock his lower arms into rope ladder straps. "Are we already dead, and this is how we're going to ascend to heaven?! Jesus Ridiculous CHRIST!!"

"Oh-oh. UMM, MR. LONGBOTTOM?!?!" Irene cried out to Samuel.

Samuel was already leaping from the ladder for Fred to Ali's intended ladder, to strap him there.

"UMM, I THINK THAT WOLF-SIZED SPIDER IS ABOUT TO FLING MORE WEBBING FROM OUT ON THE LAKE!!"

Irene pointed offshore to where a tangle of palm fronds, swamp grass and even a few embedded coconuts and fruits was moving swiftly closer. Only, there were no humans paddling it along. Instead, the ch-bah foo-fee Prince Englebert hurled into the lake was using its rear legs as oars. And it had lifted its pincer-fronted visage for its eight eyes to enjoy a better look at the prey it had yet to give up on.

"WHAT IS THE MATTER WITH YOU, *MONSIEUR* CH-BAH FOO-FEE?!?!" Prince Englebert shouted at the steadily approaching oversized spider. "HAVE YOU FORGOTTEN ALREADY ABOUT THESE?!?!" He waved his hands high over his head, rapidly moving his fingers like he'd done to tickle the creature into rolling itself into a ball.

Prince Englebert's display clearly did grab the ch-bah foo-fee's attention, to the hoped-for effect. Abruptly, the ch-bah foo-fee reversed its improvised raft's course, though still keeping a wary eight eyes on the prince.

By then, the last of the three time travelers, Officer Kevin Smith-Park of the starship, Smoke and Mirrors, had been pulled free of the quicksand. Covered in a grimy brown, sulfur-fetid layer of the stuff, he disappeared on a rope ladder up into the fog bank generated by Cloud Nine.

*

"We have a simple question for you," Prince Englebert said to Kevin, Ali, and Fred on their returning via rope ladder into Cloud Nine, eschewing any formal introductions yet.

Ali Magabu gushed, regardless, "We cannot thank you enough, whoever you are, for securing our rescue. Oh," he added, finally noticing Prince Angelbert's small yet lethal-looking machine gun.

"Forgive my saying so," gently said Bernie Coleman, trying as before not to allow the looming gun presence to rattle him. "But you gentlemen smell as if you were fart upon by a sauropod dinosaur."

"That might not be far off the mark," commented Sherman Peabody as he finished climbing back aboard, having heard what Bernie said on his way up. "My flatus emission spectrometer has detected a signature very similar to what we detected on New Britain Island."

"But I trust you realized your oversized spider was actually a spider monkey," interjected Stephen. "How it climbs about branches by its long, slim limbs; didn't receive its name by accident."

"I can guarantee you, *monsieur*, it was no such thing," insisted Prince Englebert. "I held the ch-bah foo-fee in these very hands. And it produced web filaments, strands of which I believe still cling to those we rescued."

"You're certain those weren't old spider webs a spider monkey might fling about to capture prey? Some monkeys have been known to use tools. Sherman," Stephen went on quickly to preclude any interruption, "perhaps your spectrometer picked up a simian flatus emission as well?"

"Not that I have noticed so far. And if spiders make any such gaseous expulsions, not a whole lot of research on that yet."

"He sounds like our Dr. Skepticus," Fred whispered to Ali and Kevin about Stephen. "Here's hoping that unbeknownst to us, we were accompanied by an ephemeral dragon intent on torching pants, whether or not they're stuffed full of chocolate chip cookies."

"So to reiterate, we have a simple question for you," said Prince Englebert, ignoring Fred's remark.

"And please don't mind our weapons, really," Prince Angelbert offered up in his bid to ease the obvious tension from Englebert and himself keeping their guns trained on the time travelers.

"Excuse me saying this," Ali fearlessly reacted, "but how you're aiming your weapons at us, why *shouldn't* we assume that if we give the wrong answer, or say the wrong thing..."

"The only wrong answer is a dishonest answer," firmly responded Prince Englebert. "The last person who gave me a dishonest answer-"

"Was *shot?*" Kevin interrupted.

"Oh, no," Englebert shook his head. "I tickled him until he passed out!"

"Nobody wants to mess with Prince Englebert," said Prince Angelbert. "They call his fingers 'the giggle-makers of doom,' *faiseurs de rire.*"

"We have a wise old Cameroonian proverb that says, 'Baby who squeals knows he has earned a coochie-coo.' So I trust you will answer my question honestly. That is, unless you actually want to feel these in your most sensitive regions," Englebert concluded. He played his fingers before him like Augie imagined a spider, ironically enough, moving its legs to weave its web.

"Oh no, no-no," Kevin shook his head emphatically, his eyes as wide with terror as eyes could ever get. "We'll be truthful."

"Which does beg the question, excuse me again for harping on the subject," said Ali, "but why continue putting us in your gun sight?"

"Oh, this." Prince Englebert suddenly raised his weapon away from aiming at Ali and company as though, Augie mused, he forgot how it ended up in his hands in the first place. "How far we have come, I suppose you are correct, *monsieur.* We really don't require them anymore," he said, gently setting the weapon aside. "It is out of ammunition, anyway."

"What?!" Stephen exclaimed in shock, once more squinting like he'd experienced stabbing head pain as from a migraine.

"Please let me remind you about my- about Prince Englebert's tickling powers," said Prince Angelbert as he also set aside his gun. "I once saw him locate his intended victim among hundreds at an outdoor market. Within seconds, his fingers ran up that unfortunate soul's armpits, moving with the impassioned expertise of a concert pianist. I am guessing that were that person to have been offered an assassin's swift knife across his throat instead, he might have given pause before he answered.

"Now as for why the guns in the first place, whether loaded or empty: What are the chances we would have successfully cajoled you into this immense detour without them?"

"Had you made one of us pass out from tickles, the chances were probably pretty good," Stephen responded.

"A wise answer, *monsieur*," boomed Englebert in his deepest voice and with his most mischievous look.

Scott feared he might go ahead and tickle someone into a coma just for the heck of it.

"As for our simple question for you," the tickle prince went on instead, turning his attention exclusively to the three time travelers. "And before I ask, I would like *Monsieur* Longbottom to replay the part of his surveillance film that shows the very top of something potentially enormous, and definitely shiny metallic, sinking out of sight into the swamp."

"Coming right up," responded Samuel Longbottom most obligingly. Pursuant to which the snippet of recorded video replayed on his surveillance monitor. A shiny, silver-ish portion of the tear-drop-shaped shuttle pod could be clearly espied before rushing-in swamp water sank it completely.

"The reason our guns lack ammunition," said Englebert after the snippet concluded, "is that a massive weapons shipment vanished mysteriously from warehouses in Yaounde. Around that same time, military radar followed a UFO's disappearance into the swamp below, bordering Lake Tele in the Central African Republic."

"One small detail, if I might add," said Samuel raising a forefinger. "Our steam-powered passenger drone, about which you will be learning so much more soon enough, I suspect, is evasively non-existent where radar is concerned. The powers that be ought not to have any idea we've crossed over to here from Cameroon."

"Which brings us to our question, *mais oui*," nodded Prince Englebert. "Did you three *monsieurs* have anything to do with the disappearance of those weaponries from their storage in Yaounde?"

Again, Englebert rapidly moved his fingers about before him. Where Augie was concerned, he could have been playing an invisible keyboard...or keeping his fingers limber for his next round of tickles.

It was the tickle possibility that continued to frighten Kevin as he said, "Suppose we dic have something to do with that; will you subject us to..." Kevin's eyes returned fearfully to the prince's fingers all ir a commotion.

"Only should you lie," Prince Englebert did not hesitate to respond. "To which I am as sensitive as an open wound to salt."

Ali, Kevin, and Fred exchanged telling looks, their eyes shining especially brightly, out from amidst their caked-on swamp slime. Then Kevin took a deep breath, and sighed, "We knew this day was coming, and probably sooner rather than later. So yes, the answer is yes; we had everything to do with that arms shipment disappearing without a trace, plus alternatives left in their place, such as the golf clubs."

"And you sank all of it into the swamp below?" Prince Englebert asked, dropping his hands to his side, fingers gone limp.

"Actually," Ali Magabu inserted himself, "we entrained the storage units to drag them into deep space, caravan style, where we set them on a course for the sun. What you filmed of that last shiny bit sinking into the swamp was our shuttle pod."

"We're aided by a group of extraterrestrials named the Nuah-Cherpels," Kevin resumed. "Our plan is to strategically disarm potential conflicts round the globe, hopefully redirect our planet's history on a more productively peaceful course…"

"Thereby saving us from destroying ourselves before we had a chance to join a larger, interstellar community," Ali went on.

Expressions played across Stephen's face with such rapidity, Augie gathered he couldn't decide whether to be shocked, dubious, or amused. Or some combination thereof.

Meanwhile, though, the princes retrieved their small machine guns.

The time travelers flinched with fear that the two armed strangers might beat them over the head with their weapons. That is, assuming they weren't lying about having run out of ammo, and weren't about to shoot them, forget about tickling, too furious to think straight.

But next thing Ali and company knew, Englebert and Angelbert gently laid their guns at the time travelers' feet, and backed away.

Prince Angelbert said, "We would be honored were you to also send these sailing into the sun."

"Wait," said Stephen holding one hand out as in, *Please stop*, his other hand to his forehead as in, *You're giving me a headache*. "When you talk about 'redirecting our planet's history,' does that imply we are to believe you are time travelers?"

Ali Magabu tried best he could to wipe enough of the grainy, sulfur-fetid greenish-brown crud off his shirt to reveal a smile-y sun insignia set against bright blue. "You are truly most correct, dear sir," he smiled. "I, Dr. Ali Magabu, and my esteemed colleagues here, Sergeant Fred Frankly and engineer Kevin Smith-Park, are officers from aboard the light-propelled starship, Smoke and Mirrors. We arrived here from the year 2064."

Those on whose faces a wide grin broke out, whether the princes, Bernie Coleman, or Irene McDowell, were all thinking the same thing: Whether real or farce, this was going to be good.

Everyone else's mouths simply dropped open save for Stephen's; he buried his face in his hands and shook his head. *For the guarantee of more money,* he lamented, *have I found my way into Ground Zero for Crazy?*

"Listen, I know we must sound absolutely f-n' insane," Fred hastened to follow up Ali's announcement. "If I were one of you – except maybe you with that chicken on your head; I'll circle back to that."

"Buk-buk-BUK!" went Houdini Chicken with her feathers literally ruffled.

"Jesus Clucking Chickadee! Anyway, were I one of you, I'd most likely want to see how quickly we could be fitted for straitjackets. But Ali here is telling you the truth. You see, one of our resident geniuses aboard the Smoke and Mirrors discovered these wounds left in the space-time continuum whenever wherever someone has met a tragic death, down to an ant being squished."

"I am certain that is true," said Prince Englebert with instantly inspired conviction.

"In some locations of mass casualties, those wounds are large enough to fly a spaceship through. So these peace-

and-love extraterrestrials Ali noted earlier, named the Nuah-Cherpels, they've had us hopscotching the past. We've already snuck away enough armaments to preempt numerous conflicts, including two world wars on our original time line."

"Plus accelerate technological progress by leaving behind solar panels and other such goodies from your future," interjected Kevin.

"What made that so truly easily possible," went on Ali, "was that when you travel to the past, you find everything frozen. That's because some universal consciousness we've provisionally named the quantum wave has already passed through."

"Freakin' correct, no bullshit," affirmed Sergeant Frankly. "But once we tinker with the past, it's like the spider on one part of its web notices something happening, the other part of its web. So the quantum wave backtracks to fold over our changes into new circumstances for the future."

"Only, my biggest regret, truly," lamented Ali shaking his head, "is that despite whatever progress we've made, many people's attitudes are proving harder to change. So many manifestations of bigotry and fear...I suppose we could abscond with Ku Klux Klan crosses and other symbols of hate from around the world, and leave colorfully beaded necklaces in their place. But until more people can enjoy life, and prosper too much to bother demonizing 'the other,'...I'm sure there will be much more to discuss on this matter, and given our present predicament, plenty of time to discuss it."

"So, that bigotry and fear you call it," Prince Englebert said in an unusually tentative way for him after all his previous bluster, thought Augie, "that is still a big problem in 2064?"

"Oh, no, not at all," Ali responded emphatically. "Pockets of hate still do remain. But especially since the Nuah-Cherpels have intruded on us in such a big way, well, what I am saying is that accelerating social progress in our past, known to you as your present and immediate future, has proven an especially daunting task."

"But, for example how are homosexuals treated in your present?" Englebert probed further.

Before he could open his mouth to respond, Ali noticed one of the women, who happened to be Dr. Roberta Quiñones, perk up especially much, as though her attention was not riveted enough already. "Ah yes," he said finally. "Well again, aside from a few, most isolated backwaters, that has become no real issue for us anymore. In fact our chief medical officer and one of our starship engineers constitute a happily married lesbian couple. They're one of the happiest couples you'll meet anywhere, but its lesbian nature is worthy of nothing more than a big ho-hum. Ditto for all other forms of gender identity and ambiguity."

With that, the two princes locked arms and turned away from the time travelers to favor Eclipso's team with their attention instead.

"We were going to share this with you in any event," said Angelbert. "We aren't really brothers. Camounui is actually King Payasoboo's second son after Englebert. He is rightfully the second prince. But in our society, you see, homosexuality is grounds for imprisonment, and possibly much worse."

"Very early on, my father noticed our affinity for one another," continued Prince Englebert, fondly stroking Angelbert's head full of tightly curled hair. "So he very cleverly tickled our community into believing Angelbert here was my brother. Meanwhile my real brother,

Camounui, has been amply compensated for his superficial demotion."

"This way," proceeded Angelbert, "we have been able to remain close together with none the wiser outside our family's immediate circle."

"But when vultures circle often enough, their sharp eyes inevitably notice the scurrying mouse," Englebert warned, for once not invoking another Cameroonian proverb, to Augie's surprise. "Therefore, forget my rescuing you from the ch-bah foo-fee. We would still feel in your debt, time travelers from 2064, if you were to allow us asylum aboard your starship. Or we could initiate a profound debt to you, dinosaur-hunting sweet potatoes, if you delivered us out of Africa to the United States on this strange fog-bank-producing aircraft."

"I thought you and Camounui looked like twins," Bernie Coleman noted.

"Wait," said Stephen, back to holding out his hand as in STOP, at the same time he appeared to favor a splitting headache with his other hand. Re asylum for the gay princes, he wanted to say, *More like an insane asylum, here*. Instead, though, he said, "The three of you are claiming to have time-travelled from the year 2064, only to crash your shuttle craft into a swamp. Isn't that as though I drove a thousand miles out to some coastal area, only to then accidentally run my car off the pier? Whoops?"

"I suppose that does sound truly improbable," conceded Ali.

"I notice you're carrying backpacks," said Stephen. "Anything impressively hi-tech inside them, that would obviously have originated from way into our future?"

Kevin, Fred, and Ali exchanged wondering looks over Stephen's question, concluded by Ali saying, "Maybe our holophones?"

"Holophones," Stephen repeated dubiously.

"I'll call you, Officer Smith-Park; how is that?" asked Ali as he retrieved a cellphone-sized object from his backpack.

When Kevin Smith-Park answered his own small device, a three-dimensional, ghostly image of Ali projected out of it before him. At the same time, a comparable image of Kevin projected from Ali's device.

A split-second delay echoed the brief hello-goodbye interaction Ali and Kevin carried on with each other's images before they hung up.

"Well, that is impressive," Stephen acknowledged as much as he didn't want to. "That is, assuming you didn't abscond with devices the armaments thieves left behind, rather than being those thieves yourselves. But this still begs the issue of how you travelled eighty-some years back in time, and then all the sudden went 'Whoops!' into some wayward swamp."

"We'd returned to our starship with our caravan of armaments," Kevin didn't hesitate to respond. "But then we realized surveillance cameras were covertly attached, transmitting to Earth, to whoever presumably hid them there in the first place. So we had to time travel back to Earth, back before we first arrived here, to remove those cameras and bury them near the warehouses."

"Soon as we buried those cameras," Sergeant Frankly proceeded, "we half-expected some space-time conundrum would yank us back aboard our starship Smoke and Mirrors. You see, our bodies ended up in two different places at the same time, and we're never sure how that's going to resolve the final location for our consciousness."

"Rather complicated," Ali admitted, sensitive to much head-scratching by princes and expedition members alike.

"But the bottom line is, either the conundrum or the starship was supposed to swoop us out of here," continued Kevin. "And before that happened, our shuttle pod you saw finish sinking into the swamp was supposed to autopilot us into hiding, under a sand dune in the Sahara Desert."

"Only, the freakin' quantum wave caught up to us before our man Kevin here could finish programming the autopilot," Fred slapped Kevin on the back. "We ended up crash-landing in your land that time forgot, complete with its own giant spider. Though it's not nearly as giant as what we ran across on another planet, let me tell you!"

"Just when I thought things could not get any weirder around here," said Irene. She pointedly stared down Houdini Chicken still firmly ensconced on Augie's head, prompting her to "Buk-buk-BUK!" with yet another feather ruffle.

"*Monsieur* Magabu," Prince Englebert addressed Ali, choosing to address him since he was a dark-skinned fellow like himself, "assume the conundrum suddenly snatches you away before you can help us. Assume it does make you vanish in a puff of smoke. As mentioned before, our lives here as a committed homosexual couple are probably going to be put in serious jeopardy, sooner rather than later. There are already whispers, maybe even by our sweet-potato dinosaur searchers, about my father's counselor Camounui looking like he could be my twin brother. And so, if that conundrum doesn't intrude, any possibility we could join you when your starship formally spirits you off?"

"I truly have no doubt that could be arranged," affirmed Ali. "Either you could join us on our time-travel wanderings, or there's a planet some seven light-years distant called Oomb. We've made it something of a refuge for people from the world over, a new beginning for everyone from victims of child trafficking to former drug addicts."

"But be forewarned," Sergeant Frankly growled. "The locals are mobile, mind-reading trees who ritually hang their bare butts out to dry every mid-day, in commemoration of some long-ago mass orgy that brought them worldwide peace. They also swing them at golf balls, what they call oof balls, they literally poop out like oyster pearls."

"Trees don't have butts," protested Stephen, making no effort to hide pinching his arm to wake up.

"However, if they do have butts, maybe that's where they're ticklish?" Englebert asked, wide-eyed.

"I hear you, sir," Fred addressed Stephen. "But you've got to believe me."

"It's a big universe out there that probably contains most everything you could truly imagine, and more," said Ali.

"Trees with butts definitely come under the heading of more," drily noted Stephen, a spot on his left forearm reddened by his this-must-be-a-crazy-dream pinching.

"Makes our search seem a bit ho-hum by comparison," Irene said, eyeing Scott as she spoke, thrilling him no end.

"But if you'd like to remain on Earth, in present time," Roberta Quiñones finally worked up the courage to interject, "my significant other and I, we live in a fairly open-minded university community in the United States. I am sure we could get you settled there quickly. You could even do coursework on campus."

"Or I'm sure our benefactor wouldn't object to you tagging along on our quest," offered Samuel Longbottom.

"It's just sinking in," said Alistair Frump in his usual hyper-enthused disposition. He pressed his fingertips to the sides of his forehead like he was a medium receiving a message from beyond the grave, Augie managed to muse despite Houdini Chicken's sharp talons gripping his shower-capped scalp extra-firmly. "Time travelers from 2064, is there any chance those golf-addicted trees-"

"Actually, they call it 'oof,'" corrected Ali.

"Po-ta-to, po-tah-to; is there any chance they could benefit from my golf-course-designing expertise? No, scrap that," Alistair waved his hands, brushing his question away. "If they egg-lay their own balls...and heaven knows the possibilities we're scouting out on good old planet Earth are as exciting as exciting can get!"

"Hold the freakin' phone," Fred sputtered. "Is that what you're here for? Searching for the world's very worst hazards to set up a golf course beside? That's what this flying cloud is all about?"

"Well, yes, when we're not searching for dinosaurs," Alistair responded in a tone as though it should have been obvious.

"Okay, before we get into that," said Fred, "for my own sanity if nothing else, I need to know what this is about with a chicken on your head."

"Buk-buk-BUK!!" clucked Houdini Chicken with a commotion of ruffled feathers, in protest to Fred's severe regard.

"Not really sure," admitted Augie. "Oh, and I'm guessing we'll save the rest of the introductions for later. But I'm Augie Matias, the resident paleontologist."

"So one day that chicken just landed on your head," Fred pointed at Houdini Chicken, this time knowing better than to make more cluck-cluck-inducing eye contact with the bird. "And you simply shrugged your shoulders, and have been putting up with it ever since?"

"She was one of several chickens we secured from a market in Douala for villagers to fertilize their soil," Augie explained.

"But this one refused to stay put in her cage," went on Irene. "Instead, she kept finding ways to escape until we finally named her Houdini Chicken, and let her remain with Augie."

"For the time being," said Augie.

"Buk-buk-BUK!"

"Sounds like some disagreement on that point," Irene snickered, again directed Scott's way to his heartwarming delight.

"Something very special between *Monsieur* Matias and that chicken, I do not know what it is," Prince Englebert shook his head.

But you'd be willing to tickle someone to find out, Augie couldn't help thinking.

"Not too special, I hope," said Fred.

"His wife would kill him, I suspect," ventured Bernie, amused no end.

"I'd kill myself," said Augie.

"Not to worry, dearie," Harriet said to Harry, patting his hand comfortingly thanks to the worried expression on his face. "I will not allow any chicken that close to you."

"And any rooster will have to answer to me first!" Harry lit up happily, hi-fiving Harriet.

"Okay, enough about the chicken!" complained Fred Frankly. "I've heard mention of searching for dinosaurs and developing a golf course. What the hell is going on here? Of all the gin joints in town, what exactly have we gotten ourselves into?"

"Well, Sergeant," said Samuel Longbottom, "you have gotten yourself into a steam-powered passenger drone. It's been specially financed by a Mr. Eclipso Sunray Smith for the express purpose of locating, definitively proving the survival into the present day of a least one non-avian dinosaur."

"And also, just maybe, we will locate the perfect spot for the ultimate in scenic golf courses," added Alistair Frump, "straddling that dinosaur's lost-world habitat. The caddies, of course, would double as protective security," he chuckled.

"Just a fresh reminder: There has to be a whole lot more than 'at least one non-avian dinosaur.' If the relic population was too small, it wouldn't have lasted very many generations before weakened to extinction by inbreeding," lectured Stephen Feldman.

Where Augie was concerned, clearly the subtext of Stephen's claim was: Rots of ruck if any of them think there's a chance of discovering a living non-avian dinosaur, on their present time-line or any alternate one.

"Actually, there is an exception to that," Sherman Peabody hastened to say as in No so fast, albeit with his chin still scrunched firmly into his neck. "A South American lizard known as Muller's Tegus usually reproduces via parthenogenesis. The female becomes pregnant unassisted by any male, and neary always gives birth to strong, healthy babies. And has been doing so, apparently, for millions of years."

"I'll have to grant you that," conceded Stephen.

"Anyway," went on Scott, further emboldened by Irene's rapt attention, "the other important factor is Mr. Sunray Smith himself. He made the bulk of his fortune exploiting the advanced technologies you time travelers left behind when you swept up al those armaments. And then for whatever reason,-"

"He claims his miniature alligator friend thinks it's a good idea," inserted Irene.

"That is what he says. And so he has poured his fortune into definitively establishing, once and for all, whether or not any non-avian dinosaurs have survived to the present day."

"Otherwise known as trying to prove a negative," dead-panned Stephen.

"Whichever," continued Scott undaunted, "it's not clear to me there was anyone else around, willing to go so all-in on such an investment."

"Which means that on our original timeline, before the Nuah-Cherpels enhanced our past-event alterations, nobody with such financial wherewithal would have tickled- I mean tackled your quest," concluded Ali Magabu. "It simply would never have happened in the first place.

"I must say, gentlemen," Ali turned Kevin and Fred's grime-covered way to speak, "embedded in their expedition while we await deliverance by our fellow time travelers...I can imagine truly more onerous ways to fly under the radar, as it were. That is," he looked to Samuel Longbottom and Irene for encouragement, "if you can accommodate us, and are okay with keeping us as well as our project hidden from virtually the rest of civilization."

"I would be surprised if Eclipso were anything less than absolutely thrilled over such c prospect," enthused Samuel.

"It was only with the greatest reluctance I admitted to my colleagues, my partners in sensible skepticism, that I would be participating in a living dinosaur search," confessed Stephen Feldman. "Were I to also tell them, 'Oh, by the way, there are these three guys claiming they're time travelers responsible for those mysterious weapons disappearances,' they would probably excommunicate me from the editorial staff of our magazine. In short, your secret is safe with me."

"The ironic thing is," said Sherman Peabody, "our detour that resulted in saving you three gentlemen from the quicksand as well as from the ch-bah foo-fee might end up not being so much of a detour after all."

This time, Sherman bowing his chin into his neck struck Augie in an especially peculiar way. He could imagine Sherman as a human cowcatcher at the front of an antique train engine. Only, he was pushing aside people rather than livestock, to stand dead center of them for his pronouncement.

"During your rescue operation," Sherman went on, "my flatus emission detector recorded something a half-mile away with approximately the same signature as our suspected saurian in Papua."

"What the fried fish is a 'flatus emission detector'?" grumbled Fred Frankly. "Or shouldn't I ask?"

"You shouldn't ask," said Stephen.

"To put it more crudely," responded Sherman, undaunted, "it's an application of your 2060s technology that teases out signature fart noises from a variety of creatures. An olfactory spectrometer for such a task remains but a glimmer in the chemist's eye."

"Dare to dream," snarked Irene.

However, the three time travelers were suddenly too preoccupied by something else to care. They gave each other wide-eyed looks until Kevin said, "It couldn't be..."

"What couldn't be?" asked Stephen, his voice freighted with dubious apprehension. *What absurd thing is one of those purported visitors from the future – a claim I'm far from ready to believe yet – going to offer next?*

"When we were ditching our shuttle pod," Fred explained, "we heard this freakin' loud noise. We joked about it being a dino-fart, and man did it ever stink. But I figured we were downwind of some herd of elephants, that's all."

"That's more reasonable than assuming your 'freakin' loud noise' came from a dinosaur." Stephen was quick to opine.

"Imagine a large, fully-inflated balloon, its navel untied to suddenly let all the air out. That's what it sounded like to me," said Ali, thoughtfully stroking his chin. "But also imagine it's super moistened around where the air is exiting, lending the noise a slurping quality."

Sherman's eyes lit up. "So it sounded something like: SLLURRRRPPP?" he asked excitedly.

"Actually, I think it was more of a: SPLLUURRPP!" Kevin weighed in.

"Damn!" cussed Fred. "So are we sure that muck we sank into wasn't, um…"

"I honestly cannot think of a place I would enjoy being more," Prince Englebert had to say, "than right here, listening to you disagree over the fart sound a dinosaur made."

Ring! Ring!

"Oh, I better take this," Englebert added, removing his cellphone from a pocket hidden within his colorful pagne robes.

The prince's ensuing conversation with whoever was on the other end included so much Bantu mixed with French, Scott couldn't make sense out of any of it.

No matter.

"That was head of security police for the French Cameroon government," Prince Englebert stated plainly after flipping shut his phone. "He was seeking an honest update on our investigation of the UFO. However, as that wise old Cameroonian proverb goes, Honesty is not a birthright. It has to be earned." Englebert paused for his serious demeanor to bloom into a mischievously joyful regard of the time travelers and expedition members alike. Whereupon he continued, "Sweet potatoes or otherwise, you have more than earned my honesty. As for the head of security police, however, my thinking on this subject led me to assure him we discovered nothing more than dead bodies, plus a biplane sinking into a swamp. Could have been drug runners, I proposed; certainly nothing more onerous than that. I did add one honest 'thing': there was absolutely no trace of stolen armaments."

Ring! Ring!

"Oh, probably my father. I'm sure that's the next person the security chief contacted.

"*Bonjour?*"

The prince was off on still more mix of Bantu with French that continued to leave Scott befuddled.

Before Prince Englebert could offer a debriefing on the conversation with his father, Irene bluntly asked, "So has King Payasoboo earned your honesty?"

"Ah mademoiselle, with my father that is always a tricky question. And I say that even though he has been very good about our charade to keep well hidden my romance with Angelbert here. But on this occasion it did not matter. He was focused entirely on whether your presence opens up an asylum prospect for us, not one reference to my fabricated biplane."

"What did you tell your father, Bertie?" anxiously asked Englebert's true-love fellow prince.

"I told him I believe our prospect is excellent for tickling our way into something."

"I'm sure Eclipso will prove most amenable to your entreaties," said Samuel. "You can put your fingers on stand-down."

"Say," said Alistair Frump, "I'm thinking way outside the box. Just how large an animal, Prince Englebert, have you been able to tickle into submission with those magic fingers of yours?"

"One time, a bull elephant was separated from his herd at the height of romantic desire. He rampaged towards a nearby village, trampling everything in his path, about to slam himself against a one-room schoolhouse. On the very threshold of that building, you must believe me, I tickled him rolling over onto his back. His trunk trumpeted his predicament so loudly, he attracted a female and, well, some students were not only saved from being crushed to death. They also received the most explicit biology lesson possible."

"Poof! Mind blown!" Alistair gestured with fingers splaying apart beside his forehead. "Imagine this, people: Of course, Prince Englebert, we keep your dream-team romance discreetly hidden from all the haters. But you and Prince Angelbert become special caddies extraordinaire. You accompany golfers willing to pay a premium to play the ultimate in lost world golf, winding through unexplored swamps and quicksand pits. Should a mokele-mbembe a.k.a. Awesome Apatosaurus threaten, you leap into action!" Alistair hopped up and down, unable to contain himself. "That is, you tickle our prehistoric monster so mercilessly, it rolls over harmlessly on its back for photo ops like the world's never seen before! You might also launch the odd giant spider like a Frisbee, for bonus thrills. And not to worry; should a particular dinosaur not succumb to your fingers' giggle-inducing onslaught, another caddie will be armed with enough tranquillizer darts to send a blue whale off to Lala-land.

"What do you think?"

"I think I'm going to be sick," complained Stephen, crouched down with head between his legs, extremely nauseous from what he considered overabundant absurdity.

Chapter 9

"Sorry, Captain, but I must object in the strongest possible terms, harrumph!" snorted Professor Skepticus, storming onto the navigation bridge of the starship, Smoke and Mirrors.

"You're not sorry in the least!" countered Professor Aquinas straining to follow close behind, what with perpetually readjusting spectacles on the bridge of his nose. "In fact, I dare say you would have been bitterly disappointed had you not found something to object to! Besides, when have you ever objected in any less than the strongest possible terms? When have you ever been caught saying, for example, that you object, but only slightly?"

"Given what we are dealing with currently, professors," said Yoon-hee, "I'm going to be the one objecting if you keep-"

"That's okay, Yoon-hee," Captain Helena Taylor interrupted. "We could use the comic relief."

"'Comic relief' do you say, Captain?! Well, harrumph," Dauntilus Skepticus snorted anew. "If that's how you regard my complaint, a priori to even learning its content, then I must object in even stronger terms! Yes, that's correct! Because what we are dealing with here is nothing less than a persisting case of juvenile delinquency!! You heard me! Juvenile delinquency!""

Shortly before the profoundly disgruntled Professor Skepticus pounded his magnetic boots onto the starship navigation bridge, Captain Taylor and navigator Yoon-hee Park-Smith reached a grim realization. Their starship would probably be stuck inside a wormhole for several months, at least. Yes, hyper-space applied physicist

Buddy Leung was hard at work in his lab, searching for an earlier off-ramp. But unless he pulled yet another rabbit out of his hat...

Only a few weeks earlier, Captain Taylor had flown the Smoke and Mirrors inside the wormhole, to travel past-wards for retrieving fellow officers Fred Frankly, Ali Magabu, and Yoon-hee's husband Kevin Smith-Park. That was, just in case those three guys didn't magically reappear on board after their latest history-tampering weapons confiscation. However, to the starship captain's unwelcome surprise, they found an immensely proportioned, donut-shaped spacecraft already inside there. Its gravitational pull entrained the Smoke and Mirrors, turned the Smoke and Mirrors into a dog on a leash that couldn't resist following wherever the owner headed. Even worse, entrainment meant the Smoke and Mirrors needed to decelerate well below light-speed. Otherwise, there would have been a devastatingly fatal collision with the donut-shaped, fifty-mile-circumference spacecraft of unknown origin.

One option Buddy was exploring involved the cigar-shaped Smoke and Mirrors shooting through the donut hole. But that looked as risky as trying to shoot a bullet through the center of a real donut from a mile away without grazing the inner circle's edge the least tiny bit.

Yoon-hee launched a firefly donut transmitting universal pictographs, meant to open communication with the presumed extraterrestrial spacecraft. However, lack of ambient light inside the wormhole, available for propelling that hi-tech message in a bottle, prevented it from accelerating fast enough to catch up. Unlike the Smoke and Mirrors rear lasers, the teensy firefly donut laser supplied too little photon force, unassisted by at least ambient starlight.

Yes, the Smoke and Mirrors could have accelerated enough before launching the firefly for said firefly to have caught up. But again, any such acceleration would have inevitably crashed the starship into the far larger donut-shaped craft. Which incidentally Buddy and Helena suspected of carrying an entire ecosystem as though it were a futuristic Noah's Ark.

"Did we hear someone say 'juvenile delinquency'?" asked Chief Medical Officer Dr. Deborah Davis-Murphy. She hurried onto the navigation bridge beside her significant other, Mirror Array Maintenance Officer Geena Murphy-Davis.

"You too, Deb?"

"Check this out, Captain," Deborah suggested as she and Geena turned their backs on Captain Taylor. They bent over to make their uniform-concealed butts feature prominently.

A pasty-white substance clung to both officers' rear ends, speckled by chocolate chip cookie crumbs.

"Back on Chonorah, both your pants would have been framed in one of their more prominent galleries," Helena remarked.

Chonorah was a planet where the dominant culture celebrated stained clothes as high art.

"Not sure how such a bold fashion statement is going to play back on Earth, however."

"Captain Taylor," sternly vented Deborah.

"All-call for Chris Olsen-Taylor; we need you on the bridge, pronto," said Helena pursuant to slapping a button on her lapel. Meanwhile with her open palm, she signaled for Deborah to stifle herself.

"Be there in a minute," Chris responded over the intercom.

"While coping with our newborn ephemeral dragons, looks like we'll have to come down extra hard on Tomás and Jorge," Helena conceded to Debbie and Geena.

"There you go again, endowing the gaseous anomaly with corporeal being," lamented Skepticus. "As though Ursa Minor could drop down out of the sky as a real bear! Harrumph!"

"Captain, a small object is headed at us from that IDA (intelligently designed artifact) up ahead," suddenly reported Yoon-hee.

Everyone else's attention focused on the panoramic view-screen, anxiously trying to discern said approaching object. Yet all anyone could see was a ghostly glow from starlight outside the wormhole. Silhouetted against that glow was the incredibly large donut-shaped extraterrestrial spacecraft. And something extra weird about said glow: Starship engineer Buddy Leung ascertained that none of it, not one single photon, actually entered the wormhole. Otherwise there would have been plenty of light to power the firefly donut.

"Should we attempt an evasive maneuver?" anxiously asked Captain Taylor. She echoed general worry a missile might have been launched their way. "And given our entrainment, will evasion even be possible?"

"We might as well try to escape from already being sucked halfway down a maelstrom whirlpool. But wait...huh," Yoon-hee sighed with relief. "The UFO is decelerating on a trajectory steering well clear of us. Oh," she added, surprised, "some background static has resolved into a repeating transmission!"

"Helena?" asked husband Chris bursting onto the bridge.

"What do you know about this?" Helena Taylor waved Chris's attention towards Professor Skepticus and fellow complainants, Debbie and Geena.

All three turned their backs on Chris, revealing the mess on the seats of their pants.

"Obviously there are lots of cookie crumbs," said Chris. "But the white stuff they're stuck to looks like white glue-paste, the kind that children use in arts and crafts. I assume it was left on chairs you guys didn't notice until after sitting…"

"Jorge and Tomás strike again," concluded Captain Taylor wearily. She slapped her lapel all-call button anew, saying, "Ciela, we need you on the bridge."

"Unless," Chris blurted out, suddenly energized by a new possibility, "that's saliva or some other secretion from the parent ephemeral dragons. They're leaving un-torched cookie bits lying about for their progeny, maybe."

"And they just happened to leave them on chairs?" asked Dr. Deborah Davis-Murphy dubiously.

"What a simply exciting prospect!" enthused Professor Aquinas despite the tenor of Deb's question.

"What a simply ridiculous suggestion!" protested Skepticus. "It is already too much of a stretch to suggest there is more than one gaseous anomaly that randomly drifted aboard the Smoke and Mirrors from the Fafaman atmosphere! I say enough is enough! We have done our part, alerting Captain Taylor to the need for disciplinary action against our resident juvenile delinquents. Now we ought to change our pants before one of us is torched again!"

"Captain, I've got an update on that UFO transmission," intruded Yoon-hee, to Helena Taylor's welcome relief.

"Let's have it, Officer Park-Smith."

"There are different parts. One features binary x's and zeroes fitting the profile for an autopilot program."

"Autopilot?" repeated Helena. "Might the passengers and crew be hibernating until they arrive at their destination? And their spaceship's central computer launched the transmission automatically, on sensing our presence nearby?"

"Perhaps," Yoon-hee conceded reluctantly.

"You don't sound all that convinced, Yoon-hee. What are you thinking?"

Captain Taylor's question got everyone else's attention off those pesky chocolate-chip-cookie crumbs that were pasted to the seats of certain pants. So nobody tried speaking to that again before Yoon-hee responded, "Another part of the extraterrestrial communication features a universal messaging sketch of two separate spheres. In between them, a pie chart has two of ten slices emblazoned with a simplfied depiction of an oxygen molecule. Six of the remaining eight pie slices are emblazoned with a nitrogen-"

"They are searching for a home away from home, and our Earth would likely fit the bill, atmosphere-wise. Okay, got it," Captain Taylor interrupted impatiently.

"Then on to the part I suspect they sent off before they could complete it, definitely not in a hibernating state," said Yoon-hee, unfazed. "Check this out."

What Yoon-hee posted on the view-screen next contained two sketches. A rectangle enclosed a seven-pointed star, each point of varying length. Beside it, the second sketch consisted of nothing more than a half-oval with a dot inside, facing the rectangle.

"Not sure about the rectangle," went on Yoon-hee. "But the half-oval looks incomplete to me. Maybe the author hoped it contained enough info for anyone to still figure out."

"You're suggesting the entity behind this transmission must have been working under duress?" asked Dr. Davis-Murphy.

"So much duress, this particular component was sent unfinished. That is, unless I am simply too dense to 'get it.' Maybe one of you…"

"Most definitely, there are people present here who are too dense to understand the gaseous anomaly is not some ghostly creature such as a so-called ephemeral dragon," insultingly spat out Professor Skepticus. "But where that pictograph is concerned, if it is finished, I join you in being too rock-headed to decipher it, Officer Park-Smith."

"That seven-pointed a-symmetrical star inside the rectangle," timidly ventured Geena, "maybe something they spotted outside their spacecraft? Through a rectangular porthole?"

"You folks who unwittingly sat where our young mischief-makers left their mess-"

"I most likely picked it up inside the cafeteria," Dr. Skepticus interrupted Captain Taylor with a pompous snort. He hadn't yet budged, even though he called for all of the cookie-crumb-afflicted to go change their pants.

"Same for us!" chimed in Geena, 'us' referring to her and Deborah.

"Anyway, I *am* anxious to understand that extraterrestrial messaging," said Captain Taylor. "However, it's really making me distractingly nervous, the prospect one or more of you might be about to have your butt torched, whether by a newborn ephemeral dragon or one of their parents. You especially, Dr. Skepticus; how many times have you already had to use the mend-o-tron for huge gashes in the seat of your pants? I urge you to follow your own advice about changing your pants soon as-"

"Aydiomio, Captain Taylor," Ciela Sanchez-Frankly stormed onto the navigation bridge, soggy cookie crumbs dripping off her suit pants behind her. "I thought Jorge and Tomás knew better than to play this trick on me. I'm the one who should have known better!" She turned her back on Helena to display the same cookie-crumb-strewn stain already seen on the seat of multiple other pants. "Let me assure you, I am going to put a stop to this, 'once and for all,' as that expression goes!"

"Little devils they might be, still don't want them falsely accused of something, Ciela," cautioned Helena. "There is a competing hypothesis."

"*No me diga!*" (Don't tell me!)

"That so-called 'competing hypothesis' is an entirely non-competitive absurdity," blustered Skepticus dismissively. "And Captain, no need to worry about me 'especially.' So many other people's pants bottoms are afflicted with this juvenile scourge, I rather like the odds that this time, I will personally avoid the gaseous anomaly's flaming reaction. At the end of the day, there is insufficient evidence for there being more than one such anomaly, and far less than that for it having any conscious intent as some superstitiously posited semi-visible dragon. To the ephemeral dragon I say: Ha! And I repeat: Ha!"

Whoomf!

"Ouch!" cried Geena, startled by the sudden ignition of the cookie crumbs pasted to her pants' rear end. Wispy gray smoke rose quickly from there, along with a distinct odor of burning cotton fabric.

"You see?" Professor Skepticus waved a hand Geena's direction. "Just as I expected! The odds have finally favored-"

Whoomf!

"Ouch-ouch-ouch-ouch-ouch!" cried Skepticus, suddenly running around in circles, trailing smoke from his rear end, as Deborah and Ciela's cookie crumbs also went up in flames.

While Chris used the fire extinguisher on all four smoking-hot rear ends, something dawned on Helena that eclipsed her concern for the safety of those who just got their pants torched. The very first time Effie the ephemeral dragon afflicted Professor Skepticus, Helena remembered seeing the seat of his pants afterwards. The hole burnt through there, its jagged border now reminded her of the irregularly shaped, seven-pointed star inside the rectangular box depicted on the extraterrestrial transmission. *A hull breach?* she wondered. *Or some other breach?*

Chapter 10

I'm sure if Augie were here, he'd tell me the good news is these kids writing more and more in their journals. And I'd counter the bad news is these kids writing more and more in their journals. That means extra work for me, evaluating them with an eye towards which particular skills each student needs to focus on. But yes, more data points in that regard is well worth the added hassle. On balance, the good does outweigh the bad; I wish Diane appreciated this. What did Augie tell me, ever the optimist? Physicists have found there's slightly more matter than anti-matter in the universe?

"So this is Ms. Copplestone's classroom," marveled someone out in the hallway with an unfamiliar, hoarse voice as Vicky finished piling a dozen student journals into her backpack.

"There's her name beside the door, spelled out in what I guess are supposed to be dinosaur bones," chuckled a voice Vicky recognized being from Giselle's father, Peter George.

"Very appropriate since a pile of bones, fossilized bones, is the only condition in which anyone's going to find a dinosaur these days," the hoarse-voiced man remarked as he knocked on the open door. "Ms. Copplestone?" he said. "May we enter? I know I haven't made an appointment, but this really can't wait."

"No worries," answered Vicky. She took the situation well in stride, especially with Diane Mueller not leading the charge.

"Dear Ms. Copplestone," said Peter George in his heavy British accent, "I see you are packed up to leave. Perhaps this is not a convenient time."

"It's convenient enough, Mr. George. Good to see you again. Please, both take a seat," motioned Vicky. She set her backpack aside and pulled out some chairs from student desks, nevertheless lamenting wistfully, *There goes that driving range session I was going to sneak in before picking up Liz. Have to buy her a starter set so she can join me; she does enjoy mini-golf. Oh, well, I can still work off my pent-in frustration with a neighborhood jog instead, while Liz plays outdoors.*

"Don't believe we've met, Ms. Copplestone; I'm Michael's dad, Dr. Tru." Dr. Tru offered a hearty handshake before taking a student seat, awkwardly small given his rotund physique.

"Micky, yes, it's a pleasure to have him in my class, as well as Giselle, of course," Vicky nodded Peter George's way.

"Since we lost Micky's mother to cancer three years ago, I've had to wear this additional hat as parental interface with his school," Dr. Tru explained. "Fortunately, there was an opening in my schedule this afternoon. You see, I run a general medical practice."

"Read about that in his cumulative file, and cannot express how sorry I am for your loss," said Vicky empathetically.

"Of course given my son's special needs," Dr. Tru proceeded, not acknowledging Vicky's condolences, "I was advised he should be enrolled in summer school remediation. I concluded Ms. Kowalski would be a good fit for working on Micky's organizational skills. But your curriculum specialist, I believe her name is Ms. Mueller, strongly urged me to give your sessions a chance instead. And I heard through the grapevine that the county superintendent singled you out for commendation on how you handled a student who died from a brain aneurysm this past spring."

"We felt horrible," was all Vicky could think to verbalize while her head raced with bottom-dropping-out-of-her-stomach wonder. Did Diane press Dr. Tru to enroll Micky in her class, hoping he'd be outraged over her unique pedagogy? Hoping he'd freak over the quest for a living dinosaur aspect?

"Well I have to say, Ms. Copplestone, I felt horrible too, when my son prattled on about your husband's search for a dinosaur still romping about somewhere. Then I learned that Cameroon is where your husband's nonsense is taking place. And that just coincidentally, a girl from Cameroon wound up in your class. So I reached out to her father, here."

"Yes indeed," Peter nodded.

"Ms. Copplestone, we have a problem. As I hope you noticed so you don't really need to be told, Micky struggles to organize his schoolwork. This past school year, his teacher kept reporting his desk a constant mess. Ever since we lost his mother, I have done everything possible to structure his home life. Soon as he returns from day care, I call his attention to a posted schedule for everything from snack time to soccer practice. Plus I do a whole lot more. In consultation with his therapist, I've put him on a positive reinforcement regimen. And of course, there's the remedial learning summer school."

"I'd like to point out something about my daughter, Liz, who also enters fifth grade this fall," interjected Vicky before Dr. Tru could elaborate any further. "She needs a certain amount of unstructured time in her day when she can just let it all hang out. If she chooses simply to daydream, so be it. My husband and I have found-"

"I already allow that," Tru reacted defensively. "Every weekday, between his late afternoon snack and dinner, there are forty-five minutes for him to choose from twenty different fun activities, updated each month! Everything from making his own paper airplanes to assembling puzzles! And on Saturday afternoons, for a full two hours he can enjoy a play date, or watch any television program he wants from an approved list!"

"That sounds exhausting," commented Peter George, wiping his brow with a handkerchief.

"Without his mother," Dr. Tru's voice cracked, "Micky's care *is* exhausting. Even more exhausting was how Micky's first therapist didn't appreciate my efforts one bit. He essentially recommended allowing chaos to rule at home for at least two hours every day! And for most of the time on weekends! As disorganized as Micky's studies are now, I can't imagine how they would be under such an anti-regimen! I had to let that therapist go, and get a new one. Hopefully, the new one won't take too much longer to diagnose an attention-deficit hyperactive disorder that will open the door to helpful medication.

"Along that same line, Ms. Copplestone, I might need to withdraw Micky from your class, as so far it sounds like exactly what he doesn't need."

In other words, Vicky wanted to say, *"the beatings will continue until morale improves," as that saying goes*. But she settled instead for asking, while trying to project a disinterest definitely opposite from what she felt, "What is it about my class that sounds to you like exactly what your son doesn't need?"

"To reiterate, Ms. Copplestone, I'm trying to get him on the straight and narrow path to self-organized academic development and achievement. My son certainly doesn't need wasteful detours, especially not the ludicrous proposition any dinosaurs might have survived to the present day! But this has become an extremely onerous problem because now he talks about nothing else during open-ended dinner discussion! And for five consecutive days, he has been devoting his library reading exclusively to dinosaurs. If he *is* doing any reading, that is. I'm not sure he's not just ogling the illustrations! I need him out of your class, hopefully with that Ms. Kowalski who I wanted in the first place. From what I hear, she is sure to forbid him checking out any more dinosaur books until he has gone back to actual reading on other subjects! A patient whose son is in Ms. Kowalski's class told me she has laser-like focus on grammar and math drills!"

"I'm hopeful your request can be satisfied, Dr. Tru," said Vicky while turning Mr. George's way. "But Mr. George,-"

"I insist on it!" interrupted Dr. Tru.

"You have every right to insist on it. I just wanted to hear from Peter George what brings him here as well. Last time we spoke, Mr. George, you seemed quite satisfied with Giselle's journal writing. And you said she was already showing interest at her young age in an agricultural career."

"That was true, Ms. Copplestone," Peter conceded, nervously wiping his brow again, it having already beaded up with new perspiration. "On further reflection, however, spurred by Dr. Tru here, it occurred to me and my wife, who again I must apologize most profusely for being unable to accompany me, but please do not misapprehend she is any less committed to the very best for our daughter."

"As you were saying…"

"As I was saying, Ms. Copplestone, it occurred to me there is so much to learn that we know for certain is real. I'm just not sure how comfortable I am, when all is said and done, with so much of her time taken up by this living dinosaur prospect, which at the end of the day we must admit isn't realistic, is it?"

"My husband would strongly dispute that assumption, at least until a lot more data is examined," Vicky couldn't help bristling.

"Proving a negative," interjected Dr. Tru, bristling right back. "I'm sorry, Ms. Copplestone, but isn't that all he is doing? He'd have to spend the rest of his life exploring every last nook and cranny of every last jungle on Earth before such a mission was complete."

If he's enjoying himself, and even helping a few people along the way like that woman from Papua who's now attending college in the U.K., isn't that the important thing? Vicky found herself thinking. But rather than vocalize her initial reaction to Dr. Tru, she said, "Granted. I still would like to know, though, Mr. George, whether Giselle has continued writing in her journal, and expressing interest in agriculture."

"She's conceived a grand fertilization plan. She envisions rotating a free-range chicken habitat across a farm field on a wheeled platform the size of a soccer field. Yes, this is true," acknowledged Peter. "But her excitement also grows over the possibility your husband might be on the verge of filming a living sauropod dinosaur. We can feel that becoming an obsession for her, possessing her very being. In other words, I'm not sure it wouldn't be better to consolidate her gains by moving her out of your class sooner rather than later, Ms. Copplestone."

That's when Vicky realized the click-click-click of high heels down the hall came to a sudden stop, then resumed, growing louder and louder as it approached her classroom.

Diane Mueller overheard something she definitely wanted to be a part of. "Mr. George!" she said effusively, ducking her head in. "I thought that was a familiar voice."

Which you would have ignored to just keep heel-clicking down the hall, hadn't he said something about moving his daughter out of my class, Vicky wanted to interject, but of course kept to herself.

"Ah, Ms. Mueller," Peter George stood to welcome her, Dr. Tru following suit. "Your timing is most fortuitous, as maybe you can shed light on something."

"I'm Dr. Tru, father of Michael Tru in Ms. Copplestone's remedial summer school."

"A pleasure, Dr. Tru, to see you again," gushed Diane. She gave Dr. Tru a hearty handshake she had to stifle herself from turning into a hug for how delighted she was over what she'd overheard, but would pretend she was learning for the first time. "And I'm Diane Mueller, curriculum specialist."

"Dr. Tru and Mr. George have requested transferring their children out of my class," explained Vicky Copplestone despite her suspicion Diane had indeed overheard Mr. George, the whole reason for backtracking into her classroom.

"Yes, I- Oh..." Diane could kick herself for nearly admitting she overheard the good news.

"Please understand, Ms. Mueller," Peter George said, "this is in no way meant to cast the least aspersion on Ms. Copplestone's most unique pedagogy. It is far more a matter of wishing to consolidate my daughter's gains in a more traditional learning environment perhaps better suited to her needs."

"Ms. Copplestone's 'unique pedagogy' is the last thing my son needs at the moment," said Dr. Tru on a more negative note.

Vicky imagined that were Diane not exercising so much self-control, she would have gotten all dreamy-eyed on Dr. Tru, breathlessly sighing, *Tell me more!*

Instead, though, Diane said, as dispassionately as possible, if still unable to avoid sounding disparaging, "I assume 'unique pedagogy' refers to Ms. Copplestone revolving her classroom activities around her husband's dinosaur hunt."

Vicky couldn't help stewing over Augie's expedition being characterized as a hunt rather than a search. Nevertheless, she stifled herself out of correcting Diane.

"It does, but please take a seat, Ms. Mueller." As he spoke, Peter grabbed another awkwardly small student chair for himself.

"Thank you," squealed Diane in her girlishly falsetto voice, her unbridled joy impossible to conceal any longer. And yet, she did muster a deadly serious voice to go on, "As much as we want to accommodate all parent requests, these remedial sessions do become quite full. I honestly don't know whether Ms. Kowalski has enough empty seats. That being said, it might help make something happen-"

Like getting my ass handed to me on a silver platter, Vicky again had to stifle herself from interjecting.

"-if you write your concern to the county school superintendent. Meantime, I will work closely with Ms. Copplestone to make sure she better accommodates your children's needs."

Jonathan (RIP) Valladare's mother communicated to the superintendent her gratitude for the joy he apparently found, following my Augie's exploits. And ever since then, you've been seeking to provide the superintendent with a counter-narrative that could set the stage for railroading me out of my life's calling! Haven't you, Diane? Vicky wanted so badly to vent aloud instead of keeping bottled up.

But then, what was that gentle tap she heard?

"Excuse me," said Vicky, rising from her own too-small chair. "Sounds like someone else at the door."

"Oh?" Diane Mueller couldn't help bursting out in happy anticipation.

Far as Vicky was concerned, Diane might as well have failed at stifling a fart. *Probably super excited over the*

*possibility of a third complaining parent as in: Strike three,
and maybe she can finally have me kicked out?*

In any event, when Vicky opened her classroom door,
she wasn't sure what she found more intimidating about
the woman standing there. Was it her willowy height,
maybe even taller than Diane? Or her austerely gray
pants suit, made all the more austere by her necklace of
gumball-sized, jade beads?

"You *are* Ms. Copplestone, aren't you?" the woman
asked in a tone that said, *Don't tell me you're* not Ms.
Copplestone.

Vicky had to wonder whether she wouldn't have still
agreed, even were she not in fact Ms. Copplestone.

"Oh, you're already very busy." the woman added
before Vicky could confirm she was correct. She had
peeked through the doorway and seen the three other
people already seated on too-small student chairs. "I can
return at a more convenient-"

"Ms. Malmstein isn't it?" Diane interrupted, perkier than
ever with her growing excitement.

"Why yes it is!" exclaimed Ms. Malmstein. "You must
have an encyclopedic memory, while I'm embarrassed
to have to admit-"

"Please don't worry about that," Diane interrupted yet
again, batting away the paren⁻'s concern over not
remembering her name. "I'm Diane Mueller, Ms.
Copplestone's curriculum adviser. We are discussing the
concerns of two other parents here. They wonder about
the impact Ms. Copplestone's summer school class might
be having on their children's remedial preparation for fifth
grade. Perhaps that is what also prompts your visit?" *Can
you add to the criticism already crashing down on Ms.
Copplestone's head, please?*

The whites showed clear round Ms. Malmstein's eyes as
she said, "That's exactly what brings me here!"

"So why not share with us what your child has been experiencing?"

In response to Diane's invitation, Ms. Malmstein gave Vicky Copplestone a deferring look that Vicky found surprisingly warm as she moved hastily to pull up another chair.

"Don't know if you've met Dr. Tru and Mr. George," said Vicky, sweeping her hand their way as in, *Look here.* "Their children are Micky and Giselle, respectively. And your child is…?"

"No-no-no," Ms. Malmstein shook her head emphatically. "Gwendolyn is not in your class with them. That reality makes what I have to report all the more impressive, actually. You see, Ms. Copplestone, when I brought home my daughter from day care last evening, something strange and unexpected happened. For the first time since remedial school started, she *didn't* run outside to enjoy every last minute of summer twilight before dinner. Rather, she bounded upstairs to her room. My curiosity got the best of me, so after a few minutes I followed after her, and discovered an historic first." Madeline Malmstein leaned into the seated group, as though about to share something in strictest confidence. "She was reading a book," she related breathlessly, "on her *own*, with absolutely no cajoling from me or her father. As much as I wanted to at least ask what it was about, I feared disrupting the delicate balance that brought her to that point."

"Well isn't that wonderful, Ms. Malmstein," commented Diane. "Gwendolyn is discovering the joys of reading on her own. And you did say she's not in Ms. Copplestone's group?"

"That's what I'm getting to, Ms. Mueller, if I might proceed."

"By all means," Diane gestured as in: The floor was all hers.

"Right after dinner, before her father and I could ask whether she finished her homework at day care, she bounded upstairs again. This time, my husband Jimmy joined me to take a peek insice her bedroom. That's when we discovered another first: Gwendolyn at her desk, writing something without our having compelled her!"

"My goodness that is wonderful!" Diane clapped her hands. "What was she writing? Or were you still fearful of disrupting a delicate balance? Not that I could blame you!"

"Must admit our curiosity got the best of us," Madeline blushed. "So when I asked Gwendolyn what she was writing, turned out it was a letter to you, Ms. Copplestone."

"Oh," ohhed Diane like her balloon had just sprung a leak, Vicky mused.

"If I might share it," Madeline Malmstein effused as she unfolded a paper from her executive business bag, oblivious to Diane's nonplussed reaction.

"Yes, I should very much like to hear that letter," said Peter George, "and would find myself surprised beyond all reckoning if Ms. Copplestone's curiosity has not been piqued even more than mine."

"Let's hear it," chimed in Dr. Tru as Diane turned her head aside, this time bracing for the worst rather than suppressing another chortle.

"Okay, here we go," announced Madeline, holding up her daughter's letter before her. "'Dear Ms. Copplestone,

'Hi, my name is Gwendolyn Malmstein, and I have summer school with Ms. Kowalski, but Giselle George told me she has you for summer school, and that she is learning a whole lot about Mr. Copplestone's search for a living dinosaur in her home country, Cameroon. I have never heard of Cameroon before, and that it is located in Africa, but I guess you already know that, plus a lot more.'"

"A wee bit of run-on with her sentences, otherwise very well written," Vicky couldn't help interjecting. "Sorry about that," she added quickly. "Am always on the alert for a goal each child can set to improve their writing."

Madeline gave Vicky a hard stare to react, "Yes," as in having just experienced a profound revelation. Then returning to her daughter's letter, she said, "Okay, where were we? Ah, 'When I was younger, I had a stuffed unicorn, and I named her Poosh-Poosh, and I really, really wanted her to be real. I hoped that one day I would wake up and find her running around my bedroom, but that never happened, and eventually I felt very silly about it.

"'But then Giselle tells me Mr. Copplestone thinks all the dinosaurs didn't die, and that you talked about other amazing animals that people are looking for. There's a monkey man named Bigfoot, and a sea serpent named Champ, and she said you talked about those plus more, so at the school library, I asked if they had any books about amazing animals that might be real, and Ms. Bennett showed me this one about cryptozoology. Giselle told me you used that word, and said it's the study of animals that might or might not be real.

"'Ms. Copplestone, that is the most interesting book I have ever read. I learned about the okapi, an animal we know for sure is real. It looks like a weird cross between a zebra and a horse, with stripes on its back half, but it's in the giraffe family!

"'Okay, I'm probably repeating lots of stuff you already know, but I wanted to tell you how lucky I think Giselle is to have you for a teacher.

"'Your friend, Gwendolyn,'" Madeline concluded reading, tearfully. Turning her sternest countenance on Vicky Copplestone, with the whites showing clear round her eyes again, she added, "I want Gwendolyn to be lucky enough to have you for a teacher, sooner rather than later," she concluded turning Diane's direction.

Diane wanted to find out how the hell a book on Bigfoot and the like ever wound up in the school library. But she figured that mentioning her displeasure over that wasn't likely to go over very well. Taking a different tact, she asked, "You did say Gwendolyn's teacher is Ms. Kowalski?"

"This is true," Madeline Malmstein responded warily.

"Well isn't it possible that Ms. Kowalski's rigorous battery of reading and writing drills contributed significantly to Gwendolyn being able to enjoy reading that book, and preparing such a well-written letter?"

"Ms. Mueller," said Madeline most sternly, "I spent over an hour with my daughter last night, helping her correct numerous grammatical errors on an assigned worksheet. The only thing I see Ms. Kowalski's drills contributing to is Gwendolyn saying, and I quote, 'I hate English class.'

"What you said, Ms. Copplestone, about focusing on a specific issue such as Gwendolyn's run-on sentences, I rather prefer that approach."

"I have a confession to make," admitted Vicky, her confidence growing that she had gained sympathetic ears. "I dislike the entire summer remedial school ethic. Summer should be a time for children's extra play and extra daydreaming, to refuel for facing more growing up. It shouldn't be for pestering them over their shortcomings. And there certainly shouldn't be any assigned homework."

Diane mirthfully smirked, "Well that raises a really big question, then, Ms. Copplestone. What exactly are you doing here, teaching remedial summer school, if you have so little use for it?"

"I'm particularly inspired by what, you know, another parent reported about her child," Vicky responded without having to think twice, as she tapped directly into her heart. "I want to thread the needle. I want to see if I can provide a good daydreaming environment the same time I address those remedial needs. So I've doubled down on involving students in all different facets of my husband's admittedly quixotic quest for a living non-avian dinosaur. Only two weeks in, they're already filling their journals with items of interest that have stemmed from the dinosaur search. They're writing and reading about everything from how to keep soil fertile to firefly farts. And this has not only boosted their reading skills. It has also supplied me plenty of info for zeroing in on each child's room for improvement. In fact, Dr. Tru," Vicky paused to dig something out of her backpack, "I'm taking home Micky's journal tonight. Interested to see how he's doing with the past tense. But Ms. Malmstein, thanks so much for sharing Gwendolyn's letter. Most gratified to hear a student in another class has been moved to check a book out of the library."

"And you can be sure, Dr. Tru, I'll be looking into how our media center ended up carrying a book like that so...so on the fringe," Diane sputtered out finally.

"Wait," said Dr. Tru, brushing aside Diane's assurance with a dismissive hand wave whilst leaning towards Vicky. "My son has been keeping a journal?" his voice cracked as he asked.

"For what it's probably not worth," said Vicky while handing over Micky's journal to Dr. Tru, "I can't imagine how hard it must be to raise him on your own. But I treat all my students the same way I want my own daughter to be treated when she enters fifth grade in the fall."

"So you're here to talk with Ms. Copplestone about your son's progress?" Madeline Malms-ein turned Dr. Tru's way to ask.

"He was actually here to request transferring his son to Ms. Kowalski's class," explained Peter George. "An option I'm going to take a pass on for my daughter."

"So is it possible," Madeline turned Diane's way with the whites showing clear round her eyes again, "that there could be a trade-out, his son for my daughter?"

"No it's not possible," Dr. Tru shook his head strenuously as he gently closed his son's journal. "I've reconsidered, Ms. Copplestone, and want Micky to remain in your class, with my gratitude for your dedication."

"And again, I have concluded my daughter should also continue with Ms. Copplestone," chimed in Peter George. "So it would seem, Ms. Malmstein, that Ms. Copplestone's class might be too full to accept another student."

"But I would happily accommodate an additional student," Vicky cheerily affirmed.

"And most fortunately, Ms. Malmstein," added Peter, "according to Ms. Mueller, you could write a letter to the school superintendent that explains how earnestly you desire your daughter to be transferred into Ms. Copplestone's classroom. I am certain that any superintendent would feel quite moved to read what your daughter wrote to Ms. Copplestone. Quite extraordinary, really, a student writing to a teacher not her own, about how lucky that teacher's students are to have her."

"That won't be necessary," Diane Mueller said slowly enough to contain her frustration-fueled anger. "If Ms. Copplestone believes she can manage the additional responsibility...this conversation really doesn't need to leave this room."

"Are you feeling okay, Ms. Mueller?" Ms. Malmstein turned to ask Diane with her usual wide-eyed forceful earnestness.

"I'm doing just fine, thank you," she tersely responded, checking her wristwatch. "Oh, look, I have a prior engagement to keep, if you will excuse me..."

With a strong marguerita? Vicky couldn't help wondering as Diane click-clicked on her high heels out of the room.

*

"Couldn't help noticing the big D storm out of your room earlier, well before your other visitors left," noted Mark Waltzer while Vicky turned her back on him to lock the door.

What, Vicky wanted to say, *have you been waiting out here to intercept me, ever since?*

"I was putting up my new bulletin board..."

"'Our dreams for the future,'" Vicky quoted from Mark's bulletin board. "Very nice," she commented though thinking to herself, *So is there anything you're up to not with the intent of getting me into the sack with you?*

"Yeah, thanks, but I do care; she's not making more trouble for you, is she?"

"More trouble for herself than for anyone else."

"Oh," Mark reacted, startled. "By the by, any new word yet from Augie on when he's returning from Africa?"

"Seems his current expedition has run into some corrupt bureaucratic entanglement."

"Nothing he hasn't had to deal with before, then?"

"Same old same old," Vicky responded. She knew Mark was on a fishing expedition for any means he could cause her to toss aside Augie, give in to the bubblegum satisfaction of unbridled adulterous lust, rather than keeping that particular King Kong in permanent chains where it belonged. So she wasn't going to give this fellow teacher the satisfaction of learning that in fact her Augie's latest update was a bit overdue. And that moreover, the delay did have her somewhat peeved, including what she understood rationally was needless paranoia over the possibility he would ever surrender to some other woman's sexual advances.

"There are women on his team, didn't I hear?"

"And they can't keep their hands off him, not even the lesbian," Vicky concluded with a mocking grin.

"No," Mark reacted defensively, instantly wishing he hadn't. Then quickly recovering, he added, "I just hope they have their fair share of decision-making input."

"No reason to think they don't."

"Oh, by the way, Myriam's English does seem to be benefiting now from what you said about her teaching Spanish to her partners in crime. I yield to your greater wisdom, m'lady," he concluded bowing with no small flourish.

"Good," *although I'm not convinced the cause-effect is that obvious, that this isn't what you delude yourself to believe is seductive flattery.*

"Well I'm off for my afternoon coffee boost," Mark concluded, thinking to himself, *I'll make you beg to accompany me, and sooner or later...*

"More caffeine to you."

*

"Augie?! Thank God!"

"Were you afraid this was another scam call promising to deposit a hundred thousand in our bank account? Oh, wait; that really happened!"

"Actually, I feared it might be my bookie threatening to sever my hands if I didn't turn over our house to pay off my gambling debt."

"Hate when that happens. So is Liz there?"

"Play date; I was kind-of hoping for a view-phone rendezvous, you know…"

"Likewise of course. But Cloud Nine has been having satellite connectivity issues, Samuel told me. Hopefully they'll be cleared up in time for our next televised stakeout I expect in just another day or two."

"So you're back on track after that diversion you mentioned?"

"That diversion I mentioned led to the discovery of a sheep-dog-sized spider, plus something so unbelievable… Well there are actual security concerns over any of us breathing a word about it over transmission devices."

"You *did* find a living dinosaur?"

"Sherman thinks he might have picked up one's stink trail, but that's not it. Don't think Eclipso minds the whole world learning about our discovering a living dinosaur, soon as that happens. Otherwise why would he put a *Puffington Post* journalist on the team?"

"'Something so unbelievable': One of the women on the expedition has the hots for you? That would definitely raise a security issue, namely my own *in*security."

"No way, Vicky honey. But I find your jealous noises curiously comforting. Just remember that old song: 'I only have eyes for you.'

"We, um, didn't get disconnected, did we?" asked Augie anxiously when his remarks were met with silence.

"I'm still here."

"Uh, maybe I don't say this often enough," Augie prattled on still somewhat anxious. "But imagine we finally do stumble across a thriving non-avian dinosaur community that proves so amazing, I have to watch the video repeatedly to believe it's real. That's how I wake up feeling every day, over having you and Liz in my life."

"Then maybe I should make a video of us blowing you kisses, and hope you don't dismiss it as a clever forgery,

Augie-Doggie. Meantime, try not to go extinct before that stinky dinosaur does," Vicky concluded, teary-eyed.

Chapter 11

The cigarette boat finally emerged from dense, swampy, tributary underbrush onto the opaquely brown Sangha River. That is, after two endless-seeming days of Cloud Nine dragging it along at the end of a wiry steel cable sharp enough to slice through thick, overhanging vines with hot-knife-through-warm-butter ease.

No more blood-sucking leeches...diminished dread, back out in the wide open, they might stumble across a non-dinosaur beast even more awful than the sheep-sized spider...and fearless in the face of Prince Englebert's tickling...Sergeant Fred Frankly sighed deeply, beyond relieved.

"Okay, guess I'll have to f-n' admit there's something soothing about floating down this muddy river," Fred conceded. "Better that, than worrying the next branch that pistol-whips my head might accessorize me with a poisonous snake necklace a far cry from an Hawaiian lei!"

"Yep," wearily agreed Officer Kevin Smith-Park. "Even if we're on a stink-out as opposed to a stake-out to find a living dinosaur, because a reggae-dancing, pencil-sized gator thought it was a good idea. At least, that's according to that pretzel-munching Eclipso character with his mother looking on grimly from over his shoulder like in some two-hundred-year-old daguerreotype photo."

"Given our truly most peculiar circumstances, gentlemen, I thought we were better off joining these bold explorers out on the front lines," Ali whispered just loudly enough to be heard above the occasional wild monkey, and who knew what else from along the river banks. "Better that than sitting around on Cloud Nine, wondering what's going to happen to us ultimately, how long before we can be reunited with loved ones, if that's still even possible."

"There is a wise old Cameroonian saying," said Prince Englebert. "Might as well live while waiting to die, since there's nothing else better to do."

Sergeant Frankly and Irene McDowell both would have called "b.s." on the prince, if they didn't fear that might launch him into a tickle rage. *If ever one of his wise old sayings sounded pulled from where the sun don't shine...* thought Irene.

"Please don't take this the wrong way," pleaded Augie of the time travelers. "But from what you explained, my fondest hope would be that you suddenly vanish from our presence, re-ensconced with your loved ones back aboard your marvelous-sounding spacecraft."

"Not at all," Kevin assured him. "If I were to wake up right now, wondering whether Bonsai Gator was real or only some crazy dream after too much mushroom pizza, wouldn't be the worst thing."

*

Days earlier, just before the dinosaur search resumed formally, Samuel Longbottom succeeded in re-establishing view-phone communication with Eclipso. This allowed Eclipso to interact face-to-face with the princes as well the time travelers. He welcomed the time travelers into the fold, and assured the princes he would assist their future plans after they rode out his African search for living non-avian dinosaurs. Moreover, Eclipso found Scott's proposal most agreeable.

Time travelers Ali, Fred, and Kevin had sensed something enormous as well as enormously odoriferous sitting on their shuttle pod. Ali's camcorder malfunctioned, so much for any video evidence.

Nevertheless, he thought he glimpsed something enormous through a tropical downpour, lumbering off in a roughly southerly direction. Taken together with Sherman's flatus emission detector evidence, Scott concluded that just maybe, a remnant sauropod dinosaur had resumed its migration. So he proposed changing the embarkation point for the mokele-mbembe search.

Rather than start along the Dja River, the away team would favor a swampy tributary from Lake Tele. They would follow it down to the Sangha River, where the Dja eventually fed. If and when they detected the creature, either visually or via Sherman Peabody's flatus detection device, the away team would split in two. Cloud Nine would transport half of them further south, where they would backtrack on a second cigarette boat. Maybe they could corner the presumptively migrating creature between the two boats. That is, unless it climbed ashore and stomped off through the jungle. But Harry and Harriet Letterman were sharing round-the-clock shifts with Samuel Longbottom, attending Cloud Nine's overhead surveillance camera for any such event.

"Distinguished explorers, I feel obligated to share information with you from our present, your future," said Ali Magabu after Eclipso gave Scott's suggested minor alteration to their plans his seal of approval. "It sounds truly disappointing at first, but hopeful caveats do apply. We have no history of such a search as yours, or yours for that matter. As of 2064, the modern-day survival of non-avian dinosaurs still appears highly doubtful. There are the small Pterosaurs of New Guinea, but that's it. About those hopeful caveats, though: You say the exploitation of contraptions we left behind in place of guns contributed in no small part to the fortune this Eclipso Sunray Smith amassed. And that he's been tapping into that fortune to underwrite your efforts."

"In other words," Augie broke in excitedly, "the absence of our search in your historical records is from the reality before you tampered with the past."

"Exactly," Ali nodded. "Plus, we can't overlook the possibility our contributions to a less-polluted, less-war past have proven just enough to help some remnant dinosaur, the very last one maybe even, survive long enough for you to discover. Whereas otherwise, she might have already perished long ago."

"And then we will see your discovery in the historical records on our new time line, when we finally reawaken back aboard the Smoke and Mirrors," concluded Sergeant Frankly. "Holy freakin' saurus! Can't believe I'm actually making sense of this! Will be one hell of a story to tell my two adopted runts! Who are probably this minute, eighty years from now, still trying to stick chocolate chip cookies down people's pants to get their asses burned by invisible dragons. It's a long story," Frankly added when Irene gave him a what-the-hell-is-that-all-about? look.

*

Intercepting a dinosaur on its migratory path, whether in the Central African Republic or Cameroon, came with unique political challenges. True, Eclipso had already struck deals with Central African Republic and Cameroonian officials. But someone or some village laid claim to every square inch of wherever the expedition would be treading, no matter how remote or unexplored. Should Augie and company chance across fishermen, local game hunters or some tucked-away village, government papers wouldn't mean much. Additional tributes would be expected, and even then...

Samuel Longbottom proposed they make use of Cloud Nine's concealing self-generated cloud for "a little razzle-dazzle that will leave the more superstitious swamp dwellers awestruck harmless. They see baskets full of goodies magically lowered out of our hovering mists, fear should stifle anything apart from gratitude."

"And we don't mention we're there searching for mokele-mbembe," advised Scott.

"That doesn't sound too racist," Irene bristled. "Why don't you throw in a little 'ooga-booga' while you're at it?"

Scott sensed hurt, if not outright feelings of betrayal, in the look Irene gave him. He responded defensively, "Doesn't- Doesn't matter. Uh, my experience has been that people the world over, when faced with anything they don't understand immediately, they react superstitiously. For example," he went on despite half-expecting steam to snort angrily from Irene's flaring nostrils, "there's the Bible museum that underwrote my earlier expedition in search of mokele-mbembe. At a pancake dinner they sponsored during Lent, one pancake had an eerie likeness to a face. Many of the attendees spooked themselves into believing it was Jesus Christ. If that- I'll- I'll call them a tribe - If that tribe were transplanted here, I have no doubt how a number of them would interpret seeing our proposed baskets of goodies lowered out of our steam-powered drone's generated cloud. They would conclude those gifts were literally heaven sent. But the same as at the pancake dinner, the not-so-superstitiously inclined would figure they best keep their mouths shut."

"Us 'not-so-superstitiously-inclined' are usually able to quietly content ourselves with knowing we're correct," dead-panned Stephen.

Except where that German-Shepherd-sized spider is concerned, which you're still struggling to accept was real, Irene itched to add. With what Scott found a tantalizingly enigmatic grin, she mused to herself, *I can quietly content myself with knowing that on that particular subject, Mr. Feldman, sir, you are totally incorrect.*

*

"So tell me this, someone," Sergeant Frankly said loudly enough to be heard above the nocturnal cacophony of multitudinous birds, bugs and frogs, plus the gentle swish the cigarette boat made as the current floated it quickly down the open waters of the Sangha River. "It's not entirely clear to me, or f-n clear at all, for that matter, what exactly you're supposed to do for that Eclipso character munching away on his humus and pretzels. That's assuming you ever actually happen upon a freakin' surviving monster dinosaur. Am reminded of my two runts aboard our starship: they're always chasing an officer's three-year-old daughter down the hallway. Or she's chasing them. If one of them ever caught the other, then what? They're way too young for a serious relationship, obviously."

"I always figured it's a rehearsal for being grown up, like playing doctor or cops and robbers. For your two 'runts,' that is," Irene clarified. "I'm not sure even God knows what Eclipso has in mind."

"All he's ever said is that Bonsai Gator thinks it's a good idea," said Alistair Frump. "For my own part, I'm in it to develop the world's most unique golf course. Jurassic Links!" He raised his hands like he was envisioning the sign at the course's entrance.

"The celebration of any accomplishment is always easy," weighed in Sherman Peabody, though keeping his eyes glued to his flatus emission detector screen. "But especially when that accomplishment is essentially a beginning, the hard part quickly ensues. For example, when Sylvia and I first met, we enjoyed night after night expressing our wild passion for each other. But inevitably, we faced the hard yet very rewarding work of building a relationship, with all the give and take that entails."

The rain-forest night made it difficult for expedition members to see each other despite being bunched so close together on the cigarette boat. Nevertheless, Sherman's associates avoided eye contact with one another for fear of exploding with laughter. Irene had especial trouble holding it together, given what came to mind. *Did Sylvia go orgasmic just seeing what you were hiding under your chin?*

"Sylvia is something of an adventurer," Sherman continued, oblivious to the difficulty he was making for his fellow explorers not to succumb to unbridled hilarity. "She's working her way up to tackling a climb of Mt. Everest. Meanwhile, it was all I could do, not to have a panic attack when the rope ladder lifted me thirty feet into Cloud Nine back in Papua, New Guinea. So actually, she's thrilled I've been able to set aside my obsession over the odds of various calamities, such as being struck by a meteorite or lightning, or a microburst abruptly smashing Cloud Nine into the ground. To assist Eclipso's quest, I mean, of course."

I should think tackling you makes Everest a piece of cake, Irene couldn't help thinking, as much as she kept such snark to herself.

"Anyway, I pointedly asked Sylvia what would come after Everest, what could possibly pose an even more magnificent challenge to her than that. The answer left her lips with surprising speed. And I quote, 'After that, I aim to assemble a thirty-two-thousand-piece puzzle.' She was quite serious."

"Why not a forty-thousand-piece puzzle? How did she arrive at thirty-two-thousand?" Stephen Feldman asked with that typically pained expression on his face, as though he were suddenly afflicted by some migraine-level headache, Augie imagined in the humidly close and thick darkness. "And will she tackle some other mountain first, such as El Capitán? Not as tall, admittedly, but its ninety-degree cliff face..."

"Who even makes a thirty-two-thousand–piece puzzle?" interjected Irene.

"She plans to commission it," Sherman responded, not missing a beat. "She will use a photo taken of her after she reaches the summit. Which relates to your question, Mr. Feldman; Mt. Everest is approximately twenty-nine-thousand feet tall, varying by several feet depending on geologic activity and snow depths."

"So she's equating one foot of mountainous ascent with one puzzle piece," said Stephen dripping as much with dubious regard, Augie reckoned, as he was dripping with tropical sweat.

"Those final thousand or so pieces of clear blue sky might leave your lady friend requiring the same amount of supplemental oxygen she'll need to scale Mt. Everest's rarefied heights," whimsically speculated Bernie Coleman.

Bernie had insisted on joining the cigarette boat cruise despite his delicate health, talk about bold risk-taking.

The noise Irene produced trying to stifle her amusement came out strange. So strange, more than a few of her fellow explorers looked all directions wondering from where in the night-enshrouded, unexplored rain-forest wilderness it might have issued.

"I believe her entire point is to have her next big challenge waiting in the wings," Sherman responded to Bernie. "To blunt the sort of post-partum depression one might expect in the afterglow of any surpassing achievement. If she stood in our presence, she would likely invoke a lyric from one of her favorite progressive rock bands, Marillion, when they sing, 'Happiness is the road.'"

"In other words," said Stephen, "however much in vain Eclipso's quest most likely will turn out to be, we should enjoy it in and of itself."

"But in the event of the actual discovery of a surviving non-avian dinosaur," Sherman said with as much passion as Augie had ever heard from him, "well we should consider that like the beginning of a beautiful relationship. Yes, beginnings are always the easy part; they don't say, 'The honeymoon's over,' for nothing. In this case, though, what comes next shouldn't be that hard to enjoy. Learning surprising new things about dinosaurs we simply couldn't apprise from their fossil record, discovering whether other dinosaurs are still romping about...each orgasmic brief delight over a new, deeper understanding will certainly whet our appetite for the next."

Scott and Irene weren't exactly certain where they sat in the cigarette boat relative to one another, given the engulfing, humidly close darkness. But they both peered overboard into the chirping, croaking night. And they remained peering overboard, to forestall even the smallest chance they might catch each other's eyes. They could only hope that Sherman's way of describing scientific discovery wouldn't make their faces glow in the dark with embarrassment.

"Of course," Sherman continued, blithely oblivious to how his captive audience was reacting, "there is a distinct possibility regarding this mystery we are trying to solve by either proving a negative or confirming the value of local legends. Its solution might forever remain elusively just beyond our grasp. Nature's carrot on a stick, perhaps, for luring us into deeper understandings of everything else, but. For example, when Prince Englebert here impressed upon us the practical value of a well-considered tickle..."

"Then you're saying Eclipso's dinosaur quest might be like playing a round of golf," Alistair Frump stated more than asked. "The ecstatic release, if you will, of dropping your ball into the cup only tempts you into dreaming how great the next drop will be. I.E., happiness is the fairway!"

So much happy horse manure, thought Sergeant Fred Frankly. He'd had more than enough of what he regarded as philosophical b.s., so couldn't resist blurting out, "Not to offend any of you! But in line with what Kevin said earlier, I would be as happy as the proverbial pig in a mud puddle, happiness is the puddle, oink-oink, were our time-traveling conundrum to suddenly wake me up gone from here, back aboard our starship! Even were I to then learn my two adopted runts launched a whole batch of chocolate chip cookies into orbit round the moon, forming their own pint-sized version of an asteroid belt!"

Chuhhhhmf!

Nobody had to say a word to know exactly what happened. Or at least part of exactly what happened.

The cigarette boat was brought to a complete halt, bumping into *something*.

The other part, of course, concerned what that something was.

Chapter 12

Every last person aboard the cigarette boat quietly braced for whatever the boat ran aground on to push back.

Augie felt equal parts wouldn't-that-be-so-cool anticipation and sheer terror. Any second, was an enormous reptilian visage atop a serpentine neck going to leer out at them from the rainforest darkness?

"Well I think it's safe to say," said Alistair Frump, becoming the first to brave making any least sound, "that what we've bumped into is either dead, or never was alive in the first place."

"I vote option 'b',"' said Stephen.

"I'm reading nothing on my flatus spectrometer," said Sherman. "Either our quarry took an unexpected, unnoticed detour off the main tributary leading from Lake Tele to the Sangha River. Or has somehow outpaced us. Or has been holding it in, as it were, for an inordinately long time. Or as you suggested, Alistair, is lying dead before us."

"Or all that your flatus spectrometer picked up back there was the passed gas from some far smaller reptile that scampered off through the jungle well before we got anywhere near the Sangha," proposed Stephen in what Augie had come to know as his stern, self-styled voice-of-reason tone.

"If it has been 'holding it in' ever since we left Lake Tele," said Irene, "maybe it's time we held our noses, or donned oxygen masks, just in case."

"Or pinch our noses with clothes line clips so our hands are available as earplugs," chimed in Laura, bursting the dam of pent-up amusement for some relieving laughter.

Splash!

All chuckles cut off abruptly.

With his powerful flashlight, Samuel scanned the river ahead.

Something perturbed the prevailing current so much, said current rocked the cigarette boat despite its being run aground on what the flashlight revealed was a sandbar featuring a steep sand dune.

Prince Englebert leaped from the long sleek boat onto the sand, fingers ready to tickle rather than rifle ready to shoot, Augie couldn't help marveling.

"Well will you look at the size of the depression hollowed into the side of that sand dune," remarked Alistair. "Wait." He put fingers to forehead like he was receiving a message via mental telepathy. "Ladies and gentlemen, prepare for your minds to be blown. Anybody here know the origin of sand-traps in golf?"

"Someone's ball flew onto a beach, and by the time he finally succeeded in hitting it off of there, he'd dug his own grave?" proffered Stephen in his deadpan voice.

"Nice try," laughed Alistair. "But no. Along windswept Irish and Scottish coastlines, ancestral golfers found large depressions worked into sand dunes by sheep seeking protection from gale force winds. What if, imagine a Brontosaurus did the same thing here, seeking protection from a rainforest cloudburst?"

"There's no such thing as a Brontosaurus," sternly said Stephen. "The supposed Brontosaurus fossil came from an Apatosaurus."

"Tomato, to-mah-to, Bronto, Apahto; who cares?" said Alistair dismissively. "The point is: Imagine Jurassic Golf Links featuring sand traps carved out by lounging dinosaurs!"

Crickets, literally, as well as other creatures variously chirping, croaking, and whistling in the primeval wilderness. Everything save for any slightest human noise in reaction to Alistair's enthusing over the notion of saurian-produced golf course sand traps.

Even Houdini Chicken, ever firmly ensconced on Augie's mop-top, avoided eye contact with Alistair, her head bobbing all other directions.

Irene couldn't help imagining Houdini Chicken with earphones, grooving to some funky beat.

"So am I the only one excited about sand traps possibly left behind by living dinosaurs? And maybe instead of only one island green, we design an entire series of them, hopscotching down this river? C'mon, people!"

"I could get excited about a tall glass of iced tea back aboard Cloud Nine in air-conditioned comfort," reacted Stephen.

"I was just thinking, Mr. Frump," said Irene, "that prior to this, I would have confidently bet everything I own that I'd go to my grave, never hearing about sand traps produced by dinosaurs."

"Having seen certain extraterrestrials display their soiled clothing as artful masterpieces," crackled Sergeant Frankly, "I would have easily taken that bet, young lady."

"This is exactly, *exactement*, the type of conversation I expect from sweet potatoes," said Prince Englebert, shaking his head ruefully. "Only sweet potatoes enjoy the luxury of time for such nonsense. *Mais oui!*"

"You have a point, Prince Englebert," spoke Scott with urgent impatience. "I'm not sure that while we're aground on this sand bar, our migrating mokele-mbembe hasn't already eluded our sonar, and glided swiftly underwater well south of us! Maybe it was the one from Lake Tele. Or a different one, while for all we know the one that sat on our time travelers' space shuttle took a side trip off the tributary we followed down to the Sangha. Either way…"

"Or no dinosaur at all, given zero evidence," interjected Stephen. "There's not even any-hing registering on Dr. Peabody's fart detector."

"But whatever worked a swale into this sand dune..." Ali Magabu trailed off, having hopped ashore for a closer inspection.

"Which is exactly why – thank you Dr. Magabu – we need to break into two groups right now, instead of waiting any longer," Scott insisted. "Cloud Nine can deposit one group in our second cigarette boat, well downriver a couple miles. Then Cloud Nine can tow it quietly back upriver until meeting up with this boat drifting south on prevailing currents.

"Everyone needs to keep a lookout for certain things: burrows along the riverbank, malombo fruit like I showed you that might have been left half-eaten floating in the river, that sort of thing," Scott concluded.

"You've mentioned burrows before," yawned Dr. Roberta Quiñones, off the boat on the sand bar more to stretch than to puzzle over the giant depression hollowed into one side of the dune. "You actually saw any on your earlier expedition?"

"A large one; there's a photo of it in my book."

"Oh, that's right."

"Komodo dragons burrow, turtles and snakes in the temperate zones hibernate that way; a distinguishing characteristic, perhaps, of reptiles and amphibians that survived to cross the Cretaceous-Tertiary boundary sixty-five million years ago."

Augie and company must have heard Scott mention his burrowing hypothesis at least a half-dozen times since they arrived in Africa. In fact, there was little conversation that hadn't been set on rewind. How else to remain ever vigilant, on the alert for a non-avian dinosaur over the uncomfortably warm and humid, seemingly endless hours sailing tributaries of the Sangha?

"I'm excited about your islands-in-the-stream golf course, Alistair," Harriet Letterman's voice suddenly crackled with static from Samuel's walkie-talkie, loud enough for all to hear above the nocturnal swampy jungle din.

"Um, that's great," reacted Alistair, befuddled by Harriet's timing.

"What we really need to be excited about now is splitting up," reacted Scott, ever more anxious to get the show on the road, as it were.

"Okay," Harriet's voice crackled again.

"First, we might want to spend a few minutes scouring this dune, in particular its swale, for skin samples, scales and the like," suggested Ali, already well underway in that endeavor. "Even a few grains of sand might yield evidentiary DNA."

"'Evidentiary DNA'?" quizzically repeated Roberta Quiñones. "It would take months to run such an analysis, assuming we could find a lab, but oh," Roberta read the look Ali gave her, "where you're from…"

"I'm truly sorry; our DNA kit is at the bottom of the Lake Tele swamp, inside our shuttle pod," lamented Ali. "Otherwise, we could conduct a full analysis in twenty minutes."

"Wonder why your lounging dinosaur didn't leave any foot tracks on the sand bar," drily remarked Stephen, while stifling himself from what he really wanted to snark. *What, did you also leave your magic wand and perpetual motion machine inside your futuristic spacecraft aka crash-landed twin-engine plane? I for one would like to return to Lake Tele and exhume your so-called "shuttle pod."*

"Well there are a few large depressions here and there," Ali pushed back, directing his flashlight at them. "Assume changeable river levels regularly place this sand bar underwater. Clear tracks would be hard to come by unless we arrived soon after their production."

"Even the occasional rainforest cloud burst is probably enough to erode them beyond recognition," chimed in Kevin.

"Fair enough."

*

Bits of sand and whatever else were recovered from the sand dune for eventual DNA analysis, including what looked like a dermal plate.

Stephen argued the dermal plate might just as easily, more likely come from a large turtle than a modestly proportioned sauropod dinosaur.

Regardless, the search team easily agreed on who should remain, and who would be flown on Cloud Nine miles downriver to fill the second cigarette boat.

Augie would head up the group that remained while Scott headed up the downriver group for the tow back north, hoping to catch a dinosaur in between the two. Choosing who would accompany who might have bogged down, hadn't Prince Englebert offered to tickle everyone in order to help clarify their choices.

First off, the three time travelers agreed to stick together. Based on past experience, they assumed their colleagues from the future would thereby have an easier time "rapturing" them back to their present. Laura Gómez would join them, under Augie's auspices, in the hope she could witness their departure.

Roberta said she did *not* want to be present for Ali and company's possible sudden disappearance. She said the very thought weirded her out, likewise for Irene. Both Roberta and Irene would join Scott downriver. Augie suspected, though, and Scott hoped, Irene's decision had far more to do with her wanting to stay at Scott's side, not being too obvious about it.

The two princes thought they best split up, thereby assuring no sweet potatoes would be left to deal with the locals by themselves. Any moment, someone might emerge from surrounding jungle to demand tributes for trespassing on their property.

Prince Englebert joined Scott's group, making Stephen's choice of Augie's group effortlessly easy, in aide of minimizing his tickle risk.

Alistair electing to accompany Scott solidified Laura's choice of Augie's group. She'd avoid the golf course developer's occasional lustful leer, in addition to assuring she would be present for the purported time travelers' departure, were they to suddenly disappear into thin air.

Samuel Longbottom figured he best return to Cloud Nine beside the Lettermans, in case the away teams ever pleaded for help simultaneously.

Sherman Peabody didn't make a choice. He wound up seated beside Augie by default, having been fully distracted monitoring sonar and his flatus emission detector.

Yet as the cigarette boat finally resumed its downriver drift, Sherman's attention did not remain so fully focused on his devices that he did not find the wherewithal to say, "A question that often perplexes me: Perhaps our distinguished princes would regard it as a mere frivolous luxury of us sweet potatoes, that most of the world's populace can ill afford. And they're probably correct. All the same, just what if there was nothing new left to discover? What if we already knew one way or the other whether any non-avian dinosaurs survived into the present? But moreover, we also knew everything there was to know about everything else? Then what? Let's even say you had virtually unlimited resources at your fingertips to do anything you wanted, and every last bad guy had been defeated, with peace and prosperity for all. What would make one happy then? And how many people really know how to answer this question?"

Getting you to shut the f- up would be a good start for me, Fred Frankly came very close to answering out loud. What kept him silent was the prospect of Sherman Peabody subsequently responding, *Okay, suppose I do shut the f- up, as you said. Then what? If that's a good start, what's the second step?*

"Well it's fortunate, I suppose," said Stephen Feldman while nervously eyeing Prince Angelbert's hands. He hoped the prince wasn't wondering whether the secret to happiness would be to follow his lover's lead, and tickle everyone he could on whatever flimsiest pretext, beginning with Stephen himself. "It's fortunate our lives don't last nearly long enough to risk running out of new things to experience."

"Unless, monsieur, we are reincarnated innumerable times across millions of years,' corrected Prince Angelbert.

"Ah," Stephen raised a forefinger, "but if I can't recall anything I experienced on jus⁻ my most recent incarnation, let alone a number of them…"

"I'd like to risk changing the subject back to what we're here for," said Augie. "Speaking of evidence for the existence of mokele-mbembe, there's something Scott mentioned a while back that just occurred to me. On his prior expedition, the locals told him that hippos, especially, remain far away from arywhere the mokele-mbembe might linger. Our beastie o⁼ interest purportedly has a penchant for killing hippos even though it's probably a plant eater. Well, I happened to read it's not uncommon to see hippos sunning themselves along the

Sangha River banks, if not actually in the river for a good cleansing swim. Yet ever since the tributary emptied us into the Sangha, can't say I've seen one hippo or any other large mammal, for that matter, such as an elephant."

"Wow, that must mean there's a mokele-mbembe in my garden back home," said Stephen in mockingly affected awe. "Because I've never seen a hippo there."

"Guys?" said Laura with a smidge of alarm in her voice, "Um, where I'm shining this flashlight along the river bank, oh damn! We've already drifted past it!"

"No problem," said Augie. He revved up the cigarette boat's electric-powered outboard motor to U-turn and head back north, upstream. After steering near shore and cutting off the engine to resume their quiet drift carried on the Sangha River's strong currents, he whispered to Laura, "Now what was it, exactly?"

"There!" she pointed excitedly while Prince Angelbert dropped anchor to prevent drifting too far past whatever seized the American woman journalist's attention.

"Wow!" Alistair whispered, awestruck. "Now that's the sort of location, if one of my errant golf shots ever ended up there, I'd definitely take a one-stroke penalty rather than go in looking for my ball."

"And why is that?" Stephen asked challengingly, albeit in a whisper.

"Not to put too fine a point on it, mate, but that looks exactly like what I'd imagine for the lair of a prehistoric monster."

"How so?"

"To put it another way," said Laura, "would you like us to pull the boat closer so you can jump off and explore there right now?"

Tiny pairs of eyes glowed, and an occasional lightning bug flickered, out of the night-enshrouded rainforest, a star-studded sky arching overhead. All this made for a that-much-darker darkness of the cavernous opening in the riverbank's side, Stephen did have to admit.

Laura's flashlight highlighted various lengthy roots dangling from the cavernous opening's ceiling, making the inky blackness beyond appear even more forbidding.

"No," Stephen answered finally. "But not because I'm afraid a Tyrannosaurus or your mokele-mbembe, Prince Angelbert, is crouched inside, waiting to pounce. Rather, numerous nocturnal dangers could be making that space their home. It might literally be a den of snakes."

"Mokele-mbembe is not mine, nor anyone else's," bristled the prince. "Someone tries to own it at their own peril."

"I don't think even the largest known python could have burrowed a hole that immense into the river bank," opined time-traveler Ali Magabu. "It appears large enough to hide a couple elephants."

"Who said any animal had to have created that feature?" questioned Stephen. "It looks like the product of river erosion."

"I wouldn't be so sure," said Laura, lowering her flashlight beam. "The floor of this 'feature' is distinctly above the water line."

"At this particular time," Stephen pointedly observed. "Don't think we can assume the river level is always this low."

Augie imagined a boulder-sized reptilian head looming out of the root-enshrouded opaque gloom. He could almost hear it angrily hissing at the expedition for trespassing on the threshold to its lair. But he still found mental space for fretting over coordination with his wife's classroom routine. *Better alert Vicky to prepare for a delayed video feed. Unfortunately, I don't think our likely investigation intervals here are going to match up with student attendance times like they did when we were exploring Papua.*

"Augie?" Irene's voice abruptly crackled from Augie Matias's ear piece.

"Hearing you loud and clear. Problem?"

"Opportunity; we've come across a large cave hollowed into the river bank. We've dropped anchor to investigate further."

"Same here! Hey everyone," Augie looked up to say. "Our down-river contingent has found the same feature we've found carved into the riverbank."

"You mean carved into the riverbank by erosive water currents," admonishingly corrected Stephen. "They probably stretch the length of the Sangha."

"Well let's see what we find when we explore this particular one at daybreak," suggested Augie.

"When there should be enough light to more easily spot any snakes," added Laura, smirking at Stephen.

Chapter 13

"Augie? My God, must be the dead of night there!" Vicky couldn't help exclaiming after she checked the time on her bedside alarm clock, having set down the Dickens novel she was reading. A little after ten. "Not that I'm anything less than thrilled to be hearing from you again so soon!"

"Hope I haven't caught you in the middle of something," *such as an extramarital affair.* Augie's nasal twang came out so much more nasal than Vicky was used to from him. Something in the phone connection from Central West Africa, she figured.

"It's just me with *Martin Chuzzlewit.*"

"Who's Martin Chuzzlewit? Oh, that Dickens character who comments on slavery in the United States."

"That's him, in the only Dickens novel that takes place in the United States, at least partly."

"Listen, Vicky, not sure the next time we'll be able to speak in private. But want you to know I'll have our camcorder feed starting around five a.m. your time. We're going to be exploring hollowed-out areas along the Sangha River bank. I'll try my best to provide narration, but will mostly have to whisper."

"Oooo, some dinosaur dens, perhaps?"

"Or- For once I have to give our resident skeptic the benefit of the doubt. I'm not convinced they're not abandoned pygmy hippo burrows amplified by river bank erosion."

"Well has the big news about the vaccines reached your neck of the jungle yet?"

"Vaccines?" Augie hated playing dumb with Vicky, but there was no way he could let on about the time travelers who were tagging along. During down time, they had indeed told his gang all about the vaccines.

"Has to do with the latest weapons theft that took place near the Cameroon capitol, Augie Doggie, really not that far from where you're roaming. Along with the usual humanitarian supplies and golf equipment left behind, there were boxes full of vials. They contained what Oxford researchers have just determined perfectly defang the HIV virus and malaria!"

"So now the Interveners are not only pre-empting major wars? They're also ending serious diseases?" Again, Augie didn't feel good about not making his sweetie-pie privy to information that solved the biggest mystery by far of the past century. But there was no telling who might be tapping their phone line.

The fact was, not only did Augie know all about the vaccine, and more. Eclipso had insisted on a video conference so Bonsai Gator could express through dance everyone's appreciation for what Ali and company were accomplishing with their history-altering hijinx.

Prince Angelbert and Prince Englebert missed out, though. They had to be down below off Cloud Nine, guarding the anchored cigarette boats at two different locations along the Sangha.

*

Anyway, Bonsai Gator, all six inches of him, had gyrated to a reggae version of John Lennon's "Imagine."

Watching on Cloud Nine's eighty-inch flat-screen TV, Officer Kevin Smith-Park couldn't help remarking, "Don't know about you guys," referring to fellow time travelers Ali and Fred. "But I don't remember 'Imagine' having been a complex epic symphonic rock piece, performed by all the Beatles rather than being a John Lennon solo gig. Wonder if Chris is aware of this; he either freaked out, or will be freaking out."

"...hope someday the Interveners will reveal themselves," crooned John Lennon, "So we can thank them for nursing us towards living as one..."

"Those lyrics have been altered for sure from what I recall, truly," agreed Ali, shaking his head in awestruck wonder.

*

"Anything else you need to share, sir? Or have to keep secret?" Vicky asked presently.

"Buk-buk-BUK!" went Houdini Chicken, feeling to Augie like she was trying to nestle in even closer on his head.

"Was that Houdini Chicken again? Don't tell me she's still camped on your head."

"Ummm..."

"Do I need to be jealous?"

"Houdini's not my type, believe me," said Augie as definitively as possible. But he unaccountably felt a twinge of conscience, curiously amplified by one of Houdini's claws piercing all the way through her nest to his scalp.

That's right: her nest.

Augie wondered why the flurry of gossipy whispers and chuckles when he climbed back aboard Cloud Nine earlier that night for the video conference with Eclipso. But he honestly hadn't the faintest idea it was about him until Sergeant Frankly said, "Hey, Mr. Matias, are you trying to make a fashion statement with that nest on your head?"

"That *what?!?!* Good grief!" Augie couldn't help exclaiming as he felt around on his head. To his disagreeable amazement, instead of coming across Houdini Chicken's warm feathers, he scratched his fingers on an artfully arranged assortment of especially thin twigs and branches. Somehow, that rainforest detritus had been skillfully if instinctively woven together with his mop-top hair.

Augie's exclamation burst the dam for out-and-out laughter.

Laura Gómez, barely containing herself, said, "I honestly was way too distracted to notice until these other clowns alerted me! What with the boat running aground on that sand bar, and then there was the creepily sculptured dune, and that river bank's cavernous hole. But didn't you feel something weird happening on your head? I mean Houdini Chicken had to have flown on and off your scalp several times…"

"I was obviously too distracted as well by the possibility we might catch a glimpse of mokele-mbembe. I probably discounted Houdini's comings and goings as commotion from bats, bugs, etc., what with the nocturnal ruckus."

"You had no idea your feathered groupie was treating your hair as a fixer-upper?" asked Fred Frankly incredulously.

"What can I say? Guess I'll have to sleep sitting up so I don't disturb her nest."

"You're going to let a damn freakin' escape-artist chicken run your life?"

"If she asks me to cover her gambling expenses, well that's where I draw the line. But am super exhausted from the pea-soup humidity; being back inside this air-conditioned contraption, think I could almost fall asleep on my feet."

"Spoken like a true sweet potato, if I might borrow from Prince Englebert."

Chapter 14

Augie Matias found himself hurrying down a cavernous labyrinth alongside Houdini Chicken. Only, he wasn't Augie, and she wasn't Houdini Chicken. And he was scampering naked, on all fours, across craggy rock that left him cut up and bruised as the passageway grew darker and darker. Irregularly spaced tremors didn't help, and something glowed faint, bluish-green ahead. Where were they headed? What was their destination? And why did they stall out for a most comforting nuzzle of each other's warm, downy feathers?

As Augie woke up and realized he'd been having a nightmare, he found his nose greeted, cushioned by something feathery soft. At first he wondered, *How did I get a pillow in my face, asleep sitting up?* But then, with an alarmed disgust that had him spitting to keep anything from getting in his mouth, he complained, "A dirty word, Houdini Chicken!! A-boo!! Get your butt out of my face!!"

"Squawk!" squawked Houdini Chicken, resentfully obliging a far more polite request than she would have experienced from anyone else aboard Cloud Nine. With a very noisy flutter she left Augie's face, having mistaken it for a very different part of his anatomy, and resumed settling in on the nest she wove onto his head.

"What the fried fish," vented Sergeant Frankly ducking in Augie's closet-sized stateroom aboard Cloud Nine. Houdini's ruckus and Augie's complaint woke him before he was ready. "No," he shook his head on seeing Houdini still settled snuggly into her nest on Augie's head. "Don't tell me she's been there the entire night!"

"I wish."

"Say what?" Fred Frankly did a double-take. "Maybe you two need to get a room, or a coop."

"We have a room here. I mean, look, it's not like that."

"Hey, whatever floats your boat." Frankly raised his hands as in, *I'm not here to judge, and the less I know, the better.* "I've seen enough crazy shit across four solar systems. But seriously, all kidding aside, can you please walk me through again why it makes any sense to leave her taking up residence atop your thick noggin?"

"Sure, um," Augie had to pause, defuse the defensiveness he felt over the sergeant's scurrilous insinuation, kidding or not. "We saw how much of an escape artist Houdini Chicken has proven to be, wherefore our name for her. The thinking, my thinking was that we didn't want her suddenly leaping out of nowhere smack the middle of, if we do come face to face with a dinosaur. So, since she seems to have imprinted me…"

"Yeah, where she thinks you're her mommy…"

"Or Captain Hot Stuff," Irene couldn't help snarking, having listened in on her way down the hall.

"Yeah, right," said Augie. "Whatever the reason she wants to pester me, we figured that this way, at least, we always know where she is."

"We could also know where she is, served for dinner one night, all fried up," deadpanned Stephen.

"Squawk!" complained Houdini Chicken.

Stephen felt unsettled to the point he had to tell himself her behavior was just a coincidence. *No way could she have been admonishing me over the very notion of having her goose literally cooked.*

*

"I couldn't do that to her," Augie admitted to Fred Frankly re frying up Houdini Chicken, as they were lowered out of Cloud Nine's concealing, self-generated fog bank. Both were gently re-deposited back on board the cigarette boat where Prince Angelbert pretended total focus on fishing.

Upriver from them, three men were a blur of motion, paddling their dugout canoe. After seeing someone with an occupied chicken nest on his head descend out of an odd-looking, roiled-up cloud, they figured the faster they rounded the next bend in the river, the better.

"What," said Fred whilst unstrapping himself from Cloud Nine's cable straps, "do they think Augie is some freakin' sky god, and Houdini's nest is actually his God-damn divine crown or something? Not that I wouldn't have been high-tailing it out of here, myself, if I saw our little spectacle without knowing about Cloud Nine and Houdini Chicken."

"Maybe you would have wanted to bow down to Houdini Chicken as the real sky god, Sergeant," deadpanned Stephen anew. "And assumed Augie was her beast-of-burden servant."

"I will tell you this, *monsieurs et mademoiselle*," said Prince Angelbert. "You might not have been able to discern it through the rainforest din, *mais oui*. But as you were descending out of your artificial cloud, those locals were shouting at us that we should leave while we are still able to. Nothing about a sky god. Rather, that anyone crazy enough to tolerate an occupied chicken nest on their head is someone to be fled from, period!" Prince Angelbert considered adding that Fred ought to have checked his prejudiced assumptions at the door when he first arrived there. However, he figured that would have led to unnecessary friction that not even a good tickle would alleviate. *Better that these sweet potatoes learn from the showing rather than the telling, in any event.*

*

"Isn't it impressive, we don't have to hunch over for walking through here?" Laura Gómez whispered in the company of Augie, Stephen and the three time travelers. They were taking their first tentative steps across compacted wet sand into the cavernous hole they found along the east side of the Sangha River riverbank.

Sherman remained aboard the cigarette boat along with Prince Angelbert, to keep constant vigil on both the river sonar and his flatus emission detector.

For any locals who might pass by, Prince Angelbert still pretended to be fishing.

The other away team, consisting of Irene, Scott, Roberta and Prince Englebert, worked from a second cigarette boat a few miles further downriver.

"Sure," Stephen agreed with Laura about not having to hunch over. He went on whispering, though, "Lots of sand is probably washed in here during the rainy season, making for a more claustrophobic passageway."

"But this is the height of the rainy season. I believe the driest months are December through February," Augie said pointedly. He wouldn't let Stephen's implication go uncontested, that a large burrowing animal needn't be invoked to explain the size of the passageway they were exploring. Meanwhile, his flashlight carefully scanned every nook and cranny of both the sandy ground and muddy ceiling.

The ceiling featured innumerable hanging roots of all varying thicknesses and lengths. They had Augie especially eagle-eyed for snakes giving the appearance of roots. "Um, how far in should we go before we turn around?"

"He asked nervously," added Laura to suppressed snickers from Kevin and Fred.

"I'm actually rather disappointed we haven't come across any snakes yet," lamented Stephen. "Except for the dead ones sold in that market back in Douala, of course."

"Yeah," said Fred. "You'd think some enterprising boa constrictor would have tried swallowing Houdini Chicken whole by now."

"Don't listen to him, Houdini," said Augie protectively.

Houdini Chicken let out a forlorn-sounding murmur that reminded Augie of a dove's mournful coo.

"I really would fancy a leaf viper, for example," Stephen went on with a certain mischievous relish. "They're so very brightly green-shaded, and their toxin usually only causes nonfatal hemorrhaging."

"'Nonfatal hemorrhaging'? Sounds like a f-in' bargain," cussed Fred.

"But I'd settle with a close look at what you folks jumped to the conclusion was a spider the size of a German Shepherd."

Plllp!

On this unexpected noise, the group collectively froze in their tracks. Augie found himself running his flashlight from face to face after it revealed nothing but empty passageway up ahead. "Was that what I think it was?"

"You mean a fart," answered Stephen in his sinking, here-we-go-again voice.

*

Hours later and thousands of miles away in Vicky Copplestone's fourth-grade summer school remedial class, many of her students burst into laughter. They were watching the replay made possible by Augie's teensy camcorder affixed to his shirt collar.

Coincidentally, curriculum adviser Diane Mueller ducked her head into the classroom. Hope sprang eternal for Diane that on one of these unannounced occasions, she'd finally catch Vicky at something well beyond offensively outrageous. Then once and for all, she could have her excommunicated from the school system.

"What was so funny, boys and girls?" Diane asked in her falsetto voice meant to convey much enthusiasm over the students' evident merriment.

"Someone farted!" shouted a broadly grinning Micky, not waiting for Ms. Copplestone to call on him after he joined numerous other students raising their hands.

"*Mais oui?*" Giselle nodded all around.

"*Oui! Oui!*" several students joyfully nodded.

"And where did that happen?" Vicky Copplestone asked. She figured: Better to handle the situation like she would have done had Diane not intruded. Better that, rather than emulate how she felt certain Diane wanted her to deal with student outbursts.

For sure, Diane would have severely reprimanded Micky, not only for not waiting to speak until he was called on, but also for using such crass language. Then she would have laid into Giselle and the others for only compounding the rudeness. And lastly, she would have lectured Vicky for not blowing up at them, rather tolerating their offensive behavior.

"Micky? Where did that happen?" Vicky repeated.

"It happened in someone's butt!"

"Not that!" Vicky reacted loudly to make herself heard above the riotous laughter. "I mean where did it happen, geographically?"

"But can't geography also be about where things happen on someone's body, like a person is a planet?" Micky asked half-defensively, half-mischievously.

*

"Well don't look at me!" Sergeant Frankly shouted his whisper.

"The problem is," said Augie, "there's so much echo inside here that that noise could have come from anyone…or anything."

"Oh, so now you're going to claim it was a dinosaur fart," muttered Stephen.

"Not necessarily," pushed back Augie. "Too bad Sherman's flatus emission detector probably didn't pick it up, to verify whether it was human or...other. He's too far away."

"Well for the record," said Laura, "it was not me."

"Truly not me, either," chimed in Ali. "And I would not have hesitated to claim ownership if it was me."

"That's what you want us to believe," said Kevin. "But it's not me either."

"I wish it had been me, to take the dinosaur possibility out of the picture in no uncertain terms," grumbled Stephen, "as though it could ever have been a dinosaur fart in the first place. But it was not me. Not even a silent one."

"My better half tells me that in her classroom, 'Not me' receives the blame for lots of stuff," said Augie.

*

"This sounds like a murder mystery!" giggled Vicky's remedial student Evan, clapping his hands delightedly.

"Here's around where Mr. Copplestone said they were," said Giselle. She circled the northern extent of the Sangha River with her forefinger, on a blown-up map of the Congo Basin posted beside the classroom chalkboard.

"Yes, Micky?" Vicky rushed to recognize Micky raising his hand again before he could open his mouth anew, in deference to Diane Mueller's presence. Nevertheless, she sensed that where Diane was concerned, the situation had already gotten way too far out of control.

"If they really did hear a dinosaur, Ms. Copplestone, can we call it the fart that time forgot?"

Diane stormed out of the room, heels clicking louder than ever, followed by her slamming the door shut behind her, hard.

Parents are going to hear about this, Diane swore to herself. *Her room is going to be so full of observers tomorrow, she's going to need extra chairs!*

*

"There is one person here who has yet to issue a denial," observed Stephen, back to his deadpan delivery.

"That's not fair to Houdini Chicken," said Augie. "She doesn't know enough English to defend herself."

"I wasn't talking about Houdini Chicken."

"But when I shined my flashlight on her, she did turn away," said Laura.

"What, she couldn't look you in the eye over her embarrassment? Christ almighty," Fred muttered. "Somebody please spirit me back to the Smoke and Mirrors, like yesterday, to leave this nut-job expedition."

"I'll admit," said Augie, "back on the tributary, under cover of all the rainforest critter chatter, I did slip a fart under the radar, as it were. No doubt, Sherman's flatus emission detector picked it up, along with who knows how many of you did the exact same thing. Only, Sherman is too polite to mention that. But this particular fart was definitely not mine."

"So, we're left with no alternative than to believe we just heard a dinosaur fart," drily concluded Stephen. "Well if that isn't definitive proof…"

"Actually," said Augie, full well knowing he was about to surprise Stephen, "I've noticed such an echo in here, I wouldn't be surprised if our mystery fart was produced a good distance down the shoreline, which this burrow appears to straddle. A pygmy hippo, perhaps…"

"Or someone from the other away team?" Laura asked in plain wonder over just how much sense Augie's remark made.

"Well whoever or whatever it f-n' was," cussed Sergeant Fred Frankly yet again, "have any of you freakin' fart suspects noticed what's been happening underfoot?!?"

"My sandals are becoming very wet," said Stephen matter-of-factly. "That's your rainy season river level rising, Augie, hopefully at a slow-enough pace for us to easily make our way back to the boat before we're inundated."

"Unless it's dinosaur pee," said Augie.

"Ah, yes, dinosaur pee," Stephen said most amused. "We wouldn't want to be caught in a flood of that, certainly."

"So you're not above making a mockery of this quest?" Laura asked Augie, reporter mode, while everyone picked up their pace in hurried, sloshing backtrack to where they'd left Prince Angelbert and Sherman parked at anchor in the cigarette boat.

"No reason to take ourselves too seriously, really," Augie responded. "Whether or not a living, breathing, farting, non-avian dinosaur is wandering around out here will not be contingent on whether or not we joke about it."

*

"Thought I'd check in with you upriver guys. How's it going that end?" Irene whispered softly. But Stephen had the upriver crew's walkie-talkie amped so high, they could hear her loud and clear.

"Our biggest excitement has been a fart of undetermined origin," Stephen responded in his own soft whisper, a good-faith effort not to scare off any especially shy, reclusive dinosaur, as absurdly remote a prospect as that seemed to him. "We've all but ruled out a non-avian dinosaur. Either it was one of us lying or in denial, Houdini Chicken, or a pygmy hippo's relief that echoed our way from a well-hidden location. And your end?"

"Wasn't from my end," Irene couldn't help responding before going on, "We're investigating something far more interesting than that fart, if you're correct about the choices for its origin."

"We're exploring an enormous, deep burrow that has been opened into the river bank from well above the water line," elaborated Scott, his whisper loud with nervous, on-edge anticipation. "Our flashlights reveal seeming clawed-out grooves along the burrow's inner walls. And just outside it, lots of dug-out-looking clay and sandy mud has been heaped up, forming a short, stubby peninsula into the river."

"I was reminded of the pile of dirt my childhood pet pooch pushed behind him when he dug a hole to bury his bone," chimed in Irene.

"Probably just a pygmy hippo burrow," Stephen suggested with affected casual ease. *Nothing to see there.*

"Too big and wide for that," chuckled Irene, amused at how quickly Stephen hurried way way away from any least hint at extraordinary possibilities. "We don't even have to duck our heads to avoid bumping the ceiling. Our biggest challenge so far has been not slipping on our initial downward descent."

"You're still inside there, do I understand correctly?" asked Augie, mischievously wanting to add, *where Scott can catch you in his welcoming arms should you take a tumble?*

"We are deep inside. The descent has long since leveled out, and we are trekking parallel to the Sangha, not too far from it."

"What we were investigating was obviously more river bank erosion than anything else," insisted Stephen. "In fact, we had to abandon exploring it directly, head back to the cigarette boat because of the threat posed by rising tide. Have you considered the possibility your burrow did begin with a pygmy hippo, and water erosion widened it?"

"I see a problem with that," interjected Roberta before Scott could work up the courage, forget about any poisonous vipers or frogs, to sidle up close enough to Irene's walkie-talkie again to add anything. "The wall to our left, on the river side, are as solidly compacted mud and clay as the wall to our right. And it includes those claw marks. I should think that river bank erosion would have left no wall there at all, nothing more than hanging roots like so many beaded curtains."

"There's erosion so far underneath the river bank here, I wouldn't be surprised to see the coastline edge collapse; that could form the sort of solid-wall tunnel on both sides you're describing," argued Stephen, undaunted. Moreover, Augie noticed, he conveniently ignored what Roberta said about the claw marks.

Augie's same end of the walkie-talkie, Ali had had more than his fill of Stephen's insistent pursuit of boring explanations for curious matters, whether or not those explanations were a good fit. And so, before Augie could jump in, he asked, "Can you tell us, Dr. Quiñones, whether there are roots sticking out from that tunnel wall, the other side of which flows the Sangha River? Because I should think if it is the collapsed front edge of an eroded river bank, it ought to be littered with them."

"All that our flashlight is picking up is striated clay wall," answered Roberta.

"So the only possible explanation is that a dinosaur burrowed through there," Stephen reacted in what Augie found a remarkably defensive tone.

Maybe, Augie thought to himself, *Stephen is as spooked as I am by this undercut river bank that seems to go on and on.*

As Prince Angelbert steered their cigarette boat drifting steadily downriver alongside the river bank, the bank's undercutting kept presenting with what Augie could easily picture being some impossibly large monster's impossibly wide maw. The roots hanging from topside the riverbank were stringy muscle tendons caught between the monster's teeth, awaiting a good flossing that would never be. And the pitch-black darkness past them concealed the cavernous pit which led to its whale-sized stomach.

The creepy river-scape kept Augie on edge, anticipating any moment some behemoth reptilian head surfacing on a serpentine neck. Then what was to keep it from pushing out past the veil of hanging roots, and roaring in prelude to overturning the cigarette boat? And biting its occupants dead, one by one? *It's as though there ought to be some huge, mysterious beast lurking in the waters underneath this eroded river bank. If nature abhors a vacuum, so apparently does my imagination. But Stephen is probably right; we're looking at nothing more here than the result of much water erosion. On the other hand, though, what Irene and company describe further downstream…*

"Okay, Stephen," started in Augie, while also suddenly realizing how thankful he should surely be to the brilliant Sherman Peabody. Sherman had sprayed them with a peculiar mix of local mud with ground-up local chrysanthemum blooms full of bug-repelling pyrethrum. As a result, no more stress over multitudes of bugs, tiny mite-like chiggers especially. Chiggers could have been distracting him with countless itches and sores up and down his arms and legs from their burrowing under his skin. Instead, Augie could focus more intently on how the dinosaur search was going, with nearly the detachment of Samuel Longbottom and the Lettermans back aboard

Cloud Nine. Save, of course, that his mind ran loose with notions of an attacking swamp monster. "Okay, Stephen, regarding what we're finding versus what Irene's gang is finding, maybe it's an 'and,' not an 'or.'"

"What?" Stephen squinted, once again like mere words could give him a migraine.

"Maybe you're right about what we're finding along this part of the river bank. It's nothing more than the product of water erosion. *And* Irene and Roberta are also correct, suspecting they've come across a burrow made by some huge, claw-wielding creature."

"A dinosaur."

"Not necessarily, but huge, and claw-wielding."

"Hold it," Scott's urgent voice erupted from Laura's walkie-talkie. "Looks very muddy here; could be quicksand," he went on loudly enough for Augie and company to continue hearing clearly over Laura's walkie-talkie.

"That might be leftover water from when the river bank collapsed there," Stephen was quick to resume ax-grinding.

"Only we walked a good couple hundred yards of dry ground prior to this," Scott was equally quick to push back over the walkie-talkie. "And those claw marks curve down towards the mud pit, with the burrow ending just past."

"Wait," interjected Ali from aboard the crowded cigarette boat. "Whatever creature clawed that burrow into existence, you think it might have sunk into that mud pit, hopelessly entombed itself there?"

"Scott's already sprinting back to our boat for a shovel," noted Irene.

"I don't think your huge, claw-wielding monster would have been able to sink completely out of sight in such a muddy area as you describe, even if it is quicksand," dismissively said Stephen. "A mastodon caught in the La Brea tar pits took days after its death to sink down all the way."

"For once I have to agree with you," conceded Irene.

"We might finally have something of real interest our end," announced Sherman Peabody, on the rare occurrence of his standing up in the cigarette boat, and pointing ashore. "Consider, if you will, that anomalous bulge there, mere yards inland from the river bank, like nothing I've observed up to now. Among possible explanations, one certainly has to consider something large underneath there having pushed up against the thick web of roots and natural ground cover to emerge, but without success."

"I certainly do have to consider that," said Stephen. "Of all possible explanations, I have to consider that by far the least tenable. Ridiculously unnecessary to resort to when, for example, what we see could prove nothing more than a tree stump layered over by that ground cover you mentioned, Sherman. In fact, don't those liana vines nearby look like they're enrobing fallen trunks?"

"There's one way to find out, *Monsieur Skeptique*," said Prince Angelbert as he anchored the boat close enough to shore for climbing onto the riverbank, above the cavernous erosion underneath.

Augie, Kevin, Fred and Laura quickly joined the prince on soggy land, the ground cover spongy like the cover layer over a firm mattress, Augie reckoned. But before any one of them could approach the bulge in question, all of them noticed something rather peculiar to their left.

Rocks lined a very small pond or a very large puddle, as though they comprised a primitive stone border for collecting rain water. No fallen leaves or twigs floated on the water's surface, surprising given the abundance of such detritus all around. And large tadpoles could be espied swimming about.

"This must be the work of a Goliath Frog," noted Prince Angelbert.

"You say a frog moved those rocks?" said Fred. "Damn! Just how goliath is it?"

As though in answer, a pebbly-textured golden-brown frog the size of a football suddenly hopped out from the tropical rainforest veil, planting itself squarely in front of the tadpole pool. Then it confronted the human intruders with a croak so loud and deep, Augie was reminded how an electric bass guitar throbbed through him at a rock music concert. And an unusual flap of skin under the frog's lower jaw recalled a turkey wattle.

"Buk-buk-BUK!" went Houdini Chicken, rising from her nesting squat on Augie's head to spread her wings wide.

"Are they trying to communicate with each other?" Ali called from his vantage point back down aboard the boat.

"Yeah," said Fred Frankly. "Houdini Chicken just said, 'You think that croak is something special? Well check out the noise *I* make!'"

But the frog, different from any Goliath Frog Prince Angelbert had ever seen before, especially with that aforementioned turkey wattle, wasn't through yet. Said wattle inflated, inflated and inflated some more, like Augie one time saw a bullfrog inflate its vocal sac. Although unlike with Augie's bullfrog, such ballooning-out wasn't succeeded by a quick deflation producing a distinctive bullfrog croak. Rather, the wattle kept inflating until it lifted the rest of the frog off the ground. And then the entire frog, inflated wattle and all, rose floating into mid-air.

"Fascinating," said Augie breathlessly. "She must have filled her wattle with methane or some other lighter-than-air gas. She's trying to scare us off from getting anywhere near her tadpoles!"

"Mission accomplished," said Laura. "You don't think she's going to explode, do you?"

"I wish my beloved Englebert were present to tickle her back down to size," said Prince Angelbert.

"Sure! Then maybe they could double date with you and Houdini Chicken, Augie! Whoa!" Fred exclaimed apprehensively, seeing the giant frog open its mouth wide whilst floating directly overhead.

Before anyone could say another word, the giant frog issued a deafening, "Ahhhhh-ee-ah-ee-ah-ee-ah-eeeee!" that reminded Augie of Tarzan's jungle cry in old movies. Far worse was the putrid, nauseating stench, a nightmare blend of skunk spray with rotten-egg sulphur.

The Goliath frog proceeded to swoop through the air like an out-of-control deflating balloon, sending the four humans stampeding away from the mound they'd come ashore to investigate. They ended up closer to the river, and incidentally a good distance from the tadpole pool.

"I have no idea what you have going on over there," Irene's voice suddenly crackled from Laura's walkie-talkie. "But we just heard and felt something large stomping above our heads. Oh, good; Scott's back with a shovel and ladder. Unless this mud really is quicksand, we're going to try digging through the ceiling to the surface, see if we can sneak a peek at the stomper. Whatever it is sounds like it's come to a halt nearby."

"Good luck with that," said Augie, keeping a nervous eye on the fully-deflated frog, despite it having landed statuesquely still before the tadpole pool. "Uh, we're investigating a certain mound to see whether it's pushed-up ground, or simply a covered-over tree stump, even though pushed-up ground won't necessarily mean much."

In a flash, the giant frog stuck out her ribbon tongue, and drew in a passing dragonfly.

*

Scott McDonald set up his ladder atop the muddy burrow floor, close to where the burrow ended. He stood directly underneath where his contingent of the expedition thought they heard something immense lumber across overhead. He intended to shovel a hole into the burrow's ceiling large enough to poke his head through, for an unobtrusive peek at what even he had to reluctantly admit might prove nothing more than simply an elephant or hippo passing by.

Before Scott climbed aboard the ladder, Irene and Roberta took their first tentative steps onto the mud. To hold the ladder steady for him, they had to make certain they wouldn't be standing on quicksand, or some clayey material they could still sink into up to their ankles.

Nothing to worry about in that regard, but, "Kind-of spongy, isn't it?" asked Irene, perplexed.

Scott crouched down and patted what struck him as a curious cross between wet adobe and a wet sponge. Spongy adobe. "Maybe some air pockets trapped underneath this sandy clay," he speculated.

"Are you going to keep stroking that floor affectionately, or climb on board here?" snarked Irene from where she stood beside the ladder.

"She sounds jealous, Scott," Roberta couldn't help remarking.

"Not my type. This floor, that is."

"And just for the record, I was talking about you climbing on board this ladder."

"Huh?" huh-ed Roberta. "What else would he be climb-oh."

Scott and Irene both hoped the flashlight-lit darkness still veiled how red their faces flushed.

*

"Digging into this mound, we need to proceed extra carefully," advised Augie as he pulled on his own pair of extra-reinforced latex gloves, having distributed others to Laura, Fred, Kevin and Prince Angelbert.

"For once Mr. Sweet Potato acts not so silly," Angelbert commented supportively, tugging on his gloves to assure a snug fit. "If this turns out to be an anthill, we must retreat at a pace *trés rapide* to avoid being swarmed, then nibbled down to the bone in a matter of minutes. And also beware of scorpions and brightly colored frogs not larger than my thumbnail, but which can blind you instantly, permanently, with one spit of their venom in your eyes, *mais oui*."

"Which raises the friggin' question of why we're bothering to pierce through this ground cover in the first place," muttered Sergeant Frankly half to himself, half for public consumption. "Let's say we establish there is a raised stretch of ground under there, as opposed to a tree stump or an anthill. So what? You even admitted, Augie, that doesn't necessarily mean anything."

"Something enormous burrowing underneath here…Scott spoke with locals on his previous expedition who claimed mokele-mbembe burrows into these river banks. That would certainly be consistent with what we know about the Komodo Dragon in Indonesia being an occasional burrower."

"Okay, enough of your yappin'," Fred Frankly complained. He'd heard this all before, and regretted having fueled getting to hear it again. "If it is raised ground, we're going to insert an upside-down periscope, see if we can catch a freakin' Apatosaurus doing nap time. Do I have that right?"

*

"Listen!" Scott urgently whispered as he stopped scraping at the sandy clay ceiling with his shovel, his hair caked in grit.

Roberta and Irene, holding the ladder firmly despite bits of scraped-off ceiling pelting them, did listen very intently. They heard exactly what Scott heard, a scraping noise from somewhere above him.

"The question is whether that's from another burrow," said Irene, "or from outside, totally above ground."

"We did seem to descend for a while on our trek inside here," noted Roberta. And she checked for the umpteenth time that she was securely hooked to the mountain-climber's cable, as were Scott and Irene.

Scott had fastened one end of the cable to the clayey wall on the off chance any of the muddy burrow floor should suddenly give way, or the tripod ladder overturn despite the two women's efforts.

"Well whatever's up there, sounds like my digging has its attention."

"Don't be disappointed if a pangolin pokes its snout in here, checking for ants, once you break through," warned Irene.

To heck with a possible pangolin, Scott feared he read more into Irene's empathy than was actually there.

*

"Do you hear that scraping sound?" asked Augie breathlessly. He halted his own digging into what looked more and more like a mound covered over by a mossy layer of rainforest detritus than anything else.

"Maybe we should back off, see what happens?" proposed Laura tentatively.

"Not the worst idea," said Augie. "I'm well aware we have little reason to believe it is something saurian, based on what we know about it so far, which is zilch. But it might scare as easily as any lizard or snake, even if it's twenty times larger. So how about we do just stand back a bit, wait on doing any more digging?"

"Sure," agreed Fred. "And when some pipsqueak turtle emerges, we'll be the biggest friggin' audience it's ever had, especially one *not* particularly intent on gobbling it up."

"What it should do is take a bow, then ask us to hold down the applause," said Kevin. If it wasn't for Ali's clear curiosity, he would just as soon they'd waited back aboard Cloud Nine for the Smoke and Mirrors to retrieve them. *This is ridiculous!*

*

"I know these aren't the easiest conditions," Scott said diplomatically while continuing to scrape away at the ceiling with his shovel. "But could you hold the ladder a little steadier? Keeping balance is-"

"Why are you suddenly swaying so much, Scott?" Irene interrupted to complain, alarm in her voice.

"Let go the ladder!"

"Huh?!"

"Dig your climber's hook into the wall over here! Fast!" Scott pointed at the side of the burrow wall where he'd worked in his own hook.

Scott wanted to explain his dawning realization. Namely, that what he had fastened into the wall up near the ceiling might be pulled out if the floor gave way and the three of them were left hanging in mid-air connected by the climber's cable only. He knew there wasn't time for that, though.

The muddy floor beneath Irene and Roberta's sandaled feet went from slowly to quickly sinking, producing an awful, deafening rumble. All too soon, the ladder disappeared into a dark abyss.

Irene dangled helplessly; she had not been able to swing herself over beside the wall fast enough, where Roberta had already hooked in. "Scott?! Help!" she cried.

The absence of Irene's usual snarky tone made Scott's heart go out to her even more than it already long since had as he responded, "Hang on, Irene! Can you pull her over, Roberta?!"

"Trying!! There!"

"Got it!" confirmed Irene, informing her tone with as much "no big deal" irritation as she could feign to cover for how vulnerable she'd felt...and who she couldn't help screaming out to, despite Roberta being the more practical, closer-by option.

No matter. One last echoing rumble from the unexpected sinkhole directly below left all three explorers uncontrollably screaming, "AAAA!!!" They were spooked, re-imagining that rumble as the roar from some impossibly large monster prowling the depths of the Earth.

*

"Okay, I'll have to concede that whatever that is must be larger than some pipsqueak turtle," said Sergeant Fred Frankly, rattled by the peculiar noise heard issuing from somewhere underneath the mound.

Fred and company had already backed well away from the mound, awaiting the emergence of whatever they'd heard clawing and scraping from below.

"Did any of you hear that?" Augie shouted back towards Sherman and Stephen anchored near the dramatically undercut riverbank in one of Cloud Nine's two cigarette boats.

"Echoes might amplify the burrowing sounds of a baby hippo to an extraordinary extent," responded Stephen. "However, I would be unwilling to entertain even that possibility until we learn more about any geological instability of this region. And as for a surviving non-avian dinosaur: not in the running, far as I'm concerned."

"Let me guess," said Fred. "If we saw a T-Rex suddenly poke its head out of that mound, you'd want to make sure it wasn't some wild monkey dressed up for out-of-season Halloween!"

Before Stephen could respond, a second subterranean racket, more muted than the first, sent the on-shore group even further away from the mound. They crept on hands and knees partway down the side of the riverbank, careful not to fall off the edge where the river erosion had so seriously undercut it, supposedly.

"Time for those camouflage caps, Augustine?" asked Laura.

"Definitely. Then we duck down behind this line of cycads, here. And we wait until either whatever it is emerges and we can hear it crawling around, or until it becomes apparent nothing is emerging, and the scraping was just, who knows? Maybe some snake tunneling through? And that roaring coincidentally originated from a bull elephant complaint way off in the woods? Hopefully the boat is anchored close enough to the riverbank, out of sight, to not scare off whatever-it-is. Especially if some truly extraordinary creature does pop its head out of the ground."

"I don't think sinkholes scare that easily," said Stephen drily. "I'm guessing that's the best explanation for those noises."

*

"Prince Englebert, if you will indulge me a moment, I just had a monster idea, speaking of dinosaurs, ha!" laughed Alistair in his usual hyper-enthused mode.

"Sweet potatoes were born to be indulged," responded Englebert in his usual mischievously grinning mode while

Cloud Nine, way overhead, genty tugged the cigarette boat upriver against the current.

"Then as a not-so-sweet eggplant or whatever vegetable best characterizes you, Prince, could you drop anchor, like right now? *Tout de suite?*"

Splash!

"Excellent! You see that mound up there, above the riverbank around that bend?" Alistair asked while Cloud Nine came to a hovering halt, Samuel Longbottom also obliging.

"*Possiblement* it's a burial mound for sweet potatoes who have travelled here before, with nothing better to do than chase after mythical beasts?"

Alistair gave Englebert a bespectacled look before responding, "No. Imagine if you will, there's a flag atop that mound, and this boat is a floating tee box. We make our way up and down the river from hole to hole of: The Golf Course That Time Forgot! With your further indulgence, I will work this tee into this ball of putty I smooshed onto the deck. After balancing a golf ball on top, I'll take a swing with my three wood. Guessing that mound is about two hundred yards away."

Prince Englebert grinned broadly, thinking to himself, *And with your indulgence, I should like to work my practiced fingers into your armpits until you pass out from tickles. But I am resisting that temptation so my lover and I can secure safe passage to Sweet Potato Land, where at least our odds of deadly persecution should be less than they are in our cherished Cameroon.*

*

"That frog that inflated to medicine-ball size," Sherman Peabody spoke softly to Augie and company crouched down the side of the riverbank behind a row of cycads. They wore pointy camouflage caps to suggest simply more vegetation, hopefully, to the untrained reptilian monster's eye. Except for Augie, that is; with Houdini Chicken on his head, he simply crouched down extra low. "She also moved stones into a circle to construct an artificial pond for her brood," Sherman continued. "She demonstrated once more how humans are not the only animals who build things. Wouldn't it be most intriguing to not only discover a living non-avian dinosaur, but also learn that whether in self-defense or for nesting purposes, it manipulates various objects?"

"Sure," grumbled Fred Frankly anew. "Maybe Mr. Burrowsaurus and our inflatable skunk frog can throw mud at each other while Houdini Chicken acts as ref! I mean what the f-?!"

*

"Whatever burrowed through there," said Scott as he continued slowly but steadily scraping his way up into the ceiling, "we saw the large amount of clay and mud piled into the river, from digging into the riverbank. That practically reshaped the coastline's meander. So maybe that mud floor that just gave way underneath us was excavated from further down below. What do you guys think?"

"I think you need to shut up and get us out of here!" vented Irene. Even connected by a cable to Roberta and Scott, she still didn't feel all that secure clinging to a climber's hook worked into the clay wall.

"We're almost...there!"

On Scott's excited yelp, the flashlight-lit darkness brightened considerably with sunrays slicing down into the burrow. Although, where the muddy floor collapsed was still left in forbiddingly pitch-black darkness. And the ladder was completely lost from view having plunged heaven-only-knew how far.

"Okay," Scott went on more softly, "I can almost poke my head through. We have to be quiet as possible so as not to scare off whatever we heard stomping around up there, just in case."

"But if that's what burrowed below us...I suppose there have to be lots more than one for a surviving population," acknowledged Irene.

"Lots more than one," said Roberta, suddenly re-impressed all over again with just how long the long shot was, of a surviving non-avian dinosaur. Yet ever grateful for the distraction, delaying the inevitable hard truth she needed to face back home.

×

"I hear more commotion from over there," Augie whispered to Kevin, Laura, Prince Angelbert and Fred crouched beside him. Then more loudly for Sherman Peabody back aboard the cigarette boat, "and feel it through the ground. Sherman, keep your periscope down. In case our critter of interest has eagle eye vision, don't want it scared off, seeing something it doesn't recognize."

"Augie's right. You might want to stuff that thing back inside your pants pocket," Stephen standing beside Sherman couldn't help quipping.

"Shh!"

*

"Ladies, you're not going to believe what I'm seeing the top of, down towards the riverbank," Scott whispered excitedly after he poked his head through to the surface.

"How about pulling us out of here, and we won't have to not believe you, 'cause we'll be seeing it too?" Irene whispered back harshly.

*

"Do you hear what I'm hearing?" Augie whispered excitedly. "Are those the creature's snorts?"

"If so, that's some huge-ass shit out there!" Fred whispered back, thrilled in spite of himself by the notion a prehistoric beast might be emerging from the ground not fifty yards away from them, maybe.

*

Irene and Roberta could not have exchanged more significant silent looks with Scott after he finished yanking them out of the hole he made. They crawled on hands and knees, to stay down out of view of whatever lurked the other side of numerous cycads fronting the river bank.

"You're talking about those wedge-shaped things sticking up from amidst the cycads?" Irene whispered in Scott's ear.

Between Irene's warm breath and what he imagined he might be seeing, Scott feared he would swoon.

Irene hoped the insect din drowned out her voice where "those wedge-shaped things" were concerned. And she fought an impulse to embrace Scott, relieved over their having safely surfaced from the burrow.

"Moss-covered plates on back of a slumbering Stegosaurus-type creature?" Roberta thrilled to propose.

"Maybe," squeaked Scott, teary-eyed over the possibility a life-long dream might be on the verge of fulfillment. But possible risks settled him down enough to less emotionally add, "If that is a Stegosaur or Ankylosaur type creature, we've got to beware its tail. Could swing it at us like a caveman club if we agitate it."

"But if it's taking an after-meal snooze, might not pay us any attention, like a content gator sunning itself," suggested Irene. She scanned their surroundings for any ferns or palm fronds that looked munched-on. Although if their prospective dinosaur wasn't a plant eater such as a Stegosaurus or an Ankylosaurus...

*

SWOOSH!!

"Well well well!" exclaimed Alistair with thrilled satisfaction. "One of my better fairway wood shots, if I do

say so myself! Only hope I didn't put too much draw on-
Are those Irene and- FORE!!! FORE!!!" he shouted
frantically.

"Ah, your fellow sweet potatoes must have dug
themselves out of the ground over there," calmly reacted
Prince Englebert. "Farmers won't have to exhume them,
mais oui."

*

Boink!

"Ouch!" went Augie, straining not to keel over from the
sudden pain on his head.

"Buk-buk-BUK!" went Houdini Chicken, a flurry of
flapping wings before settling back down on her head-
crowning nest again.

"Augie?! Are you okay?!" asked Laura with clear alarm
in her still-whispery voice.

"What the f- is happening?" cussed Frankly, also trying
to keep to a whisper. "I saw something drop out of the sky
into Houdini Chicken's freakin' nest!"

"Whatever is the other side of these cycads, is it
throwing something at us?!" asked Laura, her tone harsh
despite her continued effort to maintain a whisper.

*

"It moved!" pointed Scott.

"Those hisses including a cluck like a chicken; sounds
angry. Should we back off?" asked Roberta, beyond
thrilled. A clucking dinosaur made perfect sense, given
how birds most likely descended from them.

"Thought I heard the strangest noise from afar, probably
some monkey or bird," added Irene.

"If it's agitated enough by our presence," went on
Scott, "any second now it might retreat into the river, and
we'll miss our chance to catch a full glimpse."

*

"All that angry hissing," said Augie, "any second, whatever it is might turn tail and head into the jungle. Either that, or crawl back underground if that's where it came from. I say we need to sneak a peek, right now."

*

"Slowly, slowwwwly," counseled Scott. He waved his arm at Irene and Roberta to join him creepy-crawling towards the line of cycads.

*

"Let's do this," whispered Augie in his softest whisper yet. "On the count of three; one, two three…"

"AAAAAA!!!!" screamed Scott and company as Augie and company suddenly popped up their heads from behind the cycads.

"AAAAAA!!!!" Augie and company screamed right back.

"Buk-buk-BUK!!!"

"It appears our two groups of explorers spooked one another," clinically observed Sherman Peabody. Immediately thereafter, he returned to monitoring his detection equipment as in, *Nothing more to see here.*

"But I could have sworn I heard hisses and snorts as from a huge beast," said Laura, feeling more mystified than humiliated.

"Hey, that's what I thought I heard as well from down here on this boat," admitted Stephen. "I've tried to keep my guard up for misperception. Nevertheless, I wanted to believe as much as the next guy, that some prehistoric monster could still be roaming around out there. Just goes to show how easily you can mistake one thing for another thing when you're desperate for that other thing to exist, as when my childhood U.F.O. sighting turned out not so 'U.'"

"Wait, so when we were whispering to one another," said Scott, the import sinking in to most glum effect, "you guys thought you heard huffing and puffing from..."

"And vice versa, apparently," said Augie. "But my head's still sore. Guess I'm lucky Houdini Chicken's nest cushioned the blow from whatever that was..."

"Yeah, what the freakin' f- was that?" asked a totally disgruntled Fred Frankly as he reached up into the nest on Augie's-

"Buk-Buk-BUK!!!"

"Ouch!" cried Fred. "That f-n' chicken just tried to take a bite out of my finger! But think I felt a golf ball in there! What the f-?"

"A golf ball?! Seriously?!" exclaimed Irene beyond exasperation.

"Maybe your reclusive dino happened across a golf driving range," snarked Stephen.

"Anyone there see where my ball landed?!" shouted Alistair from the approaching cigarette boat, steered by Prince Englebert tickling the controls. "Sorry if it fell too close! I didn't realize how far upriver we'd gotten, pacing our team's burrow exploration!"

"It landed on my head, but fortunately Houdini's nest there cushioned the blow," explained Augie.

"Sorry 'bout that, mate, and way to go, Houdini Chicken! She's helping the cause!"

"Yes, she's protecting Augie from you," drily said Stephen.

"There's still the matter of whatever clawed out that huge burrow we explored," said Scott somewhat defensively.

"And whatever left behind a blockage that turned into a sinkhole," added Irene supportively.

"Did you collect any soil samples from your supposed claw marks? For analysis along with those so-called sandtrap samples?" asked Stephen wearily. Scott frustrated him, how quickly he pivoted away from the sobering lesson Stephen thought they should spend serious time reflecting on before they resumed their quest. It was as though nothing had happened to call their likelihood of success into question.

"Ready to go," said Scott, patting a zippered pouch full of clay dirt strapped to his belt.

"Ladies and gentlemen, there's also the matter of-"

Splash!

All eyes turned downriver to where they thought they heard the splash happen, round a sharp bend that blocked their view.

"Well now it's two matters, actually," picked up Sherman from the interruption.

"You've determined why some men and women feel compelled to launch surrogate testicles – you call them golf balls - such long distances?" asked Prince Englebert. "To accompany those surrogate penises and sperm otherwise known as guns and bullets?"

Augie sensed the prince trying to tickle them with his words, since actual physical tickles were likely to be met by so much angry if laughing protest. *Is tickling what he lives for?*

"Truly a mystery what Dr. Peabody has just replayed for me from his sonar," said Ali by way of insisting his fellow explorers give Sherman their full attention.

"Yes," said Stephen, faux enthusiastically. "What are we going to completely misperceive next?"

By then, Scott, Irene and Augie had already hopped aboard Sherman's cigarette boat to see what his latest fuss was about.

"There," Sherman pointed at the sonar replay for their benefit. "Those swirls, what are they?"

"Weird," commented Augie. "Looks like the sonar has picked up the wriggles without picking up what's doing the wriggling. I would guess something serpentine, reptilian. But there's no 'there' there."

"A ghost snake kicking up sand?" speculated Irene.

"How could a ghost have that kind of impact on material objects such as sand?" asked Scott.

"Let me see," Stephen finally surrendered to requesting as in, *Do I really have to correct all their mistaken perceptions for them?* Exhaustion made him sound even wearier, thanks to so many hours dealing with pea soup humidity. Although, the efficacy of Sherman Peabody's bug spray had spared him innumerable bites, stings and attempts to lay larval eggs under his skin.

"There you go," he said after checking out yet another replay of the sonar. "Those are simply swirls of sand stirred up by eddies in the river current."

"Wait," protested Irene. "Play it again, Sherman, and freeze...right there. How does your eddies thing explain *that*, Mr. Skeptic?"

Irene directed Stephen's attention to two swirls exactly parallel to each other.

"Caused by a water snake passing overhead? Or an eddy resulting in something analogous to a double rainbow?"

"What-ifs and maybes; the bottom line is, you really don't know. And as for your water snake passing overhead, why didn't that produce a sonar image?"

"But I do know you people spooked yourselves into hearing a huffing, puffing dinosaur, rather than each other simply whispering amongst yourselves."

"Well this does add to my growing collection of inscrutably mysterious videos..."

"Which provide zero evidence for any surviving non-avian dinosaurs," Stephen completed Augie's sentence. "'Inscrutably mysterious'? C'mon!"

Splash!

This second splash from down river sounded fainter, presumably from further away. But it proved no less effective at drawing all eyes but Stephen's that direction.

Stephen simply rolled his.

"Is this a good time to interrupt?" Harry Letterman's voice suddenly crackled from Laura's walkie-talkie.

"Not so loud, honey," Heidi Letterman could be overheard counseling her husband. "You might scare away a dinosaur."

"Okay, no so loud," Harry whispered, but up so close to his mike, it came out even louder than his question.

"No problem," assured Laura in full loud voice. "The only creatures we've scared off are each other. What have you got?"

"About one mile downriver from your present location, Cloud Nine has spotted and filmed mysterious splashing, twice," reported Harry.

"Harry is correct," said Heidi. "But nothing was visible. Something made a big fuss without showing itself!"

"Are you sure the hippo or whatever it was didn't agitate the water so much," spoke Stephen loudly enough to be picked up on Laura's walkie-talkie, "it was lost from view amidst the foam and waves?"

"We're reviewing a magnified replay right now," said Samuel Longbottom, "and I'm still not seeing what caused that splash-fest."

"Perhaps a mineral spring, an aquifer bubbling up mid-river," Stephen speculated.

"Well, there's no 'perhaps' or 'maybe' about this," said Sherman, his eyes glued to the screen on his flatus emission spectrometer. "Coincident with that first splash we heard, our spectrometer recorded the same noise signature we detected near Lake Tele, and back on that fateful night on New Britain Island."

"*Maintenant*, off we go? See if we can approach one of these entities that can so profoundly agitate the physical world around them without plainly revealing themselves?" asked Prince Englebert excitedly, flexing his fingers made for tickling.

You're off, alright; totally off your rockers, Stephen wanted to say. However, his intuition warned him that might be one jaded-sounding remark too many, liable to draw Englebert's ire. Then no telling what Mr. Tickle Fingers might do. So he merely rolled his eyes, again.

"Are those drums I'm hearing in the distance?" asked Irene. "They sound like Morse Code."

"It's yet another unusual talent of your lone surviving dinosaur. That is, along with being able to move about invisibly," Stephen couldn't help commenting wryly.

"We do have a species of bullfrog, maybe as rare as the mokele-mbembe, that sounds like that, *mais oui*," noted Prince Angelbert. He was intent on not allowing the irritatingly close-minded American, as he perceived Stephen, to get to him as drums another direction answered the first drums. "But those are actual drums, beaten by the Lokele."

"It is *vraiment* amazing how fast they can transmit a message," said Prince Englebert with one of his trademark sly grins. "Were I to tickle one of you to death, the news would reach the west coast in an hour or less, *mais oui*."

"*Mon cher* Bertie!" shouted Prince Angelbert in his most admonishing tone. He wanted to add, *Are you forgetting we depend on these sweet potatoes for our deliverance from persecution?*

But *mon cher* quickly added, "Merely an abstract example several miles distant from anything I would seriously consider doing."

"You princes have any idea what their drums are communicating?" asked Sergeant Frankly, anxious to move the conversation away from the subject of tickling, and careful not to refer to Angelbert and Englebert as "f-n' princes."

"A local witch doctor," responded Prince Englebert, "says tree spirits have told him about us."

"'Told him about us,'" Stephen repeated dubiously, though quickly adding, nodding the time travelers' direction, "I know; among your many claims, you dealt with telepathic trees on some other planet."'

"The tree spirits said there are great lovers among us, including two dressed as royalty," Prince Englebert continued. And he spread his arms wide to fully display his most colorful dashiki robes, while Scott and Irene looked away from each other. "Those spirits went on to suggest, *trés* enigmatically, that this group must waste time in order to not waste time, ultimately. And that they are led by one inspired by someone else, not necessarily among us, who, and I quote, 'thought it was a good idea.'"

Most of the searchers exchanged significant looks, recalling Eclipso's claim Bonsai Gator thought their quest "would be a good idea." Did the prince overhear one of them mention this aboard Cloud Nine?

Meanwhile, though, Stephen Feldman obliviously reacted, "Okay, wasting time looking for a surviving dinosaur to stop wasting time looking for a surviving dinosaur; I can buy that if sooner rather than later, you all come to realize the hours would be much better spent collecting bugs here, perhaps identify a few new species."

"I know exactly what you're thinking," announced Prince Englebert ominously. "You think I am- What is your expression? – bullshitting you. But you are afraid to call me out, being sweet potatoes. You fear that calling me out might provoke Prince Angelbert and me to abandon you, leave you lost here, having to deal with the Bantu, the snakes and many other et ceteras on your own."

"Their 'Cloud Nine' can always bail them out, *mon cher*," Prince Angelbert advised his lover.

But not paying attention to that, Augie defensively reacted, "No! Yes! I mean, I want to believe you're being truthful, but maybe that's still the sweet potato in me, as you put it!"

"We have an old Cameroon saying: It is more important that sweet potatoes thrive where they thrive best, which is underground, of course, where they can't be seen, than that they can't be seen when they are doing their best. In other words, it is more important you are honest to yourself than how you are to anyone else, *mais oui*," Prince Englebert nodding, grinning.

"I have my own special saying: My lover is full of Cameroon sayings, some of which are not Cameroon sayings at all, but rather are pumpkin seeds he has harvested from his calabash butt!"

Chapter 15

"Who would like to explain for our visiting parents why Lucas can't stop laughing? Gwendolyn?" Vicky Copplestone chose from among several shot-up hands. This, while keeping a nervous eye on Gwendolyn Malmstein's stick-figure mother. Vicky strained to read her crossed-arm countenance as anything other than severely judgmental.

Meanwhile, Lucas had laughed himself into a quiet stasis. The redness round his eyes could have been from grieving rather than tear-producing hilarity.

"We saw what happened in Africa overnight, while we were sleeping," Gwendolyn stood to turn and address with considerable pep a small group of parents who'd gathered on adult-sized chairs in back of the classroom. "But we're about to have a live feed-"

"Wait," interrupted Micky's father, Dr. Tru. "You're going to continue wasting this morning's remedial class watching the boob tube?"

"Our first live-stream update from Mr. Copplestone's expedition in several days," explained Vicky. She'd set up the adult chairs before leaving school the previous evening, as she fully expected a peanut gallery. How could her students not excitedly inform their parents they might see a living dinosaur on her TV the next day?

Unbeknownst to Vicky, there was even someone from a local newspaper embedded with the parents. That journalist reached an agreement with the principal to save the school lots of embarrassment and unwanted media attention. She would report out, only were Vicky's husband to make some astounding discovery sure to cause a big sensation anyway, well beyond a small group of remedial students getting in on the act.

"Whatever happens on 'the ooob tube,'" went on Vicky, "I'm confident your kids will comment on it at length in their journals, as they've been doing all along. But go on, Gwendy."

"So there were these two teams searching for a dinosaur. Not dinosaur bones! A walking, breathing dinosaur other than a bird," Gwendolyn bubbled. "One team explored a big hole in the ground beside a river. We learned the Komodo Dragon makes holes in the ground in Indonesia, so why not a hole-digging dinosaur?"

"I can dig that!" said Micky.

"Stop!" protested Gwendolyn, impatiently stamping her foot over several giggles triggered by the resident wise guy's remark.

"Okay, that wasn't that funny," intervened Vicky to settling-down effect.

"Thank you, Ms. Copplestone. So, Ms. Copplestone's husband led the other team to search caves eroded out of the riverbank. But there was this strange mound they decided to investigate."

"After a giant frog croaked a big stink on them!" added Lucas.

"So it was a goliath frog protecting her babies," explained Gwendolyn in what Vicky found a most amusingly admonishing tone. "So when Ms. Copplestone's husband and his team investigated the mound, they heard strange noises from underneath, like something was trying to dig its way out. So...am I saying 'so' too much, Ms. Copplestone?" asked Gwendolyn, suddenly feeling self-conscious.

"You're doing great, Gwendy. But why not try other transition words, such as 'next' and 'after that'?"

"Thank you, Ms. Copplestone. So after that..." To a few chuckles, "Gwendy" buried her face in her hands, but quickly collected her wits to go on assertively, "After that, Mr. Copplestone's team hid behind some plants to see what came out. Maybe it would be a dangerous animal, maybe even a meat-eating dinosaur, or a plant eater not happy about people invading its territory.

"Um, *next* they thought they heard a monster huffing and puffing. Sounded like whispers to me, and, and..." Gwendolyn couldn't speak any further, practically choking on suppressed giggles. Her face turned beet red.

"'On the count of three: One, two...'" quoted Micky from the video.

"The two teams scared each other!" cried Lucas, back to out-of-control amused.

Click! Click! Click! went the familiar high-heel racket from out in the hallway, growing ever louder as Diane Mueller rapidly approached the door to Vicky's classroom.

Vicky imagined the claws of a prowling velociraptor wouldn't have sounded that much different scraping against the linoleum floor.

Lucas's resurgent mirth sent most other students clear round the bend into uproarious laughter that peaked just as Diane click-click-clicked across the classroom threshold.

Murphy's Law rides again, Vicky lamented.

"Can one of you tell me what's so funny?" asked Diane in a tone of *Don't leave me out of it*, her pleasantness fueled by the concerned looks on parent faces over so many students coming that unglued. "Prissy?" she called on Priscilla Fineman, one of several students to politely if excitedly raise their hands.

"For me, the funniest part was this guy who wants to build a golf course along a river that might contain dinosaurs; he hit a golf ball that landed in the nest a chicken made on Mr. Copplestone's head..." That's as far as Prissy got, shaking her head and making wild gesticulations with her hands before her amusement left her speechless.

"When someone reached in for it, Houdini Chicken almost snapped his fingers off," said Micky picking up the slack. "Maybe she thinks it's an egg she laid!"

"Nobody, certainly not , can deny how profoundly amusing her students find Ms. Copplestone's class," Giselle's father Peter George confided to Micky's father, Dr. Tru, seated beside him in back of the room.

"They're entertained, that's for sure," nodded Tru. "But I'm not clear this is the most productive use of classroom time, despite what I've seen my son writing in his journal."

Gwendolyn's mother, Madeline Malmstein, seated just behind the two fathers, frowned an agreeing nod. And Diane also overhearing the conversation said, "Well let's not rush to any conclusions until we see where this is headed."

Of course, Vicky thought to herself, somewhat fatalistically if also disgustedly, *my expected comeuppance is the dish, every morsel of which she wants to savor most leisurely.*

Chapter 16

"A gentle reminder, my most esteemed colleagues and time travelers," said Augie, pretending the entire group was his target audience when only one very specific person, one of the time travelers, was his real concern. "In minutes, my shirt-collar mini-cam will go live-stream so my wife's fourth grade remedial summer school class might vicariously tag along. Vicky appreciates most deeply when you are careful with your language, steer clear of any obscenities. She never knows when an unsympathetic observer might drop by, or one of her students might complain to their parents. Talk of dinosaur farts is no issue, apparently. But..."

"What the f-, Dr. Matias?!" cussed Fred Frankly. "You think it would take a Sherlock Holmes to figure out you're talking to me?! F-n' bullshit!!"

"Remember, Sergeant, these folks have been carefully shielding us from the outside world's attention until Captain Taylor can spirit us out of here," counseled Kevin. "Don't think it's asking too much-"

"I know," interrupted Fred, taking it down several notches. "Sorry there, Dr. Matias. My nerves are frayed between our bizarre predicament, and dealing with this pea soup humidity. I ought to be more battle-hardened than this!"

"We're all feeling a bit off. At least I know I am," admitted Augie understandingly.

Eclipso's expedition crew did go to the trouble of having the time travelers pack away their starship uniforms in favor of supplied camouflage outfits. The idea was that any adults watching Augie's feed to Vicky's classroom wouldn't think any more of them than as simply additional hangers-on, lured by the prospect of history-making adventure.

"What really concerns me," said Stephen Feldman, ever vigilant for opportunities to throw cold water on the entire operation, where Augie was concerned, "is all this time and energy expended on such a hopelessly quixotic-Okay," he interrupted himself with a bristly tone, "I see many eyes rolling already. But what has this come down to, mere hours after you spooked yourselves into fearing each other as some prehistoric monster? You're well on the way to freaking yourselves out over nothing again, concerning a splash that could have been from literally anything. And about that fart, if your flatus emission detector is to be trusted, Sherman..."

"It is."

"Okay, very well. You've recorded a distant fart that distinguishes itself from an iguana fart only by its intensity. You have no way of knowing it isn t merely the gaseous expulsion from a monitor lizard or other large reptile that doesn't have to be a dinosaur. That's all you've got: A splash, and a fart, both easily explained without bringing a dinosaur into the picture."

"That's not all we've got," protested Scott.

"That light," Laura pointed into the rapidly darkening dusk, grateful for the distraction from a clearly simmering argument, but sincerely puzzled nonetheless.

"Must be a flying Iguanodon," sniped Stephen, though he did search the sky for what Laura mentioned.

Prince Englebert climbed his wiggly fingers heavenward like he would tickle the light once he located it, if he could, Augie imagined.

Irene visualized the prince's fingers as spider legs climbing a web.

"Ah, there we are," the prince nodded as his eyes if not his fingers firmly latched on to the slowly moving object. "I don't know whether any of you sweet potatoes are familiar with the kongamoto, but that might be one."

"Last year, a Bantu villager in Cameroon told me his great grandfather described it as a bat the size of an elephant. It was much leaner, of course, and with a very un-bat-like long pointy crest on back of its long pointy head. Sounded like a Pteranodon to me," said Scott.

"With a glowing belly from bioluminescent bacteria, *mais oui*," nodded Englebert agreeably.

"Sounds like the ropen we might have seen that fateful night on Great Britain Island, before the storm arrived," said Augie.

"An elephant-sized bat with a glowing belly, of course that could only be a prehistoric flying reptile," Stephen sniped some more, with acid sarcasm.

"Well for what it's worth," said Ali, "unless that's a shuttle pod from, um, a science fiction story I recently read, um…" Ali was about to say, *from our starship*, but abruptly shifted gears to fib. The stateside class might be eavesdropping, he remembered nearly too late. He had to be careful not to reveal either directly or indirectly he was there from eighty years in the future. "It's flying so low-altitude, any vehicle such as a biplane or helicopter should truly be making a clearly audible racket, even with this nocturnal creature din. But I'm not hearing any such noise."

"Again, the only possible candidate is a prehistoric flying reptile."

"I'm not necessarily saying that, sir," Ali snapped at Stephen. "If you could only have seen what we've seen, um, of course I'm talking about that dog-sized spider on the shores of Lake Tele…" Ali Magabu was about to mention peculiar beasts he'd seen on other planets. But at least this time he was able to remain truthful.

Stephen would have repeated his assertion the dog-sized spider must have been a matter of mistaken identity, even for Prince Englebert who tickled it into submission before hurling it far away like a Frisbee. But before he could, the mystery light was lost from view behind a stand of tall palms. Immediately pursuant to which, a distinct splash! issued from that same general direction.

"If it is a giant bat or kongamoto with a bioluminescent underbelly, maybe it dove into the Sangha for fish?" speculated Roberta Quiñones.

"There it is again," said Alistair, pointing to the once-more-in-view light moving off into the distance, vanishing there in a haze from trans-evaporation. "Say, maybe it's one of those so-called UFOs?"

"Oh, a correction," said Stephen once again in full snark mode. "You've narrowed it down to either a Pteranodon or an extraterrestrial spacecraft."

Kevin bit his lip to stifle himself, though he swore that later, when Mrs. Matias's classroom wasn't watching, he would tell Captain Skeptic about the antlered Tictoctickians with their flying saucers. No matter Stephen's noises to the effect he wasn't convinced Ali Magabu and company were really time travelers, despite some magically impressive hi-tech contraptions they carried in their backpacks, such as a holophone.

"Harriet? Harry?" Irene was meanwhile calling into Laura's walkie-talkie. "Have you guys picked up our UFO?"

"And it *is* an unidentified flying object, make no mistake, until we know exactly what it is," lectured Stephen. "But that doesn't mean it won't turn out to be something with which we're already well familiar."

"Our radar did pick up a slow-moving, low-altitude object that paused over the Sangha River," reported Harriet.

"Half of it split off, and fell into the river," continued Harry, "if I might complete my sweetie's debrief."

"He completes me."

"And she would have completed me, had I answered first."

"I hear you," said Irene. "So, um, what did you pick up, visually?"

"Exceedingly difficult to wrap my mind around exactly what we were seeing," admitted Samuel Longbottom. "From our view, it was part spindly, part angular, part this, part that. No single shape predominated."

"But did it dive into the river?" asked Irene. "We heard a splash when we lost it from view, followed by our seeing something continue off into the dusk."

"Here's the strange thing," went on Samuel. "Exactly as Harry described it, half of it split off and dropped into the Sangha, without ever re-emerging that we noticed."

"How's this for a crazy idea?" interjected Roberta. "We do know a host of various bugs that mate in mid-air, such as certain dragonflies."

"Sure," acknowledged Stephen. "They can't wait to get a room."

"Some of you have already experienced a giant spider back on Lake Tele. Maybe there are also some relic, prehistoric behemoth dragonflies. After two of them finished mating in mid-air..."

"One of them went to shower while the other smoked a cigarette; yeah, that's a crazy idea alright," said Irene. "Mission definitely accomplished."

"Not so f- errr- fantastically crazy when you consider these cow-sized parachute ahtpah spiders, uh, in a sci-fi story I read," Sergeant Fred Frankly spun his own abrupt change-up with the fury of a spider spinning a cocoon around a bug caught in its web, Ali mused. Every possible cuss word filled Fred's head over how carefully they had to pick and choose their words. with the outside world listening in.

*

"Ewww!" went Vicky's children collectively, clearly as much grossed out as amused over the mating-in-flight possibility.

"It is not for me to simply stand up and object to Ms. Copplestone's proceedings, at least not yet," Peter George whispered to Dr. Tru seated beside him, under cover of the prolonged "Ewww" chorus and Vicky's consequent admonishments in aid of tamping it down. "But freighting every not-instantly-recognized light in the sky or bump in the night with the prospect of something most fantastical? That would certainly seem to tread frightfully close to inculcating superstition."

"That is worth considering," nodded Diane with feigned disinterest, while grateful for the darkened room concealing her ear-to-ear grin.

However, Vicky could still discern it, and found it positively reptilian.

*

"Again," went Stephen, prompting Augie to think to himself, *"Again," indeed, with your doomed-to-the-mundane pronouncements.* "Two dragonflies that large, or two insects or arthropods of any kind that size, their exoskeletons would weigh far too much for them to survive, let alone fly. Those prehistoric dragonflies you alluded to, Dr. Quiñones, surely with your expertise you know they were far smaller than our UFO must be, even split into two. Which is why I'm still extremely doubtful about that supposed dog-sized spider."

"Couldn't they have been two large raptors, ospreys perhaps, mating in mid-air?" proposed Alistair.

"That possibility has never transcended myth status," pointed out Irene. "There's zero substantial evidence birds can mate in flight," she added while studiously avoiding eye contact with Scott.

"Glad someone else did the boring reality honors this time, for a change," said Stephen.

"Not so fast! What say you, good people back aboard Cloud Nine?" asked Alistair with self-fancied boldness. "You have the video to review, I trust. Could that have been two large birds doing the birds-and-the-bees thing?"

"We do have it on video and are reviewing it as you speak," confirmed Harry Letterman over Laura's walkie-talkie. "But nothing we see looks like a bird. And like Mr. Longbottom said, hard to wrap my head around what shapes those were."

"My Harry is especially cute when his ears turn bright red!" gushed Harriet, flushing Harry's ears an even brighter red.

"Something I want to go back to," erupted Scott, turning all eyes his way. "What you said, Stephen, about us 'freaking ourselves out' over what you keep insisting is nothing new under the sun…"

"Okay."

"And let's set aside that light, and what fell from it into the river; I'm willing to grant it might be nothing more than a large raptor that lifted off with more snake or fish than it could handle."

A raptor the size of a small biplane, hmmm…. Samuel Longbottom listening from back aboard Cloud Nine decided not to express his doubt aloud, so as not to interrupt Scott.

"I want to revisit our admittedly mock-worthy scaring one another on the riverbank. Yes, we made total fools of ourselves, no question about that. But the fact remains: that burrow we were exploring was way too large to have been dug by a pygmy hippo, or even a full-sized one. And it included a muddy clay stopper that suddenly fell through like a sinkhole, leaving us to hang in mid-air.

"Of course, that doesn't necessarily mean it was produced by a dinosaur," Scott hurried to acknowledge, beat Stephen to that particular punch. "However, this purportedly is mokele-mbembe country. And I will remind you that that beast is described having an elephant's torso, an alligator's tail, and a snake-like neck, the morphology of a sauropod dinosaur."

"You don't know that some enterprising locals didn't put out that description to boost tourism. Which is to say, after they saw speculative dinosaur depictions," pushed back Stephen. "Are there any known accounts of mokele-mbembe that predate the first artist renderings based on dinosaur fossils?"

"The answer is no," said Irene after giving Scott a gentle shove as in, *Let me handle this.* "But it's also true that western colonialists didn't hear any descriptions of the okapi until the 1880s. And those turned out to be unerringly accurate. Of course, nothing is considered officially 'discovered' until some white guy has verified it."

"Until anyone, white or black, has provided solid evidence for its existence."

"Which the locals had provided for years, again starting in the late 1800s with their bandoliers made of okapi skin," blistered Irene. "But then a British explorer named Sir Harry Johnston received credit for the 'discovery' in 1901."

*

"That woman makes a very good point, actually," commented Peter George to Dr. Tru, watching the back-

and-forth between Irene and Stephen on Vicky's television.

"All I know is that your children are frozen in front of a TV, for a discussion that probably goes over their heads," Diane Mueller reacted, unwilling to concede anything worthwhile happening. "Shouldn't Giselle and Micky be doing grammar exercises instead?"

*

"We are picking up a disturbance in the river only six hundred yards ahead of your present location!" Harry couldn't help exclaiming into the Cloud Nine intercom connected to Laura Gómez's walkie-talkie.

"Not so loud, dearie," Heidi advised her hubbie, though her husky voice transmitted at the same volume as his. "You'll scare away the dinosaur, if it is a dinosaur. They're probably even more bashful than you."

"I'm not seeing anything yet," reported Stephen in his monotone, excitement-dampening voice, far as Augie was concerned. He was peering intently at the water's smooth surface through infrared lens goggles. Everyone had already donned them to deal with the rapidly encroaching nightfall.

"Whatever it is should come into view as you round the next bend in the river," said Samuel Longbottom seated beside Heidi and Harry Letterman.

"No flatus emission signature of interest is issuing from there currently, or from anywhere else at the moment," reported Sherman, ever vigilant with his flatus emission detector.

"I truly doubt such a creature expels gas nonstop," said Ali.

"Especially if it's trying to impress a member of the opposite sex," snarked Irene with a fleeting glance Scott's way he pretended not to notice, and which she pretended not to notice him pretending not to notice.

"Or the same sex," added Roberta.

"Nothing would surprise me, after what I've, err, imagined sci-fi wise," Fred verbally somersaulted yet again, away from what he interded to say. He cussed himself anew over forgetting for the umpteenth time that with eavesdroppers from a suburban Maryland classroom, he needed to be careful not to even hint at his time-traveling circumstances.

"Actually," interjected Sherman, "the whiptail lizard doesn't need to impress anyone of the opposite sex. Her ovulated eggs contain the right amount of chromosomes, all on their own. That form of reproduction is called parthenogenesis, and probably would come in most handy for a lone relic dinosaur. As I've mentioned before. There's always an attendant risk of weakening the gene pool, though."

"Sure, and over several millennia," said Stephen, "you would expect any lone surviving dinosaur past the Cretaceous-Tertiary boundary to in-breed itself out of existence."

"Assuming no viable males around with whom to mix things up, even from another species," said Sherman. "Some biologists believe inter-species mingling led to the whiptail lizard's special ability in the first place."

"I know about that, and can confirm what Peabody is saying," said Dr. Roberta Quiñones. "Moreover, even though they don't have to mate in order to lay fertile eggs, female whiptails mount one another nevertheless."

"So tell us, Houdini Chicken," Prince Englebert addressed Houdini Chicken contiruing to sit squat in the nest she wove attached to Augie's scalp, "does the dissertation by Dr. Quiñones inspire you to fertilize and lay your own egg? Rather than waiting for Dr. Matias to assist you in that matter? Or do you prefer warming a golf ball that, sorry to say for you, will never hatch?"

Houdini Chicken turned her head this way and that; Scott could easily imagine her clucking in response, *Who? Me?*

"If that was your attempt at humor, Prince," said Fred, "you already laid an egg."

"Well I guess someone's not afraid of being tickled," Irene whispered under her breath to Scott.

Scott appreciated the rapidly descending night, as he was sure his ears turned red, just over Irene whispering under her breath to him about anything.

"Something that occurs to me," said Sherman, his attention not the least bit sidetracked by Prince Englebert's playful remarks. "A large beast waddling across this river, its flatus emissions would be lost from detection underwater, at least where their signature noise was concerned. Of course, some rather large bubbles might rise in its wake…"

"I see it! There!" Laura pointed forward excitedly.

"A duck; congratulations," deadpanned Stephen.

"That's no duck," countered Scott, nearly as irritated by Stephen's dismissiveness as he was excited over what he was seeing. "That's a head, alone, at least the size of a full-grown duck!"

"And no duck it's ever been my distinct pleasure to meet could ever stretch its neck out of the water like that, to the length of a giraffe's," chimed in Irene. Despite her snarky tone, she clutched at Scott's elbow, fearful she might pass out over the momentousness of what she beheld.

*

As her students let out a collective gasp over what Augie's infrared camera revealed from thousands of miles away, Vicky Copplestone couldn't help notice Diane Mueller's deer-in-the-headlights visage.

Whatever surfaced like a submarine periscope in the Sangha River riveted Diane's attention, as much as anyone else's.

Nevertheless, Vicky found herself bracing uncontrollably for disappointment. Her hubby's quixotic dinosaur-related quests in the past, after varying intensities of high hopes, had always foundered on inconclusive results, at best.

*

Multiple camcorders wielded by Eclipso's explorers provided multiple angles on whatever-it-was rising further and further up out of the Sangha River.

Stephen Feldman labored furiously, mentally, to understand what had surfaced out of the placid river in ways he could accept. Indisputably, it was not a duck.

Augie was reminded of water falling away in rivulets from a surfacing submarine, until... "You guys notice what I'm noticing?" he whispered with breathless excitement.

"I assume you're referring to the larger, wide body to which the presumed neck is attached?" asked Sherman.

"You must mean the elephant's head from which its trunk is extending," said Stephen in another of his righteously intoned, reality-check pronouncements. He had finally wrapped his head around what he was observing without threatening his world view.

"Harriet Letterman," Irene called over Laura's walkie-talkie, "from up there in Cloud Nine, any of you noticed an elephant make its way down into the river?"

"No elephants or hippos," responded Harriet.

"Maybe some overhanging forest canopy obstructed their view," proposed Stephen. "Or the elephant was lost in late-day shadows."

"About this elephant of yours," said Irene dubiously, as more and more of the body to which the long, neck-like object was attached swelled from the river into awe-inspiring view in the rapidly fading dusk, eerily enhanced by infrared goggles. "Let's say it did manage to trundle down a nearby river bank without any of us noticing it, either from ground level or from overhead in Cloud Nine. It also swam or walked underwater so many hundred yards with its trunk totally submersed, holding its breath and keeping any water from going into its trunk?"

"Elephants are known to be able to swim underwater for long periods of time, using their trunks as snorkels," Stephen took no small amount of pleasure explaining.

"If that's an elephant's head," said Sergeant Frankly, "it's the largest, um, fantastic elephant head, must be the size all by itself of a full-grown bull. And anyway, where are its ears?"

Its ears; Stephen was stunned into consternated silence as even more of whatever-it-was rose from the river. So much water slid off its back, the noise reminded Augie of a small waterfall on a hiking trail just north of Frederick, Maryland.

"This creature's immensity, if creature indeed it is," remarked Sherman, completely distracted from his data-gathering instruments by the looming, silhouetted spectacle, "means that surviving sauropod dinosaurs have nothing to apologize to their Cretaceous ancestors for, where size is concerned. What we are beholding can stop looming any bigger right now, and its proportions already appear comparable to the Argentine Titanosaurus."

Splash!

This noise so close to the cigarette boats, accompanied by fetid river water spray, made Augie's heart skip a beat. *Did a behemoth sauropod dinosaur just lift its tail out of the water, then slap it down hard?*

But no; the splash was from Prince Englebert leaping off one of the cigarette boats. He held onto the anchor rope he'd latched onto just before taking his plunge, to keep himself doggy paddling alongside the streamlined hull. "If we are indeed beholding a surfacing sauropod dinosaur of classic immensity even for prehistoric times," he started to explain, "then my subduing it with tickles should set a record bound to last for several generations, *mais oui!*"

"Tickle my ass, isn't that monster far enough out of the water for you to be recording its f- errrr- foul flatus emissions by now, Peabody?" asked Fred Frankly.

"One thing before you push off, *mon cher*, seeking a ticklishly behemoth belly to play your fingers across like performing a piano concerto," harshly whispered Prince Angelbert his true love's way. Looking directly down on Prince Englebert from the deck of the cigarette boat, he continued, "Please conjure on this: Should you perish in your admittedly historic attempt, should that magnificent beast's response to being tickled be to so quickly re-submerge, it flattens you like a *crepe*, then what about us? What about our dream of opening a special fashion boutique that caters to human beings of diverse sexual orientation?"

Prince Englebert rotated his glance from Prince Angelbert to his tickle fingers, to the immense shape looming ahead, around and around, clearly conflicted on his next course of action.

"What about our love?" went on Angelbert, feeling encouraged to further press his case by his true heart's desire having not yet let go of the anchor rope to approach what very well might be a surviving sauropod dinosaur. "Isn't it enough that you so tickled the world's largest spider into submission, you were able to hurl it away like a football goalie throwing the ball back into play? And which would you prefer? That I be howling like a banshee over your untimely demise, or over your once again coochie-cooing me into submission?"

"Reptile farts generally occur far less frequently than our own," finally responded Sherman after much careful deliberation over Sergeant Frankly's question, and heedless of Prince Angelbert's distress over his lover's reckless intention. "Reptiles tend to accumulate the various gases generated by digestive processes until they can't hold them in any longer, possibly a survival mechanism evolved to avoid notice by fellow predators. If that's what is happening with our sauropod specter out there, maybe we need to brace for something quite colossal. In fact, it might be a good idea if-"

PFFFTTTTTT!!!!!

The deafening noise suddenly issuing from the direction of the "sauropod specter" went on and on, PFFFTTTTTT!!!!

For how quickly Prince Englebert leapt out of the water into his lover's cigarette boat, Augie couldn't help being reminded of daughter Liz thrashing her way out of a swimming pool when a lifeguard blew the whistle over an approaching thunderstorm. But despite how terrorizing he found the persistently whiny noise, in a back corner of his mind Augie was having that all-too-familiar sinking feeling from prior cryptozoological pursuits.

And yet, he still found himself torn between cupping both hands over his ears to shut out the seemingly endless PFFFTTTTTT!!!!, and pinching his nostrils shut in case a stench was about to wash over them commensurate with the racket. I.e. silent but deadly didn't necessarily mean noisy but odorless.

PFFFTTTTTT!!!!

"What the..." Fred Frankly was stunned silent by the ensuing spectacle as seen through his infrared goggles.

The presumed sauropod had emerged so far out of the river, its legs in addition to what had to have been a tail nearly forty feet long came into view, more and more of its legs until impossibly…

"Freakin' Jesus-saurus, walking on the f-ing water?!?!" exclaimed Fred. The fear that swept across him and all the others might as well have been a mighty earthquake, shaking them to their core, even Stephen Feldman,

But not Augie Matias; his sinking feeling came center stage for him.

"What were you going to do if its anus wasn't thundering like the trumpets of Jericho?!" Prince Angelbert shouted at Prince Englebert, to be heard above the persisting PFFFTTTTTT!!!!!!

"I would be far less than honest with you if I said I know for sure!! But I quickly realized, *mais oui*, that this shrill bombardment is a warning: I was about to lose you!"

Grinning ear to ear despite the continuing din from the presumed longest and loudest fart ever, Angelbert pulled Englebert close, to whisper in his ear, "*Mais non, mon amour*; the real warning was that you were about to lose yourself."

"No, that's impossible!" blurted out Stephen. His inability to cope with what he was seeing in any explain-it-away manner had finally built to the can't-hold-it-in-any-longer stage. Like what Sherman described regarding reptiles with their accumulated digestive gases, he had to let it rip.

The presumed creature's legs finished rising up out of the Sangha River into infrared goggle view so that, as Fred cussed over, it appeared to be walking on water. But it didn't stop there. Rather, it slowly lifted into the thick, muggy air. And after a momentary hover, it actually spiraled further into the darkened sky.

"Good God!" exclaimed Scott. "Where are its wings?!?! How is this even possible?!?!"

PFFTTTT!!!

"Well here's a curious thing," said Sherman as clinically detached as Scott sounded emotionally unhinged. "My flatus emission detector isn't identifying that shrill whine as any sort of flatus whatsoever."

"So maybe it's propelling itself on air deflated from its torso, like a bullfrog deflating the sac on its throat?" suggested Ali. "That would be a truly most amazing evolutionary adaptation, if true."

"DUCK!!!" Kevin screamed as with a WHOOSH!! nearly as loud as the PFFFTTTT!!!, the flying sauropod dinosaur, supposedly, swooped down so close above the explorers, its tail slapped the nest woven onto Augie's scalp.

Reacting to the draft from the oncoming tail, Houdini Chicken evacuated her nest in plenty of time to avoid being battered, in a feathery commotion with an especially agitated-sounding, "Buk-Buk-BUK!!"

The two eggs she'd laid, of course, were incapable of any such behavior. They were shattered to bits, leaving Augie's head dripping with yoke like so many lamb-leg boogers, he couldn't help grossly imagining.

The golf ball that had become the third egg in the nest bounced from the one cigarette boat deck to the other, followed by a distinct plop! when it landed in the river.

Alistair became so distracted, he forgot about the seven iron he wielded as admittedly lame defense against the gargantuan flying thing they were confronting. The golf club conked him in the forehead as it fell lax in his hand. And he toppled over onto the deck.

PFFTTT!!

"Whatever that is," went on Sherman clinically, "sounds to be finally of diminishing intensity. But it has already lasted far longer than an infamously long-lasting, silent-but-deadly hippo flatus emission, and even longer than a human's world-record two-minute-plus emission."

"Houdini's eggs, a real shame, that," said Scott. "At least they weren't actually fertilized. Wasn't as if..."

"I feel comfortable assuming-"

Before Stephen could finish drily expressing full confidence Augie didn't fertilize Houdini's smashed-apart eggs, the noise from the apparently flying sauropod dinosaur suddenly re-intensified almost to its original volume, PFFFTTTTTT!!!! And an updraft sent the supposed creature directly skywards for its final nose-dive.

"CROUCH DOWN, PEOPLE!!!" cried out Prince Angelbert, there being no time to steer the cigarette boats out of the way if the monstrous whatever crash-dove their way.

Augie crouched into a fetal position on the deck of the one boat, his head and shoulders sticky sopping wet from the smashed eggs.

Houdini Chicken fled her nest to snuggle against him.

Meanwhile, Scott also curled into a fetal position, down low in the other cigarette boat. And he felt someone protectively drape herself across his back. Irene.

SPLASH!!!

Fortunately impacting with nothing more than the Sangha River, whatever-it-was's titanic splash nevertheless rocked both boats so violently, they nearly tipped over. Water drenched everyone, not the worst thing for Augie to the extent it diluted the egg-yolk stickiness.

As the boats settled down, curious monkeys saw noses one by one slowly hang out over both railings.

Houdini's beak came last.

Everyone was taking a cautious peek into the Sangha.

Steady river currents were already smoothing out the roiling tumult from the monstrous something's crash-dive.

"Is Houdini Chicken okay?" crackled Harry Letterman's voice over Laura's walkie-talkie.

"We could make out the rest of you from our magnified overhead surveillance," Samuel Longbottom jumped in to explain, lest anyone entertain the mistaken notion Harry cared more about the chicken's fate than anyone else's. "But- oh, there! She's peeking over the side of the boat into the Sangha like the rest of you!"

"Must be a case of chicken see, chicken do," drolly remarked Irene. Her voice sounded especially nasal from pinching her nose as did everyone else.

Even Houdini Chicken lifted one three-clawed foot to her beak.

What precipitated so much nose-holding were several bubbles rising and popping from where the flying object of sauropod morphology crash-dove.

After a good half minute, the normally risk-adverse Sherman Peabody let go his own snout. Pursuant to confirmatory sniffs, he remarked, "If those bubbles are carrying the beast's flatus emissions, they possess no noticeable scents whatsoever, let alone foul methane and/or sulfur. That means they likely are not flatus emissions at all."

"Then what?" asked Laura. "The creature can breathe underwater?"

"Perhaps," said Sherman noncommittally.

Before anyone else could join the conversation, the river's surface where the presumed monster crash-dived suddenly boiled with something enormous surfacing. Someone could have just turned on a football-field-sized Jacuzzi, Augie found himself thinking.

Quickly thereafter, a hundred-foot-long object bobbed up into infrared goggle view, taking the classic shape of a sauropod dinosaur. Completely sprawled out, a whiny noise accompanied it, the petering out version of the much louder noise they heard earlier as the presumed beast made wildly erratic flight across tropical night skies.

Prince Englebert stood to his full height on the bow of one cigarette boat, his tickle-ready fingers bravely at the ready. *You'll have to get past me to go after anyone else here!*

Alistair, revived from knocking himself out with a seven iron, could only think to ask, "Our prehistoric friend didn't crash-land to its death, did it?"

By then, the monstrous shape floating on the river's surface had its bulges flatten out. and the whiny sound finally ceased.

Air has finally finished evacuating a leaky balloon, Augie realized most regretfully.

Something small left the surface of whatever-it-was, zooming off into the darkness. A very large bug had stopped briefly to check out the floating carcass?

"Don't tell me," Scott said, joining Augie in rapidly growing certainty they'd been had.

Meanwhile, Prince Angelbert retrieved a pole from the floor of the cigarette boat, normally used for dislodging from a sandbar. And he prodded tentatively at what looked like the floating carcass's tail.

After the prince's poking-about produced no reflex reaction, he worked the pole underneath the presumed tail to lift its tip out of the water. Clearly, it was far thinner, far flatter than any such actual tail of that size could possibly have been.

"Ahh, yes," said Stephen, luxuriating in his skeptical attitude once again finding full vindication, where he was concerned. "That must be the famous Balloonodon. It lives like a cicada for so many years underwater rather than underground. When it surfaces. it has only so many minutes to fly about looking for a mate before it deflates."

Chapter 17

"Okay," Vicky tried to say loud enough to soothingly blanket the chorus of groans. "I know many of you are disappointed, and I'm certainly disappointed too. But let's sort this out. Giselle?"

"There was a humongous dinosaur balloon, like could have escaped from the Macy's Thanksgiving Day Parade? And a leak sent it flying all over the place? I mean, why would anyone do that?!" Giselle vented. "What's the point, people?" she looked around the classroom to ask, standing.

On the television screen, Augie Matias could be seen pulling twigs from his hair one by one, some dripping with egg yolk, via Laura's infrared lens.

Pfffttt!

Dead silence greeted this unmistakable sound. Everyone but its source took a moment to process that it originated from within the classroom rather than the television.

"What was the point of *that*, people?" Micky finally asked, met by uproarious laughter.

Vicky noticed Diane Mueller was among the few adults not laughing. She had a certain fixed, wide-eyed expression frozen on her face that seemed equal parts shock…and terror she'd be found out. Vicky imagined that had the room been fully lighted, Diane's complexion would have been seen gone ghostly pale.

"Not me!"

"Not me!"

"Not me!" defensively cried out student after student.

"That 'not me' character has committed more crimes around here," mockingly observed Vicky. "But unless a dead body suddenly shows up somewhere, no need for any confession."

Under cloak of further laughter, Peter George confidentially asided to Diane, "I must admit this nonstop succession of amusing events leaves me most non-amused over how much time my Giselle is losing for her academic catching-up."

"Let me guess, Mr. George," Diane said bitterly. "There's also a big 'but.' What is it this time? Ah, I've got it!" Diane raised her voice so much, caught up in her frustration, she garnered the rest of the classroom's attention. "For the longest while, that expedition over there in West Africa looked like it might actually have stumbled upon a living, breathing, monstrously sized dinosaur! And Ms. Copplestone's students had a front row seat, thanks to the wonders of a modern-day technology continually upgraded by mysterious benefactors!! And things just kept getting more and more amazing as the beast loomed larger and larger until it was flying wingless! The single greatest wonder of the entire animal kingdom, propelled like a rocket as from rocket fuel, but by its own gas!! Beyond amazing, until it deflated enough for them, and us, to realize it was just an extra-large balloon springing a leak!! So now you're going to argue, aren't you, Mr. George, that such a dramatic demonstration of how if it looks too good to be true, it probably isn't, is worth a whole semester of reading and math lessons! Am I correct?!? And now they can write about it for days on end!! Am I missing anything?!?!"

"Actually, Ms. Mueller, I was too caught up in my worry for any such qualifications to amend it whatsoever. To be honest with you, I had returned to considering that perhaps my Giselle should be relocated to a different class after all. But the eloquence by which you have clearly so justly defended your colleague's pedagogical tactics, I can only say: Bravo!! And offer both you and Ms. Copplestone a personal round of applause for jobs well done!"

Other parents and the visiting journalist quickly joined Peter George to enthusiastically clap their hands. By the time Vicky's students also joined in, they were giving her and Diane Mueller a standing ovation.

Click! Click! Click! Click! SLAM!!

Chapter 18

On a short wooden dais, Eclipso Sunray Smith's diminutively proportioned mother gently opened a comic book for Eclipso seated at his swamp-embedded conference table.

Augie watched intently on the panoramically proportioned TV screen aboard Cloud Nine. He found himself reminded of a gospel reader opening a prayer book, up near the altar at the church his parents attended back when he was c comic-book-collecting lad of eight years old.

"Holy f-n Christ," Fred Frankly swore softly, "does she also wipe his ass for him?"

"Shhh!" shushed Samuel Longbottom in a rare display of irritation.

Bernie Coleman reckoned he would have been feeling rather irritable, himself, had he followed Samuel's example, and worn a cardigan sweater for his venture off Cloud Nine down into the sticky humid African rainforest.

What caught Stephen's attention, meanwhile, was pencil-tall Bonsai Gator posted like a sentry beside Eclipso's dais. He was the only gator Stephen had ever seen stand perfectly upright.

As if his posture was not astounding enough, Bonsai put a fore claw to his snout like he was urging quiet.

Either he's imitating what he saw Samuel do on their TV monitor, Stephen tried to assure himself, *or he's grabbing at some bug felt tickling his nostrils. Either way, most unfortunate that so much of his behavior is ambiguous enough for especially gullible and suggestible people to read far more into than can possibly be occurring. But I did choose to comport with these bozos, on the promise of an even larger fortune than has already been deposited to my bank account.*

"In this forty-first issue of *Turok, son of stone*," said Eclipso after his mother flipped pages to the comic book scripture of choice, "we have 'The Phantom Honker' featured on the cover."

Eclipso's mother held up the comic book for his attentively dumbstruck audience. The cover depicted Turok aiming a bow and arrow at a green-glowing theropod dinosaur.

"Turok discovers that a supposed ghost dinosaur is actually a man enrobed by a dead dinosaur hide covered in phosphorescent cave dust. What becomes clear by story's end is that he scared food out of his tribe to hog all for himself. This brings us to consideration of your most recent adventure."

Eclipso's mother folded close the Turok comic book, and unobtrusively removed both it and the dais from his presence.

"For the second time now, quite obviously," Eclipso went on, "someone or some group of someones has gone to great lengths to make us look like fools. But to what useful purpose?"

Stephen Feldman stifled himself from voicing what came instantly to mind. *Why go to great lengths to rub your noses in your foolishness, indeed. Very short lengths would have sufficed.*

"Yes, Mr. Peabody," said Eclipso, seeing on his TV monitor Sherman Peabody raise a forefinger as he was usually wont to do.

"A detail I find most interesting," said Sherman, his chin once more pushed so far down against his neck, Augie easily imagined he was addressing his belly button instead of Eclipso. "The sauropod balloon, if you will, consists of entirely biodegradable material. Left to float down the Sangha, aside from the pieces I sliced off, it will dissolve to ingestible cellulose bits in mere days. There is a short ring tube that would not have dissolved, through which I'm guessing our pestering pranksters filled it with a helium-oxygen mix. But that's part of what I retrieved."

"Thought I saw an enormous bug fly away from the inflatable before you cut into it," said Laura. "Or was that something else?"

"Truly frustrating we couldn't have tracked wherever it was headed," remarked time traveler Ali Magabu, thoughtfully stroking his chin. "I noticed as well."

"Sorry you came so close to believing your impossible dream was about to actually be realized," said Stephen, "only to have those hopes, um, deflated." To his credit, Stephen felt a bit remorseful about belying his attempt to express sympathy with a pun. But he also wished Bonsai Gator would stop shaking his head at such inopportune moments as he did presently.

"My big question," said Eclipso, ignoring his skeptic-in-residence, "is whether it is too much of a coincidence both of our first two searches have been so dramatically pranked."

"I would say three's the charm...or curse," proposed Irene.

"All pranking aside, let us not forget we have already accumulated quite a bit more than no evidence at all, where the possibility of succeeding at Eclipso's quest is concerned," argued cryptozoology museum curator Bernie Coleman in his characteristically very non-arguing voice. "Among other delightfully tantalizing curiosities, there are those farts Sherman Peabody recorded that, while similar to an iguana's expulsive noises, imply a much larger creature. And if I might backtrack to our escapades in Papua, New Guinea, let us also not forget that something, we still don't know what, tore a hole in

Augie Matias's pants, something that had to have been rather towering,-"

"Like a palm tree," deadpanned Stephen interrupting.

"Yes, of course; a palm tree felt to have been huffing and puffing rather warm, fetid breath on him, isn't that correct, Dr. Matias?"

"Unless a special gust of wind tricked me into a major misperception," allowed Augie.

"Well there was also that spider the size of a German Shepherd," Dr. Roberta Quiñones interjected. "Certainly makes a lurking sauropod dinosaur seem more plausible."

"Given some of the freaky shit we've come across on other planets, wait," Kevin stopped himself mid-stream. "Your wife's classroom kiddies aren't still listening in, are they?" Augie shaking his head in the negative, he went on, "I'm up for anything after watching gun-toting stag emerge from a flying saucer, and mobile trees swing their butts at teed-up golf balls.

"It's a long story," he added on receiving several puzzled looks.

"So, the hole in Augie's pants and certain 'flatus emissions,'" Stephen made finger quotation marks, "could only have come from relic dinosaurs."

"C'mon, man! There was more than that!" exclaimed Alistair Frump in a rare moment of pique. "What about that swale we found worked into a sand dune? That had to have been produced by something far larger than those pygmy hippos you keep mentioning! Or the sheep who unwittingly invented the original sand traps along the coasts of Scotland and Ireland! And please don't try blaming it all on an elephant, mate! Because there is also that tunnel Scott and Irene explored that contained claw marks an elephant couldn't have made!"

"What *looked like* claw marks," fired back Stephen. "Maybe someone was already trying to sculpt a golf course here."

"On the Sangha River in the middle of- Okay, not nowhere," Alistair conceded with a nod the princes' way. He caught himself just before he made what he would have been the first to admit was a stupidly prejudiced remark. "But it's certainly nowhere that anyone in their right mind had previously seriously considered designing a golf course."

"Well you're seriously considering it."

"But that's me, Alistair Mark Frump, blazing previously undreamt-of new frontiers for golf!"

"I feel the same way about tickling," nodded Prince Englebert empathetically.

Anyone standing or sitting anywhere near Englebert on the Cloud Nine navigation bridge felt apprehensive, the way he moved his fingers as though attempting to make thin air giggle.

Even Bonsai Gator crossed his stubby front legs to cover his tiny armpits. It was as though Englebert might be paranormally capable of remote tickling, like certain psychics were purportedly capable of remote viewing, Augie mused.

Stephen strained to account for the anxious look on the small reptile's snout as having nothing to do with a tickle threat. *There must be something else he's noticing. Maybe there's something in Eclipso's Ankylosaurus-shaped mansion that the video cam is not picking up for us, such as a large dragonfly. Bonsai Gator doesn't have a turtle shell to retract his head into, and so...but I wish he'd just stop, and behave more like a normal gator...*

"Now I understand you two romantically involved gentlemen are considering an exceptionally generous offer from Dr. Quiñones and her significant other to bail on our quest. You plan to set up shop in College Park, Maryland, chasing after your fashion design dreams, is that correct?"

The way Eclipso considered his latest humus-dipped pretzel, seemed to Augie he was scrutinizing it as though it were the embodiment of the princes' dreams. Either that, or Eclipso could have been admiring a most elegant diamond's every facet.

Moreover, Augie was struck by what he could do nothing other than assume was a most curious illusion. Namely, the pretzel seemed to spin in mid-air, out of touch with Eclipso's chubby fingertips.

In addition, Augie couldn't help noticing that Eclipso's mother, standing diminutively behind him as always, had her fingers in a commotion. Ready like Prince Englebert to launch a pouncing tickle attack? Or working invisible marionette strings?

"We deeply, profoundly appreciate the ambitious tenacity of your dinosaur search," embarked Prince Angelbert on the most charitably diplomatic response he could conjure. "*Certainement*, there are far more harmful projects you could have enjoined. For example, the massive deforestation across parts of the African continent in aid of even more harmful projects, poisonous fossil-fuel mining for one. Not that your project appears harmful in the least," Angelbert strained to qualify. "In fact, the discovery of surviving dinosaurs might assist in halting certain deforestations."

"Your Goliath Frog pushes large stones about to create breeding pools. Is the confirmed presence of such amazing wildlife not enough already to inspire better preservation of tropical rainforest environments?" asked Stephen. "If not, why would a herd of surviving dinosaurs help in any more significant way?"

"I agree about the unique magnificence of Goliath Frog behavior," said Scott. "But I would also have to sadly admit that doesn't hold the same cache for most people of a surviving non-avian dinosaur."

"I'm still trying to get past you're not going all skeptic on us again about the pond-building part," snarked Irene.

"I did see that ring of stones with my own two eyes."

"And you're comfortable assuming the frog put them there?"

"I happen to have read about Goliath Frog behavior well prior to this trip."

"Oh, well," dripped mock-haughtily from Irene's lips.

"Having lived my entire life in this eco-system," said Prince Englebert, "I am well familiar with what people think they see after ingesting certain psychotropic substances. For example, a modestly sized monitor lizard peeking out from behind a bush can easily appear to have his head the size of an elephant's...under the influence. Still, where cache is concerned," he moved his fingers as though, Augie mused, the mere concept of cache could be subject to tickles, "*peut-etre* the possibility alone of dinosaur survival could be made to appear plausible enough to end certain rainforest degradations. Who knows?"

"I would put it more poetically, *mon cher*," Prince Angelbert gave Englebert an affectionate wrist squeeze. "Let's imagine the beauty of the prospect alone of dinosaur survival. Let's imagine that prospect cosmetically applied in reports from here to the outside world, like makeup and eye shadow applied to hide wrinkles and liver spots and such. *Peut-etre* such allure could be created as to seduce outsiders into a more useful, less-deforesting relationship. Such a relationship would doubtless prove *trés* transient, in my estimation. But just like fading sexual beauty, it would last long enough for a love relationship to blossom and intensify, based on a deepened appreciation for nature."

"I hope my fellow prince is not in any way implying the more superficial aspects of my own allure are already on the wane for him. My fingers might want to weigh in."

"In other words, this would be like the female praying mantis munching the head off the male after mating; she might have used her allure to attract him into that situation in the first place. But something useful, the continuation of the species, resulted," said Stephen, clearly delighted by the grotesque spin he gave Prince Angelbert's poetic outlook.

"I will put it this way," pushed back Prince Angelbert. "Opening our clothes boutique will require an effort *trés formidable* on my part, simply to stay focused on our customers, and not have my eyes constantly wandering your direction, *mon cher*. But *certainement*, the birth of such an establishment can be considered the love child, if you will, Monsieur Eclipso Sunray Smith, of your seduction by the possibility of dinosaur survival. With no heads bitten off into that bargain."

"Ah, *mais oui*," Englebert sighed approvingly. "I can already imagine greeting our customers with: 'I promise you will not be able to leave this store before something has tickled your fancy.'"

That something being you tickling their fanny, Irene stifled herself from snarking. "I wouldn't put it that way," she said instead. "Might make it sound like you're holding them hostage until they buy something."

"Nothing would be further from the truth, I assure you," said Englebert placing hand over heart like he was making a pledge. "But I must confess to having thought about tickling fancies in the more literal sense, *cher* Angelbert. Massage parlors are already so popular; why not a tickle parlor?" The prince's fingers got all agitated again, like he was itching to give away an abundance of free promotional tickles, Augie feared.

"There are obviously several details of our joint business venture to hammer out," diplomatically said Angelbert, though fuming over his lover broaching this tickle parlor absurdity, as he regarded it, with him for the very first time in front of an audience. *Why put me on the spot like this? What, did he seriously think anyone in their right mind would seek to shame me into going along with such a scheme? Nobody wants to be tickled!*

"I'd rather tickle out those details than hammer them out," said Englebert, oblivious to his lover's simmering seethe.

"Love will see us through, *certainement,*" asserted Prince Angelbert with a smile plastered across his face, and avoiding eye contact with Prince Englebert.

"I hope your quest for a successful thriving business does not disappoint you how you suspect we will end up disappointed. But what about our time travelers?" Eclipso looked towards Ali, Kevin and Fred on his television screen, gesturing at them with a humus-dipped pretzel. "What are your current plans until or unless you are spirited by your fellow starship officers back to the next century? Or should I say forward to the next century?"

Before Sergeant Fred Frankly could open his mouth on behalf of himself, Ali Magabu and Kevin Smith-Park, a downbeat from Eclipso's end of the communication, from back in central west Pennsylvania, announced a reggae version of the Beatles song, "Wait." The Beatles tribute band, Yellow Dubmarine, sang about a long time before "coming back home," and sent Bonsai Gator into a languid boogie across Eclipso's swamp-embedded conference table.

In a rare moment of restraint, Fred did *not* say exactly what was on his mind. *So we have here the reggae-*

dancing world's smallest gator, and that Eclipso guy presiding over him, hooked on humus-smeared pretzels and making people rich for indulging an impossible mission. In other words, we've entered a black hole of crazy probably as good as anywhere for remaining incognito. I mean, who the flying f- is going to believe any of these assorted characters if they leak to the outside world, "On our dinosaur hunt fueled by a pencil-sized dancing gator who 'thought it was a good idea,' we happened across time travelers responsible for switching out our large weapons caches for twenty-first-century technology"?

"I think the plan is simply to keep hanging out with you guys, if that's okay," Fred went on to diplomatically say to nods from Ali and Kevin. "No insult meant, but were one of your posse to rat on us to the outside world, well, coming from a search for living dinosaurs…"

"No offense taken," Eclipso assured Fred.

Eclipso's mother standing guard behind him had her mouth in ruminative motion, even though it looked to Augie like Eclipso was the one who just took a bite out of his gestured pretzel for extra emphasis.

"I would just as soon nobody took us seriously, so we wouldn't be plagued by pranksters," Eclipso explained.

"But isn't being pranked actually indicative you're *not* taken seriously?" Stephen asked testily.

"I take it as a sign we're considered worth disrupting," Eclipso countered.

Bonsai Gator nodded with seeming approval while continuing his languid boogie, irritating Stephen no end, on both counts.

"I for one truly regret we were not able to salvage our DNA scanner from our shuttle pod before it sank into the rainforest muck," said Ali Magabu. "With it, Mr. Peabody, you wouldn't have to be waiting weeks to discover whether those small bits you recovered from that mid-river sand dune swale have anything to do with the object of your quest."

"Yes, and also a shame, coincidentally, that none of you can produce such a device for our examination. Or anything else, for that matter, that might lend some credence to your extraordinary claim you arrived here from the next century," Stephen needled with relish.

"Were I in your shoes, Stevie boy, must admit I'd probably doubt our claim myself unless and until we suddenly vanished into thin air as our fellow time travelers or a space-time conundrum retrieved us. Which could happen any second, hopefully," admitted starship engineer Kevin. "But c'mon, that holographic com device we demonstrated has to give you pause!"

"Holograms are not unknown to us," said Stephen shaking his head. "It's not a far stretch to believe you pieced together your device in the present day."

"What I'm hearing, truly, is that you would have said the same thing about our DNA scanner, had we produced it for your scrutinizing pleasure," acidly observed Ali.

"For what it's worth," Eclipso jumped back in to short-circuit the tit-for-tat, "I take you three gentlemen at your word, and enthusiastically welcome your further involvement in our quest spurred on by Bonsai Gator here. Moreover, I am imposing a multi-week break for everyone to refresh, regroup, recommit, and carefully consider our next move, in the wake of the latest sabotage by unknown entities. During that time, I cordially invite you to accept my hospitality at Ankylosaurus Mansion. While you consider my offer, I have a question for you, Dr. Augustine Matias, that simply can't wait any longer. What happened to Houdini Chicken, and her nest on your head? Not that I'm anything less than pleased you don't have to deal with that any longer."

"She ran off with another rooster," Fred couldn't help saying.

"That explains why I overheard Augie in the shower room, singing, 'I'm going to wash that nest right out of my hair,'" piled on Irene.

"Sergeant Frankly has it correct," laughed Augie. "We accompanied the princes back to the village presided over by Prince Englebert's father," he went on, albeit unsettled by Bonsai Gator reacting to his confirmation of Frankly's answer with what seemed a knowing, that-makes-sense nod. "We brought him fish they caught on the Sangha River as a going-away present. Anyway, Houdini Chicken returned to being firmly ensconced on my head, despite her eggs having been crushed by the deflating dino balloon's tail whiplash. But then this rooster showed up, putting on quite a show strutting about and cockadoodling."

"Augie's own cockadoodledos were just no match for his," chortled Irene.

"Hell, he didn't even try a single cluck," added Fred Frankly. "He just stood there all forlorn while Houdini Chicken hopped off his head and followed the new guy in town to a new love nest."

"I just couldn't perform," Augie shrugged his shoulders, going with the silly. Although, soon as those words left his lips, an appalled look crossed his face and he added, "Wait; that didn't come out right."

What Augie could never admit, even to Vicky back home, was something about that lingering last look Houdini Chicken gave him before, with a commotion of flapping wings, she headed off with the rooster. It seemed oddly full of wistful regret that spooked him to his core.

*

Scott McDonald required immense courage to approach Irene on their way out of Eclipso's conference room. More courage, in fact, than he suspected he would require to approach a surviving relic non-avian dinosaur, if it ever came to that.

Irene and Scott were headed for the bus that would take them back to a parking garage near an airport in Baltimore, Maryland.

After they boarded the bus, Scott knew he might have to go for weeks before the next opportunity to speak with Irene confidentially. Such a dire prospect emboldened him. Almost causing him to bail out, though, was a new song played purportedly for Bonsai Gator's dancing pleasure. It was a spacey version of "I Want You (She's So Heavy)" by the Beatles, as performed reggae style by Yellow Dubmarine.

But courage did win the day. With a feigned nonchalance belied by his halting delivery, Scott asked, "So what are your plans, Irene, this summer? I mean, until we meet again? I mean, reconvene for Eclipso's quest?"

Irene's feelings for Scott irritated her similarly to how Bonsai Gator's nonverbal behavior irritated Stephen. Bonsai's behavior could be so easily construed as evidencing his comprehension of overheard human conversations. And in Stephen's estimation, such comprehension couldn't possibly be real. *Could it?* Stephen feared this unknown as much as Irene feared the prospect of falling in love.

Ever-mischievous regardless, Irene affected a most wistful voice to say, "If only I had a pin-up poster calendar of Bonsai Gator. I could make eyes at him as I excitedly mark off each day until I once again see him rise from the swamp embedded in Eclipso's conference table, to dance more Beatles reggae. But alas..." Sigh.

"Um, do I guess correctly that someone special in your life is going to be very happy to see you back home?"

"You must be talking about our local KKK, who will be very happy for all the wrong reasons," bitterly spat out Irene, instinctively set on assuring Scott there was not seriously "someone special." But also wanting to emphasize his pathetic puppy love was an unimportant trifle, where what she had to endure was concerned.

"The KKK? You mean the Ku Klux Klan? I didn't even know that was still a thing," Scott admitted sheepishly.

"Did you feel local eyes on you at that Cameroon market in Douala? Even before Houdini Chicken came into your life?"

"So that wasn't my imagination. But figured I dressed so differently from them, and as I guess you're maybe getting at, I was one of the few white guys some of them have ever seen…Anyway I had the same feeling on my earlier expedition out there; nothing bad, though. More curiosity than anything else, it seemed."

"'More curiosity than anything else,' exactly," nodded Irene. *Unlike with the goo-goo eyes you always make at me*, she refrained from adding, but did go on, "Mr. McDonald, I would give anything to be regarded with 'more curiosity than anything else' back home in Frederick, Maryland. However, lots of other African Americans are to be seen there regularly, so nothing unique about me, far as that goes. And nothing unique about how I'm treated, compared to how those other African Americans are treated. Our whole lives, we've had to endure hatefully suspicious looks from folks who if they had their way, would put us back in chains on a plantation."

"Sorry. I don't know how that feels."

"Yeah, I'm sorry too, especially about those haters who consider themselves good church goers, and would love patronizing your Bible museum if they haven't already."

"Not all church goers are ike that," Scott couldn't help bristling.

"And what does that matter if they don't push back against bigotry?"

I'd be thrilled to push back against bigotry, walking arm-in-arm with you into church, Scott couldn't work up the gumption to say, leaving him to give Irene a deer-in-the-headlights look that had her adding, "Sorry! It's just so frustrating that there's no special hate-o-meter we could use to identify certain people when they're not wearing pointy hoods and burning wood crosses."

Chapter 19

At first, Adriana Sousa feared answering the urgent knocks at the door to the makeshift mining-town shack near Serra Pelada, some two hundred miles south from the mouth of the Amazon River in northeast Brazil. Based on overheard local gossip, she could easily imagine one of the *garimpeiros* stalking her, and now trying to move in for the rape. He'd had even less luck than her husband panning for gold, and gone broke, homeless. There was nothing left for him than to revert to savagery, satisfy one of his most basic primal urges. No matter that Adriana's four-month-old pregnancy was starting to show.

Bam! Bam! Bam! Bam! Bam!

"Open the door, *mulher*!" tearfully screamed the door knocker in Portuguese. "It's your husband, Sebastião!! Hurry!!"

Uau, Adriana thought to herself in amazement as she hastened to unlock the door for her *Tião. The sun has hardly set; this is a good hour earlier, at least, than he normally makes it home. Oh-oh, this must be something even worse than when he and his fellow garimpeiros search for a prostitute to pass around with bonus wages he doesn't think will be missed.*

Sebastião burst through the entrance, and sprawled out on the mud-packed floor, exhausted, like he'd been spilled out of an overturned bowl.

Assuming the very worst, Adriana most unsympathetically asked, "Okay, how much gambling debt did you accumulate, and how dangerous are the gangsters you cheated?! Before I pack up and leave this hell hole for good?! *Bruto!!*"

"No! It's not that way this time!" cried Adriana's *Tião*. He struggled to even prop his head up off the ground, to face his wife staring down at him judgmentally.

For Adriana, all his caked-on mud from another day mining made the whites of his eyes seem looking out at her from another world, a place of sheer terror he was desperate to escape, to return to the safety and security of her loving embrace.

"Look," he scrambled to fish a small cloth purse from his pants pocket, and extend it towards her. "My earnings from today, not one centavo wasted on anything! It's all there!!" he wept.

"This is a lot more than usual," she admitted after a brief rummage through the purse without even bothering to count the coins one by one. "What happened?" she asked nervously. What she'd experienced earlier was gnawing at her as in, *There couldn't be a connection, could there?*

"I'll admit, *certo?* Cal was driving a bunch of us in his pickup to Julio's for *cachaça* and cards and who knows what else. But then in the headlights we saw a dinosaur cross the road!"

"You mean an iguana."

"Iguanas don't stand on their hind legs unless they have a tree to lean against!! And while it wasn't very big for a dinosaur, it was far bigger than any iguana we have ever seen! And it had these bright feathers down its back that rose like quills on an angry porcupine, as it froze and looked at us in the headlights!"

"So you're this upset because you believe you saw a dinosaur?" Adriana could feel the bile once more rising inside her, of familiar growing anger. And yet...

"That's not anywhere close to the worst of it!!" wept *Tião* with such insistence, fear finally eclipsed Adriana's anger. "Cal had to slam on the brakes to keep from hitting it!

Then the ground quaked! So much that the pickup overturned! I crawled out from under it just in time to see something incredible, thanks to the one headlight that still worked. This dinosaur head emerged, as large as in a monster movie, and the small dinosaur ran inside it moving from side to side, like this!" The way *Tião* moved his head to demonstrate reminded Adriana of an old film showing a snake following a snake-charmer's flute. "Cal was walking like drunk in front of it! I screamed for him to run! RUN!!! But then the monster dinosaur head disappeared, and Cal along with it!"

"Let me check your breath," Adriana managed to say despite her teeth chattering. After a perfunctory sniff, she announced, "As I suspected; you must have had a whole bottle of *cachaça, bruto*!! That bottle of *cachaça* could have been a bottle of juice for our child!" She patted her subtly swollen belly.

"But we never made it to Julio's!! And you admitted yourself there are more coins than usual in my purse!"

"This is nothing!" Adriana asserted after giving the purse a shake. "So light, could be a butterfly you caught in there!"

No longer trying to prop up his head to one side, *Tião* rolled over on his back and draped an arm across his forehead. "And you're serious that my breath smells of that much alcohol?"

"You must have drunk yourself so senseless, they tossed you out of the bar into a ditch from where you somehow crawled home. And in your wasted stupor, I do believe you imagined everything you just described. Is probably God's way of warning you need to stop drinking, and let go this foolish search for a fifteen-pound gold nugget! Nobody there would let you cash it in anyway, even if you dug it out of the middle of your plot! Now stand up, go take a shower and I'll prepare a better meal than you deserve for all your crazy foolishness!"

As *Tião* stumbled to his feet, he sniffed the palm of one hand after blowing on it. "I'm so wasted, I can't even smell my own alcohol breath?"

"You're so wasted, you mistook a bottle of *cachaça* for a dinosaur! And when you fell off your stool and were thrown in the street, you hallucinated that Cal's pickup overturned!"

"Incredible!" *Tião* muttered to himself as he staggered out the back of their corrugated-roofed hovel, to slowly empty a bucket of water over his head in the shower stall. There was more he didn't tell his wife, about the bag of two rocks nearly the size of two small coconuts Cal dug up that day. He suspected both were large gold nuggets, and was certain Cal intended to share their cash value with him once they both made it several kilometers away from the mining village, en route back to Belém. But then the pickup overturned in the earthquake. *Tião* didn't accept he could have ever gotten so drunk as to imagine that. He and Cal were both intent on remaining as sober as possible to skip town. He was sure Cal's stumbling-about so near to the monstrous reptilian head sticking out of the ground had nothing to do with drunkenness. No; Cal was searching frantically for his canvas sack containing a possible vast fortune in gold. The truck overturning must have tossed it who-knows-where.

For all *Tião* knew, the sack was swallowed by the monster, alongside Cal. The bottom line: Clearly, he needed to bring his pregnant wife as far away from there as possible, start over again. Adriana might have believed what she told him about his getting that drunk, to the point of her imagining fermented sugar cane booze on his breath. But he was easily willing to play along with the idea this had been a transformative experience from which he'd now emerge seeking an enduring redemption.

What *Tião* did not know was that Adriana flat-out lied about the alcoholic breath. Moreover, she suspected the significant tremor she experienced about an hour before he returned home was the same tremor that overturned Cal's pickup. As for that dinosaur stuff, she couldn't deal with it. And whether or not her *Tião* believed the story she spun about his alcoholic hallucinating, like he'd ingested too many mushrooms, no matter, so long as he was scared into living a better life…

www.ingramcontent.com/pod-product-compliance
Lightning Source LLC
Chambersburg PA
CBHW030408020726
47493CB00003B/989